HOTSHOT CHEF

BOOK 1 - UNDER THE SPANISH SUN SERIES

JA LOW

Cover Design: Simply Defined Art

Updated Editor: More than words

Photographer: Wander Aguiar - www.wanderbookclub.com

Model: Robbin

❀ Created with Vellum

1

QUINN

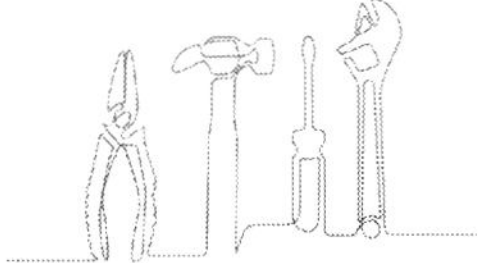

"I think we should take a break," Chad says effortlessly as he gets into the waiting car at the airport as if he hadn't dropped a bombshell in my lap. We've flown in from Waco to Los Angeles for an urgent contract meeting called by the producers of *Farmhouse Reno,* the television show Chad and I started.

"Excuse me?"

Did I hear him correctly? Is he breaking up with me? My stomach rolls at the thought.

The car takes off before I get to answer him and maneuvers into peak-hour LAX traffic. This is going to be one long assed car ride as the sounds of horns blaring go off around us.

Chad turns, and I can see the condescending twitch behind his blue eyes as he looks at me. "This shouldn't be a surprise to you, Quinn."

What the hell is he talking about? Of course, this is a surprise to me.

"It's become quite clear that we want different things in our lives. We're on different paths," he explains.

What bullshit is this? No, we're not. Only last month we were sitting down planning the next five years of our show.

"We've outgrown each other."

Outgrown each other? We've been dating for eight years. We've built up this sizable brand together around my interior design and his laboring skills. We have a café, a farm, and a multi-million-dollar television show based around us—as a couple—a happy, loving couple.

"I don't understand?" I say. Looking over at the only man I have ever loved, I wonder what the hell is going on with him.

We met in college, each one of us there on scholarship. He there for football, the star quarterback until he tore his knee just before graduation, and I for cheerleading. Even after all these years, the man gives me butterflies when I'm around him. Chad's still as handsome as he was in college, all these years together have been good for him. He has some extra crinkles around his eyes, he's a little more sun-kissed, and his hair is blonder. They only add to his handsomeness.

Chad reaches out taking my hands in his. "I do love you, Quinn. But …"

There's a but? There shouldn't be a but. There's never been a but before.

"… I think after all these years, we aren't the same people we were when we met in college."

No shit. We are famous renovators. People know who we are. That is a stark difference from who we were in college. Even if we haven't got all this it's normal for people to change after being together for eight years, it's called growing up. I didn't think we had changed that much that we should be breaking up over it.

"We want different things."

No, we don't. We wrote the exact same things down in our five-year plans the other week. That sounds like we want the same things.

"I want to take the show in another direction where there are going to be more opportunities for me. While you don't want to touch a thing, you want to keep it the same for the fans."

Is this because I didn't agree with his idea of doing celebrity homes? Chad thought we needed more glitz and glamor on the show whereas I wanted to keep helping everyday people. My stomach turns at the realization that we are in negotiation for this new season and now he is finding a problem.

"You want a break because I don't agree over where you want to take the brand?" I ask. I'm feeling blindsided by this turn of events. I pull my hands away from his, his blue eyes crinkling at my gesture. The man who I thought I was madly in love with not five minutes earlier seems like a total stranger now.

"It's a business decision, Quinn. You, of all people, should understand this." His tone is curt.

What the hell?

"Understand us breaking up is a good business decision. Have you lost your fucking mind?"

Chad's eyes widen at my use of language. I rarely cuss because he doesn't like it. The whole Southern gentleman that I thought was sweet is now fucking annoying.

"I wasn't expecting you to be so emotional about this, Quinn," he chastises me.

"Emotional? Five minutes ago, I thought I was happily in a partnership, and now …" I look him up and down in disgust, "… it seems I was wrong." Anger prickles my skin. My throat closes up as I try oh-so-hard not to shed any tears, but it's becoming harder and harder to keep my *emotions* at bay. The first dreaded tear falls down my cheek.

"Oh, come on, Quinn, you can't tell me you are surprised by all this. We haven't been in a great spot for years."

What? I thought we'd been great, busy, but great. I was happy. I never once thought about breaking up with him.

"I am," I tell him. "I had no idea you were so …" trying to

piece together my thoughts, I continue, "… so, over this." Waving my hand between us, the tears fall quickly down my cheeks.

Hold it together, Quinn.

"Sweetheart." Chad's face softens as he reaches out and wipes away my tears. "I'm sorry." He sounds almost caring. "There hasn't been a good time to tell you how I've been feeling."

But on the way to the network meeting is?

"How long have you been feeling like this?" I sniffle back the tears

"Since the start of last season."

Wait, what?

That's been almost a year. He's had ample time to tell me his feelings. I pull away and wrap my arms around myself in a protective measure.

"I didn't tell you sooner because we had to finish the season, and I knew you would be emotional and ruin the show. That's why I didn't say anything sooner."

Emotional?

The season finished months ago. We were taking an extended break instead of going straight into the next season. We haven't stopped these past five years since starting the show, it's been a whirlwind. Our first holiday was him on a boy's trip to Mexico. Thankfully, my sister Aspen organized a girls' weekend in The Hampton's for me when she found out about Chad's trip. We still haven't had that couple's holiday like he promised me.

I'm still so confused by him. We were pitching a second show to the network during today's meeting which would be about following our journey designing and building our dream home on the farm. Guess that's not happening. *Was that all a lie?*

Then my mind goes somewhere I never thought it would ever go.

"Is there someone else?" I ask him. My heart aches at the

thought that he's met someone else. It has to be the only reason he's doing this.

His right eye twitches, which is a tell for when he's about to lie.

"No. Of course not."

Liar!

"I would never do that to you, Quinn. It's not about anyone else. It's about me."

Liar ... liar ... liar.

"We've been together since we were nineteen. And sometimes in life you grow apart."

We hadn't grown apart enough for you to stop sleeping with me. As far as I was concerned, we were good, stressed, busy, but good. Since

stepping into this car, I don't know what to think.

"I'm sorry to spring this on you before going into the network meeting, but I couldn't hold it in any longer."

That's because you're chicken shit and told me all of this in front of our driver knowing my Southern manners won't allow me to make a scene.

Chad gives me that megawatt smile, flutters his eyelashes, and pops those dimples. Like he always does when he wants to get his own way, and everyone falls for it. And the bastard is doing that right now to me, hoping I'll forgive him. Like I always do. Not today, buddy.

"Please, stop talking or I will do something I regret," I say, holding up my hand and facing it in his direction.

Chad's mouth falls open, surprised by my words.

I need a moment of silence to collect myself otherwise I might punch him in his smug face, and I'm too southern to go to jail.

We sit in silence for the rest of the drive to the network.

2

QUINN

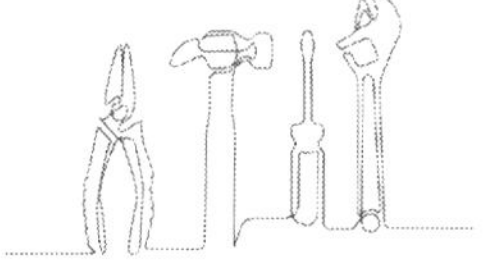

That motherfucking asshole.

The lies spewing out of his mouth during that meeting were all well-rehearsed. I realize he's been planning this for a long time, keeping me sweet so I wouldn't catch on to what his master plan was, which is to get rid of me and turn our show from a duo to a single star. Chad's ego is out of control. Never thought the sweet, humble guy I met in college would turn into this money-hungry, egomaniac chasing all the fame, fortune, and probably women that Hollywood is sending his way.

"We were growing along different paths," he told the executives.

He's the one on a different path. A path that gives him his own show, Executive Producer rights, and branding deals all of his own.

The meeting was all about *him, him, him.*

Sucker punched for the second time today, and I stood there like a deer in headlights while Chad steered the course of the meeting. The network praised Chad and me for being all Gwyneth Paltrow and Chris Martin with our conscious uncoupling breakup. They were worried it would turn into a nightmare of a breakup like so many before us.

And like an idiot I sat there, nodded, and put on a brave face when all I wanted to do was crumble into a heap. I'm so angry with myself for letting him bulldoze me. My brain shut down and I became mute. This was probably his plan from the beginning. Telling me in the car, he knew it would freeze me, and then dropping all his bombshells in the network meeting, I would be so shocked by everything that I wouldn't contest anything he was saying.

He played me, and I let him.

"Oh my god, Quinn. I've just heard," Lettie says, letting me into her Hollywood Hills home. She's my best friend as well as an executive at the network. She wraps her arms around my body and pulls me tightly against her. I need a friendly face right now. "If I'd known what was going down, I would have been there. I would have stopped it."

"I don't know what the hell happened. I arrived in Los Angeles as one person, and now I'm going to be leaving as another."

I've known Lettie for years. She's the entire reason Chad and I had our own show. She discovered us on *YouTube*. Lettie thought we would be perfect for her network and pitched us to the executives—that was almost six years ago. She was the producer for the first two seasons. We became tight growing up on the job, and now she's Head of Lifestyle for the network.

"Where the hell was Tammy?" she asks about our agent.

"She was there and agreed with Chad," I tell her. That was shocking. It was as if all these people were talking around me, and I was invisible.

"What the fuck! She works for you too. She's supposed to be looking after your interests as well as his," Lettie answers angrily.

"At the end of the meeting she quit representing me."

Lettie's mouth falls open with shock. "I can squash his plans. Say the word, Quinn, and I'll do it. I have the final signature," she says, walking over to her alcohol cabinet and pulling out a bottle of tequila. Lettie begins pouring shots for each of us. I'm going to need it to deal with this clusterfuck. "Chad is a fucking douchebag," she adds, handing me the shot.

"Thanks, and I know," I say, taking the shot before throwing it back, loving the way the tequila burns down my throat soothing my pain. "It's like I'm awake in a nightmare that won't quit, and I don't know how to wake up to make it stop."

Lettie pours us both another large glass of tequila. "You need something bigger than a shot to unpack all this bullshit," she says, handing me the crystal tumbler.

I stare down at the clear liquid in the glass and swirl it around as if magically it will help solve my problems.

"It's early days but trust me, Quinn, he did you a favor," Lettie says.

Not sure how he did me a favor by taking everything I worked so hard for all these years.

Lettie ushers me into her sunken living room with its gorgeous views of Los Angeles' twinkling city lights to talk. It's a vast difference from our Texas ranch where the only things twinkling are the stars above. I slump against the sofa and take a big sip of the tequila. Feeling the weight of the world on my shoulders.

"Now, tell me what the hell went down today in that board room meeting. Because I don't understand how the pea brain of a man was able to get one over on you."

I let out a heavy sigh and tell her the entire sordid tale. How Chad made a presentation about *him* taking over the *Farmhouse Reno* brand and that he would concentrate on more of his famous friend's ranches and country homes instead of everyday people. The network lapped it up as he worked the willing room. Chad talked about what he wanted, his dreams for the brand, and he spoke about multi-million-dollar brand endorsement deals he had been working on. The executives had dollar signs in their eyes over everything he was saying.

And I sat there and watched everything we had built get torn to the ground and did nothing. Hating Chad is a given, but I hate myself too because I did nothing to stop him. Let them all steamroll over me as if I were complicit in this endeavor. I have no one to blame but myself for how that meeting went.

Chad planned this coup so well. It's masterful really what he was able to achieve today. He must be laughing to himself about how well he did in duping me like he did.

I'm ashamed of myself, I played into Chad's plan and reacted precisely the way he wanted me to do. I nodded and smiled in all the right places, while internally, I wanted to murder him. In the end, I walked out of that meeting with nothing, and Chad got *everything.*

"Babe, I'm so sorry." Lettie reaches out and takes my hand in hers. "You didn't deserve this." She curses, taking another sip of her tequila.

"My whole life has disappeared overnight, Lettie. Not even overnight, my life blew up in one single day," I say, throwing back the last of my drink. A small giggle bubbles to the surface as I think about how my life has imploded. Then another giggle and another until I am manically laughing over the entire situation. I'm losing my mind.

"Fuck him, Quinn. How dare he waltz in there and take everything you have built away from you. I can't believe those fuckers sat there and let him railroad you into Chad's master plan. I mean it, I can cancel his contract if you want me to?" Lettie grins over her tumbler.

"Aw … you'd do that for me?" I say with a smile as I hold my hand over my heart. The petty in me wants Lettie to rip up the contracts we signed and tell Chad to fuck off.

"Damn right, I would. Fuck the patriarchy," she says, raising her glass in the air as she shouts, making me laugh.

"As much as I would love for you to cancel him …"

The look on his face if Lettie did cancel his contracts and he lost everything just like I have, now I would pay to see that. But the thought of imploding Farmhouse Reno, my baby, my love, she doesn't deserve it. And as high up as Lettie is at the network, they won't let her blow up their golden goose, even if it doesn't resemble what it used to be.

"… the bottom line is the show makes them too much money."

Lettie gives me a sad smile as she wraps her arms around my shoulders. "Alas, this is true."

We sit there in silence, and I'm sure Lettie is plotting all the ways she can murder Chad without going to jail for it because I know I am.

Lettie then lets out a long sigh. "I don't want to be the bearer of bad news, but it's something you really should be thinking about. You're still under contract with the network. That doesn't stop because you are no longer on the show."

"Wait, what?" I question her.

"There are two contracts, and I'm assuming what you signed today was getting out of the contract for Farmhouse Reno not the network. From memory you still have one more year left," Lettie explains.

Panic races through my veins hearing this.

"What does that mean?"

Lettie jumps up from the sofa and stands in front of me, her chocolate-colored eyes glowing with excitement as a wide smile falls across her plump lips. "It means you have a chance to take Chad down with a show of your own."

Huh. What? My own show. No way.

She continues, "He thinks your show is a success because of *him* and only him. He thinks he can maintain a highly successful show with thirst traps for all the bored housewives sliding into his DMs."

The amount of over-the-top DMs he's gotten over the years has been a little out of control. Of course, I see the sexual appeal. I mean, we played into it on the show. Chad works in the sun without a shirt. There are even some scenes where he wets himself down with a hose. I thought that was borderline eye-roll worthy, but the viewers loved it.

"And let's be serious … most of the demographic who watches Lifestyle is female. So, it's understandable."

This is true. But I have an equal number of female followers on my socials regarding my designs, and I don't need to resort to a bikini to increase my followers. I would never anyway.

"But … you, Quinn Miller …" Lettie looks me up and down. "You have this gorgeous apple pie, Daisy Duke wearing, wholesome country look going on, and men find that entirely fuckable."

Yeah, I think the tequila has gone to her head.

"I'm not fuckable."

"Fuck that shit. That sounds like something Chad told you, so you wouldn't see there were plenty of other options out there for you other than him."

Lettie reaches for her cell, then taps away and turns it around to me. She thrusts it into my face.

The screen is a little blurry after my second glass of tequila so I can't see what she is showing me.

Lettie takes the phone away from me before I even get a chance to focus on whatever is on display.

"Let me read it to you." She clears her throat. "Quinn Miller is the girl you take home to Mom."

Aw, that's sweet.

"Then blows you in your childhood bed like a porn star."

Um … what the hell?

"I don't know how Chad lets Quinn walk around in those

cut-off shorts. They mold to her ass perfectly. I'd want to throat-punch any contractor who dared look at her." Lettie raises a brow.

"Our contractors are lovely. They wouldn't do that," I say, shaking my head. I try to get that horrid visual out of my head.

Lettie continues, "Quinn Miller has the best rack on TV," she reads out with a chuckle. "I think I would staple gun my hand to some wood if Quinn Miller walked past me in those denim cut-offs, and I don't even think I would feel it or care." This comment makes her laugh out loud.

"Not sure what this is proving." I'm now questioning the sanity of my friend.

"It's proving that you have a very happy male following." Lettie waves her cell at me.

"No. That proves I have a heap of online creepers," I say, taking a sip of tequila, erasing their words from my mind.

"Creepers who watch your show probably jerk off to you wearing your shorts."

Eww. That whole thought makes me want to gag. I throw a cushion at Lettie, who bursts out laughing as she catches it.

"All I'm saying is you're Chad's competition, and he doesn't even realize it," Lettie explains.

Chad's competition?

"You're a star, too, Quinn," Lettie states.

"Not a porn star. I don't know if I want all this anymore," I tell her, looking over the rim of my glass. "I never wanted it in the first place," I state, waving my hand around her gorgeous home. "Give me my farm. My horses. The stars. That's all I need to be happy."

"That's all good and well except you're still under contract and the network will not let one of their stars go back to the country and do nothing. You have a year left, and they are going to want their pound of flesh from you," she explains.

This doesn't sound good for me. "What the hell am I meant

to do?" The panic I've been trying to keep back begins rising again. Not only has my life imploded, but now I'm going to be forced to work on something I don't want to because I signed a damn contract.

"Lucky for you, you have me. And I'm the fucking best. We have all night to come up with something, and I can assure you it's going to blow Chad Bailey's stupid show out of the water."

I'm not so sure about that.

3

SEBASTIEN

"Welcome," Lettie Johnson greets me warmly in her office.

She's the most intimidatingly beautiful yet cutthroat businesswoman I've ever met. And I'm about to tell her I'm not interested in signing on to the next season of *Hotshot Chef*.

"Please, take a seat," she says, giving me a warm smile. I do as I'm told. "Wow …" she steeples her hands together when she sits behind her desk, "… what a first season."

"It was … surprising." I'm not sure what else to say. I thought doing this reality television show about me opening up my restaurant in Los Angeles would be a bit of fun. I could make some money, and it would be great publicity for the restaurant, and it was. My profile has exploded in the States so much more than I could ever have dreamed, perhaps even more than I was expecting.

The Americans are more enthusiastic about my celebrity than the Spaniards. It's taken me a while to get used to that excitement. Add in that I'm friends with the Dirty Texas guys—one of the largest rock star groups in the world—and their families, which has helped propel my profile into the stratosphere. Now the first season is done, complete, over with, and I'm burned out. I haven't stopped working for eighteen months. I wrote a recipe book to accompany my show, which was a best seller. I had to fly all over the country doing signings for that too. I've done all the morning network shows and cooked for them. You name it, I have done it. Now, I want my life back.

"I hear you aren't interested in signing on for another season?" Lettie leans back on her chair. Her dark brown eyes narrow in on me.

"That's correct. I'm a little … um … how do you say … burned out."

"I can understand that, Sebastien. You have worked constantly for the show and the network. You have been a model employee. You never complained. You always did what we asked no matter how absurd it may have been."

Yeah, the naked cooking segment was pushing it, and thankfully they backed down on that.

"But …"

Of course, there's a damn but.

"The network has made you rich, and you have helped their bottom line immensely."

Here we go, the network is friendly to you if you do as you're told, but if you don't fall into line, there will be hell to pay.

"I understand all that, Miss Johnson, but I want something else. I want to go back to Spain. I've bought an old vineyard and would love to do it up and live a quieter pace of life. Get back to my grassroots. I want to cook because I love it, not because I have to," I explain, being completely honest with her.

She remains quiet for some time, and I can see the wheels turning in her mind. This woman is plotting something.

"Tell me more about your vineyard," she asks, smiling widely at me.

My eyes narrow. I feel like I'm falling into some kind of trap here, but I take the bait. So, I explain to her about this rundown old vineyard just outside of Barcelona. The old couple had no family to pass it on to, and now they're ready to retire and live a more peaceful life. I saw it on the internet late one night when I couldn't sleep and purchased it sight unseen. It grows Cava grapes, which is Spain's version of French champagne. It's set high atop a mountain and looks out over rolling green hills of vines.

Paradise.

There's a heap of old farm buildings on the land that need to be renovated—it's a perfect project for me to get away from tinsel town and all its trappings. I'm not going to lie, I've enjoyed everything LA has thrown at me—especially the women—but too much excess isn't good for you, especially when you lived up to your public image of a bad-boy chef. I've lost myself here in LA, and I don't like the person I've turned into by being here.

"I love everything about it." Lettie smiles.

I can see if I want to escape, she wants something in return.

"I'm not interested in filming it," I quickly add.

Lettie chuckles. "I know." She nods at my statement. "It's a shame because it sounds exactly like what I'm looking for."

"I appreciate everything you and the network have done for me." Because I am genuinely thankful. This was a great opportunity and something I would have kicked myself about years later if I had never done it, but it's changed me, and I want to stop that change before I don't recognize the person I used to be.

"I understand, Sebastien. We will be in touch to finalize everything," Lettie tells me.

"Thank you," I say, still unsure if I'm free or not.

"I understand this town isn't for everyone, Sebastien. I also understand when someone says they need a break, they mean it."

"Thanks for your understanding," I reply, feeling relieved about how this meeting has gone.

"Enjoy the rest of your day, Sebastien. We will talk again soon," she dismisses me.

And I hightail it out of there before Lettie changes her mind.

I'm free!

4

QUINN

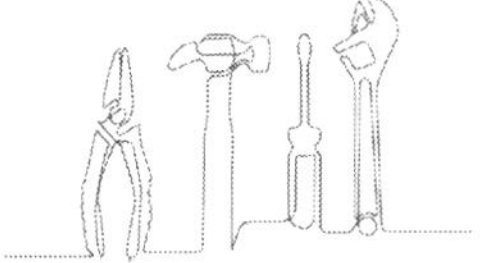

"I don't want to go," I whine to Lettie in her office.

"You have a contract, remember?" she reminds me.

Urgh, fucking contracts. They have been the bane of my existence this past month.

"It's only a meeting. A pitch. You can say no. But they might find something worse to give you to do instead," Lettie explains.

"Why won't you tell me what it's about. You know I don't like surprises." I glare at my best friend.

Lettie laughs. "Trust me, you're going to like this one."

I don't think I am.

My life has gone to crap after my last meeting with the network. Chad had been doing some creative accounting with our money and assets and has somehow been able to transfer practically everything we own into his new trust account. The documents I signed stupidly and naïvely about updating our LLC years ago were to do with Chad putting everything we own in a new company where he is the sole proprietor. Tens of millions of dollars of assets were transferred into his name. Everything we worked for over these past five years together, everything we bought, he now owns legally. All because I trusted him and signed where he asked me to. Yes, I'm the biggest idiot.

As soon as I found out, my family sought legal counsel, and I'm lucky my parents had the means to help me find the best. But because stupid me signed the papers that decreed him the owner of everything, I had in essence signed my rights away without even knowing. *Sneaky fucking bastard.* He played me from the start of all this, and I was too in love to notice. I could fight it in the courts, but my lawyer advises that it would chew up more money while tying me up in legal battles for years. A bitter pill to swallow there, my parents told me they would help me fight it, but I couldn't ask them to pay hundreds of thousands of dollars in legal fees because of my stupidity.

Chad was able to take everything from me—my farm, our home, my horses because they were all under the company's name. He graciously left me some of the cash in our bank accounts. Obviously not the five-million-dollar two-year deal he just signed with the network. I walked away with half a million dollars, which is nothing compared to what we had earned.

Fucking men!

Oh, and the real kicker!

Once I gave up my fight the very next day, he issued a statement to the world that we had broken up more than six months ago and hadn't publicly announced anything because season five of Farmhouse Reno was still showing and we didn't want to ruin it. And now the season is over we can be honest with the world and let everyone know that we are over. Then in the same breath, he announced he is now dating again. Danika DeVille, a gorgeous, young, bikini influencer, I think that is what she does. There's a heap of shots of her in bikinis and not much else on her socials. She's young, maybe twenty-one.

Everything makes sense now. That's why he wanted his brand to go in another direction. Why he thought we were growing apart. All because of her. Also explains the sudden increase in his gym workouts. He said it was because he wanted to give the ladies what they wanted for the next season, but really, he was trying to impress this girl. Was I truly that blind? I've read peoples' comments on stories about Chad and Danika which Lettie tells me I'm insane to do, but sometimes I can't help it. I'm hoping it will explain what the hell happened between us. There's a mixed bag of Team Chad vs. Team Quinn.

Once the news broke about Chad and Danika the two of them went on the charm offensive and started a PR tour about their love because he started to get too much negative press about our breakup. The bastard has been telling everyone the real reason we were taking a break after the last season of Farmhouse Reno wasn't because we needed a holiday it was because we had split up and needed to work out what to do next.

What a fucking liar.

He said that was the reason for the separate holidays that his boys wanted to do something to help cheer him up because he was heartbroken over the decision to split, so they decided to head to Mexico.

Bullshit. We were still together.

Then I found out that is where he met Danika. She's the younger sister of one of his *'new'* friends. He said he wasn't interested in meeting anyone as his heartbreak was too raw to ever be able to love again, but Danika was his anchor during that hard time and sewed his broken heart back together again. He was surprised that he could love again so soon, but Danika is that special.

Gag.

His new PR team is turning his cheating into some sort of love story with new beginning vibes.

What the hell is wrong with him? How does he think this is okay? Sprouting all these lies. Does he not think I can contradict everything he is saying? *He knows you, Quinn. And he knows that you won't come out publicly and cause a scene. That you don't like the attention. He's counting on you being a wallflower like you always are.*

Fuck him.

He's right though. The media intensity has been so crazy that I spend my days camped out at Lettie's house hiding from the paparazzi. The constant requests for interviews, the jokes by comedians about our relationship, the memes. I can't escape the worst thing that's ever happened to me because it is everywhere. This man has taken so much from me and yet he wants more.

Mentally I've shut down and refuse to answer anyone's questions about the breakup. I'm shell-shocked. Raw. Broken. Exhausted. I'm not in a good space to go on a media tour arguing over what really happened between the two of us. I know I should. I feel weak and pathetic for not sticking up for myself, but I know it will only fuel Chad's need to be right even more. He would love it if I came out and tried to fight him. The media attention that would produce would make him dizzy with excitement. So, I'm going to do what will probably annoy him even more and be silent. The more silent I am the more people will forget about him. That's my plan, it may not be a great one, but it's all I can handle now.

Chad called Lettie and told her that I needed to come get my stuff because Danika was moving in and if I didn't get it, he was going to throw it away. I left my entire life back in Waco, thinking I would step right back into it when we got back from the meeting in LA. How wrong was I?

Thankfully after a distressing phone call to my sister Aspen who lives in New York and my parents, they came to my rescue and packed up my entire life one weekend when Chad wasn't there. There was a long list of things they couldn't take and a mediator was there to make sure they didn't take anything more than they were allowed. What a fucking dick. They shipped it all back to my parents' place in Dallas where one day I'll go through it, but for now, I can't, it's too much for me.

Not only have I been fighting with lawyers over what Chad took from me, but I've been talking to them about trying to get out of this one year left on my contract with the network, and no matter which way you look at it the contract is ironclad. My soul still belongs to the network, and I owe them one more year.

So, I have no choice but to head to this meeting with Lettie today otherwise, they will call good on their contract, and I will owe them a lot of money. Money that I don't have thanks to Chad. The one saving grace is Lettie was able to negotiate the same salary that I was getting on Farmhouse Rescue for this new project, which will help ease the burden of being forced into doing something I don't want to do for a year. It can't be worse than what I've just been through, can it?

Lettie ushers me from her office toward the conference room where the meeting is being held. Her assistant hands me a bottle of water as I enter. I see five of Lettie's junior executives sitting waiting for me. *Why so many?*

"We are just waiting on one more," Lettie advises me as she takes a seat at the head of the table.

I unscrew the top of my water bottle and take a sip, hoping my nerves calm the hell down while we wait for this mysterious guest.

The door to the conference room opens, and I hear footsteps. They stop behind me, so I can't see who it is.

"What is going on?" The deep, accented voice echoes through the room.

He does *not* sound happy.

"Take a seat, Mr. Sanchez," Lettie says, giving him her most professional smile.

He does as he's told and takes the seat beside me.

Turning my head, I notice it's Sebastien Sanchez. The Hotshot Chef himself sitting beside me. Geez, I thought he was attractive on television, but in the flesh, I don't believe I've ever seen someone as handsome.

Where Chad is that All American country boy, Sebastien looks like pure and utter sin. I can see why he has a reputation —women must throw themselves at him all the time. I mean, *in my mind*, I'm seconds away from jumping him. I would never ever do it for real. He probably has a huge ego. Also, I'm still too damaged from Chad. I'm not ready to take that giant step and be with someone again. It's not like Sebastien would be interested in me anyway. He has all of Hollywood knocking on his door.

Sebastien turns his head, and his eyes widen ever so slightly as he takes me in. The chocolatey velvet abyss of his eyes gives me the once over, and his lip curls in disgust before turning back to Lettie.

Dick. What crawled up his ass?

"I don't understand why she's here?" he asks, sounding angry.

Hey. What have I done? I turn and frown at him.

Lettie's eyes narrow on him, not impressed with his attitude. "Since our last meeting, Sebastien. I've had another look at your contract. Not sure if you have read it since you signed it, Mr. Sanchez."

Sebastien stills beside me, and tension fills the room.

"I know you said that your contract was coming to an end—"

"Yes. That's because I have finished the first season of my show. That is *all* I signed up for," Sebastien counters.

"This is true." Lettie smiles wolfishly. "There's a clause in the contract that you may not have remembered signing because let's be serious, not everyone reads everything in their contracts," Lettie states. Her eyes flick over at me before returning to Sebastien.

That's not fair. And yes, I know I'm an idiot for that.

"What clause?" Sebastien asks, sitting up straighter beside me.

"There is a clause in the contract that states if season two of

Hotshot Chef isn't commissioned, you are unable to do another program with any other network until your contract has expired."

There's silence in the room while Sebastien takes in the news.

"That's fine. I'm not looking to do another show. I'm moving back to Spain," he adds.

"Yes, I understand your plans," Lettie says as she moves in a little closer, resting her elbows on the table. "But you are still contracted to the network for, then you are free."

"Wait, what?" he questions, his voice raising before a slew of Spanish curses cross his lips under his breath. "I'm not doing another show with you. I told you I'm burned out. I hate LA. I don't want to be here anymore, and now you are telling me I must stay for another year?"

You can hear the distress in his voice, and I feel bad for him. I'm in the same boat, buddy, so I get how you feel. I'm not sure why I am here, I don't think I should be listening to this private conversation.

"You signed a two-year contract with the network, Mr. Sanchez. You have fulfilled one of those years. Now you want to renege on the last year. That is going to be a very costly move."

I feel bad for the guy. Both of us have been screwed over with contracts. I think this is a lesson neither one of us will ever repeat again.

"Stay here for another year? I'm not a prisoner," Sebastien states, standing up abruptly as his hand slams down onto the conference table with a hard slap, rattling the jug of water and its glasses.

"We understand this isn't what you want," Lettie informs him.

"No fucking shit," he says, biting back angrily.

Lettie doesn't falter at his anger. "We have a proposition for you that I think will be beneficial to you and the network."

"No. No. No," Sebastien says, shaking his head beside me. "I don't want to hear it. There's nothing you can offer me that I want. Sue me. But I'm not staying here," he tells her.

"I'm sure that is *not* the route you would like to go down, Mr. Sanchez," Lettie warns him coldly.

I felt that warning to my bones, and it chilled me.

"Are you threatening me, Miss Johnson?" Sebastien glares.

"No. Just making sure you understand *all* of your options first." She gives him a sunny smile as if she hasn't dropped a bombshell into his lap.

Sebastien grumbles something in Spanish beside me, but I don't catch it.

"Go on, then ..." he says, waving his hand in the air as he takes a seat and folds his arms tightly across his chest.

"Thought you might come around," Lettie says with a smile. "We are offering you the chance to go back to Spain to work on your vineyard project."

"And you want to film me doing that?" Sebastien adds sarcastically.

"Yes."

"And the catch?" he questions her.

A grin falls across her face. "The catch is Quinn Miller is going to help you," she says, turning her attention to me.

"What?" I answer.

"With her?" Sebastien answers, sounding annoyed.

That's rude. I turn and glare at him, I'm not happy about this either.

"Both of you have a lot more in common than you think. Quinn here is stuck just like you, Sebastien." Her eyes narrow on him, then me. "We think this will be a great idea. It's a great pairing. Quinn is one of our network's biggest stars. Plus, she is a phenomenal interior designer and renovator. I think it's probably something you might need on your project," Lettie states with a grin.

"I don't want to live in Spain," I say, speaking up.

"And I don't want to stay in America," Sebastien adds.

"The network thinks this is a brilliant alternative. The Hotshot Chef and the Reno Queen in a crossover show. It's a ratings winner," Lettie exclaims enthusiastically.

"It's in Spain," I exclaim again. As in the other side of the world.

"Exactly. You need to get away from here. We could give an *Eat, Pray, Love* vibe to your story. How Quinn Miller finds herself again after her breakup from Chad Bailey."

My jaw falls wide open. Did my friend use my personal life as part of the pitch? Tears begin to well in my cycs, and thc feeling of betrayal by my best friend hits me. It's humiliating enough as it is going through this breakup, but using my heartbreak as a TV show is too much for me. Standing quickly, my chair scrapes across the floor as I hightail it out of the conference room. Pushing my way out the door, I rush down the corridor to the bathroom, where I slam the door shut and lock it as I collapse in a hot mess on the cold tiles.

Moments later I hear the bathroom door squeak as someone enters. "Quinn," Lettie says as she knocks on the door. "Babe."

"Go away," I yell at her through my tears as my entire existence feels like it's being pulled out from under me, again.

"Quinnie," Lettie whispers through the door. "I'm sorry, okay. That wasn't right, bringing in your personal life like that. I got carried away being the boss and forgot to be a friend."

I suck in a shaky breath listening to her words.

"Honestly, I think this will be good for you."

"How?"

"One … you can get away from Chad and this new woman. You know with this new show he's going to be a publicity whore. He's going to make sure he and Danika are the network's newest darlings. You don't need to see that."

This is true.

"Two … it's Spain."

I don't know anyone in Spain. I'd be all alone. It's lonely enough being in Los Angeles. Spain is so far away.

"Three … don't you think it will annoy Chad that you are doing a renovation show with another man. A handsome man. One with an accent. Who can cook. This would be the biggest fuck you to Chad."

Chad would hate it. He thinks no one would want to work with me or that I would want to work with anyone else. He thinks his show would be the biggest thing on the network. I mean, he stole it thinking I would never be strong enough to challenge him. And Hotshot Chef is huge, the ratings on his show would always give ours a run for its money. Maybe there is some truth in what Lettie is saying. Putting the two of us together would be the biggest surprise pairing on the network and something Chad wouldn't see coming.

"Four… Sebastien is hot as fuck," Lettie adds with a chuckle.

"I'm not interested."

"I know, babe. He's nice to look at. Who knows, maybe he has a hot brother or something?"

"He's an asshole."

"We caught him off-guard with the meeting," Lettie explains.

"He looked at me as if I wasn't good enough to be in the same room as him. I got rid of one egomaniac, I don't want to be saddled with another."

"Quinn, I get it. That wasn't a true reflection of Sebastien's personality. I wouldn't have thought this was a good idea if he was that much of a dick." Lettie tells me.

This is true.

Standing, I unlock the door and let her in. She pulls me into a big hug, which I welcome.

"And five … they are going to pay you *so much money* to do this show," Lettie tells me excitedly.

"You know I've never been about the money."

"Blah, blah, blah, ethics, morals, I get it. This is Hollywood, that doesn't get you a gold star. The best thing is they will pay you more than they did Chad," she says with a grin.

Lettie has my attention. This might be petty Betty of me, but this information warms my broken heart.

Suck it, Chad.

"That's how much they want you and Sebastien to work together."

"They seriously think that dick out there and I are going to be a good match?"

Lettie nods enthusiastically.

"Fine. I'll listen to what y'all have to say as I trust you. Him, I'm not sure about."

"Good. Now fix yourself up and get your butt back in there," she says, giving my ass a hard slap and disappearing back to the conference room.

5

SEBASTIEN

This is already a shit show before we've even begun.

I'm not interested in working with Quinn Miller, the overly sweet country bumpkin from Texas. Her storming out being a diva is proof of that, plus I've seen the news of her ex with that model. To be fair to Quinn she is hotter than the other woman. She's more natural, less LA than his new squeeze. She's giving me that wholesome American vibe, it's not my thing, but I can see the appeal to others.

"Be nice." Lettie points at me as she takes a seat.

Moments later Quinn walks back into the room. Her eyes are puffy from where she's been crying. Is she going to cry every time someone mentions her ex?

Quinn clears her throat as she retakes her seat. "I'm sorry about that," she says, giving me a small smile which is unexpected.

"Entirely my fault, Quinn," Lettie apologizes.

My mouth falls open, Lettie Johnson apologizes. I look out the window to see if the world is ending or if there are pigs flying because I've never seen her apologize in all my dealings with her. Who the hell is Quinn Miller to have that kind of power over her?

"Would you mind giving us all a moment," Lettie addresses her staff. They all pack up quickly and get the hell out of the room.

Once the conference door is shut and the three of us are alone, Lettie's demeanor changes, it softens even.

"Have you heard of the show *Farmhouse Reno*?" Lettie asks me.

"Yes," I answer. It was airing around the same time as my show, and I remember my agent always focused on who had the highest-rated show.

"What you might not know is this power couple have broken up."

"So, I've heard," I say. Not that I follow the gossip, but it was everywhere.

"He's been playing hide the salami with another woman long before he should have been," Lettie adds.

I look over at Quinn, and she's nervously playing with her hands. Okay, the dude was a cheater. What does that have to do with me? Maybe he was doing that because he was sick of dating Miss goody-two-shoes. I bet she tastes like cinnamon and apple pie. And she's probably as vanilla as vanilla ice cream. She looks like the kind of girl that has sex with the lights off, missionary, and doesn't like dirty talk.

My eyes lower when I notice Quinn has sunk her top teeth into her bottom lip—a very plump, luscious bottom lip. Most women would do this to be sexy and alert your attention to their lips and all the things they can do with them. She's doing it because she feels uncomfortable and yet somehow, I am now imagining what it would be like to have those perfectly plump lips wrapped around my cock before dirtying up that perfect face.

Wow. Where the hell did that come from?

I need to get laid, and it's not with sugar and no spice, Quinn Miller.

"I'm going to be unprofessional for a moment," Lettie warns. "I want to crush Chad Bailey for what he's done to my best friend."

They are best friends. Now it all makes sense. Honestly, I didn't think Lettie had friends, she seems like the kind of woman to have minions.

"What you don't know is the bastard played my friend. He took everything from Quinn. Everything she worked hard for over all these years, he fucked her over and left her with nothing."

"Lettie," Quinn warns her friend before turning her attention to me. Those bright blue doe eyes land on mine, and for a moment, I'm stunned, unable to move my attention away from her.

"None of this is your problem, Sebastien, … *at all*," she tells me. "Honestly. It's utterly mortifying that you are even hearing about how much of a shit show my life has turned into. I mean, you're Sebastien Sanchez." She gives me a self-deprecating laugh as she shakes her head.

She knows who I am. I didn't think she would.

"Chad Bailey thinks he's the big man on campus, and I want to bring him down a peg or two … off the record, of course," Lettie says, her steely eyes warning me. She doesn't need to tell me twice. "And I feel like you're just the man to do it."

"Me?"

Lettie nods. "Yes, *you*. I'm prepared to give you everything you want. I will honor your wish to leave Los Angeles and go back to Spain."

Now she's talking.

"But only if you will be part of this show. Give me one

season, that is all I ask, Sebastien, and I will give you your life back. I can guarantee it will be the last you ever hear of me or the network."

The show. Always the fucking show. I sit there in silence knowing she has me over a barrel. I have no other option than to accept the deal and work with Quinn. *At least you would be back home.*

"We will pay for all renovations. You won't have to pay for a thing," Lettie adds.

They must be desperate for me to sign offering me this carrot. If they did pay for the renovations, it would mean more money toward other things, but does that mean I don't get a say in how I want it renovated?

"Do I get a say in the renovations?"

"Of course, along with Quinn's input." Lettie nods.

I look over at Quinn, and she gives me a weak smile. I've seen her work, she's good, but it's also not my style. Guess if it's horrible I can change it once everyone's gone.

"Sebastien, you don't owe me or the network a thing, but I will warn you they will not budge on your contract, and they *will* call it in. They *will* put you on some stupid ass show here in LA that some dumbass junior executive has pitched to them to get their money from you, and unfortunately, it will be the same for Quinn." Her attention moves to her friend. "I'm here to make sure that doesn't happen."

"So, you're saying the network will let me move back home to Spain. They will pay for all renovations if I let them film the process and work with her?" I ask, looking over at Quinn before turning my attention back to Lettie. I need to double-check because it sounds way too good to be true.

"That *'her'* is the only reason you are getting this deal," Lettie states sternly.

Right, I get it, Lettie. You're Team Quinn in this scenario.

"And you're okay with it?" I turn and ask Quinn.

"Like you … I don't have a choice," she says sternly before folding her arms across her chest, which draws my attention to her impressive cleavage. Perfect mounds hidden behind a basic white t-shirt tied in a knot showing off tanned skin and a flowy skirt. Her blonde hair is pulled up in a high ponytail. She looks like she is wearing minimal makeup too.

"Do you *not* want to work with me?" I ask, a little offended.

"Um, no. Why would I when you've been nothing but a dick to me since you arrived today?" she bites back.

Wasn't expecting that bit of bite from Miss Apple Pie. I wouldn't say I've been a dick just caught off-guard and backed into a corner.

"I disagree, maybe you're being sensitive."

"Is he serious?" Quinn turns and asks Lettie.

"Right, I think this conversation has gone off track. Looks like the two of you have gotten off on the wrong foot with each other. That's my fault. How about we change that? Dinner and drinks tonight to see if you two can at least be civil with each other if we are going to make this show work," Lettie suggests.

"Fine," Quinn agrees, rolling her eyes.

"I'll set us up in the private dining room of my restaurant, that way we can talk without being disturbed," I suggest.

"That sounds like a great idea. We don't want news of this venture between the two of you getting out. I want to surprise everyone with it, especially Chad," Lettie adds.

"Also don't need the gossip channels thinking we are together either, now that you're single," I tell her.

Quinn's blue eyes narrow on me, and I swear steam would come out of her ears if it could.

"I've heard about your reputation. I don't need to be associated with all that," she says, looking me up and down.

"Might dirty up that Miss Apple Pie image the world has of you and do you some good."

Quinn's mouth falls open at my comment.

"Great," Lettie says, clapping her hands together. "We will see you tonight at eight."

6

QUINN

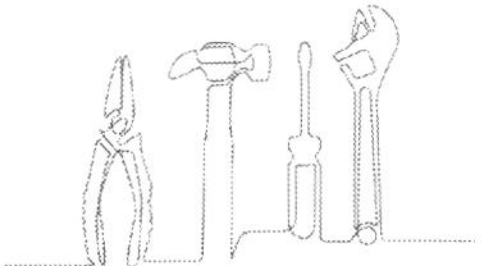

"I'm running late. I'll be there in an hour or two," Lettie says, calling me from her cell.

"An hour or two? What the hell, Lettie. You can't leave me with that man for that long."

"Sorry, babe, there's an emergency at work. I would be there if I could."

I know she would. I'm just annoyed after the meeting earlier today. The man is horrible. Not sure how he is able to hook up with all these high-profile women when his personality is the pits. *Probably because they aren't talking.*

"What the hell am I supposed to do with Sebastien Sanchez for that long?" I moan.

Lettie laughs. "Seriously?"

"Yes."

"Don't think many women would find hanging out with him in his private dining room hard."

"Ew, you think he sleeps with women in there, where we will be eating? That doesn't seem hygienic."

Lettie bursts out laughing. "I keep forgetting you're newly single."

"Even when I was with Chad, I wouldn't have thought to have done that."

"Really? You never went to dinner with him and wanted to rip his clothes off so much you said screw dinner and had him instead of food?"

"No," I answer hesitantly. Have I ever wanted to rip off Chad's clothes? I guess. Did we ever have sex in a private dining room? No. For that matter, I don't think we ever had sex outside of the bedroom. Hmm. Have I been missing out on adventurous and public sex? I think I've been missing out on a lot of things.

"Oh," Lettie answers.

"You're about to say I've been missing out, aren't you?" I say to my best friend.

"Yeah, you have been. Passionate, frantic, dirty, could get caught at any moment sex is hot. Think about it," Lettie says.

"Not with Sebastien Sanchez, thank you very much," I add.

"He'd be a great rebound."

"No. We are about to work together. Plus, the man has a huge ego, no thank you."

"It's not the only thing I've heard that's huge." Lettie chuckles.

I hate her.

"I don't need to know that."

"Thought you should in case you know, you want an orgasm or two," she says, teasing me.

"Hey, I told you that in confidence." This is what I get for drinking too much tequila and spilling all my secrets to Lettie. I may have confessed that most of the time Chad never got me off that I would have to finish with my vibrator when he was snoring away beside me. Lettie was disgusted by the lack of orgasms that I was having.

"You can't deny the man is hot," she challenges me.

"I have eyes. But he's a lot older than me."

"Hey, he's eight years older, the same age as me, and I'm not old. And remember with age comes experience," Lettie adds.

"Is that what you tell your cougar baits?" I say, joking about her penchant for younger men.

"Screw you. Go eat some nice food, drink great wine, and enjoy the company of a hot man that can hold a conversation that doesn't relate to beer, trucks, or football."

I like beer, trucks, and football though.

"Why are you trying to push me toward this man? Don't you think anything other than being professional is against network policy?"

"You haven't technically signed anything yet for this new show."

"Lettie, I'm not interested in him or anyone for that matter. I can't move on that easily from Chad no matter how much I may want to."

She lets out a sigh. "I know, babe, I'm teasing. You and Chad were together for a long time. Just because that ass wipe found it easy to move on, doesn't mean you will find it easy. Even though I do think getting under someone else will help you get over him."

"You may be right, but I have to work this out myself." Starting over is scary and daunting and overwhelming.

"Okay, I get it. I'll stop pressuring you to move on, but you better be wearing something sexy tonight, even if it's just for you," Lettie states.

"I'm wearing a little black dress."

"Show me. Turn on FaceTime," she demands.

Fiddling with my phone, I turn it on and show her what I'm wearing.

"Are you going to a funeral?" Lettie shrieks.

"I thought this was cute," I say, running my hand down the silky fabric.

"It's not. I'll call you back," Lettie says curtly before hanging up on me.

What the hell?

Moments later, my cell rings, and it's her again.

"A dress is on its way. It should be there in fifteen. You'll thank me later. I've got to run. Have fun tonight. Bye." And with those few words, she's gone.

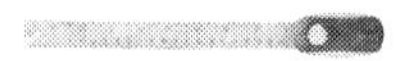

Stepping out of the chauffeur-driven car is hard in the tight-fitting, low-cut, red mini dress Lettie sent over. It took her a solid twenty minutes to convince me to wear it. I'm so far out of my comfort zone it's not funny. Chad hated it when I dressed up in something he thought was inappropriate. If the hem was too short on a dress, he would ask me to go change it to something more appropriate. I can just imagine his face seeing me stepping out in public in this dress. He would have a heart attack. And that thought alone was the reason why I am wearing it tonight.

Lettie also suggested that I go through the front entrance instead of taking the back entrance to Sebastien's restaurant. That I should hold my head up high and get photographed looking hot and single. She reassured me that it would be great PR for me and would annoy the hell out of Chad which again is why I am doing this. Yes, I know I shouldn't worry about what my ex is doing, but it's human nature when you've been cheated on to make the other party realize what they are missing. I don't want Chad back at all, he's done his dash with me, but I want him to see that he hasn't broken me.

He thinks he has won with his new life, but he's forgotten that means I get to have a new life too. I'm rebuilding from the ashes, and that means I can be whoever I want to be. And tonight, I'm going in there and being someone else for the night.

"Quinn. Quinn." A paparazzo springs out from nowhere and thrusts a camera and microphone into my face. "What do you think about Chad dating Danika so quickly after your split?"

His lens zooms in, trying to capture as much emotion on my face as he can. If he gets a tear that will be a payday for him. I won't give him the satisfaction.

"I wish them well," I say, giving him my brightest smile and mustering all my inner strength.

Another paparazzo calls out and asks for me to pose. A couple give me compliments on my outfit.

"Any truth in that Chad and Danika were seeing each other before you and Chad officially split?" someone asks.

I still at the question and turn to the paparazzo, asking, "You do the math," before taking another step toward the entrance.

"Are you dating Sebastien Sanchez?" someone else asks.

"I'm here to taste his delicious food and to support a network colleague while I'm in LA. Have you tried it, yet?"

There are a couple of chuckles.

"You're dressed as if you're on a date?" another adds.

"Thought I would change things up," I say, giving them a wink.

"Guys, come on, will you stop harassing my customers," Sebastien says, coming out of nowhere and intervening.

The paparazzi continue to click away ignoring Sebastien.

He puts his arm around my shoulder and ushers me inside.

"You, okay?" Sebastien asks.

"Yeah, I had it. I didn't need you swooping in to save me," I tell him, shaking his hands off me.

His eyes flare at my comment, he wasn't expecting that. He seriously thought I was going to thank him. Now he's given the gossips fodder by coming out and rescuing me like a white knight. They are going to think something is going on.

"You were supposed to have arrived through the back entrance like we had planned," he states gruffly.

"Lettie thought it would be better if I was photographed walking in through the front entrance in this dress. Show them that I'm not in my bed crying over Chad Bailey."

His chocolate-colored eyes continue to narrow on me. “Is that why you wore that dress?” he asks, his eyes trailing over me.

I don’t like what he is implying, it’s exactly the way Chad would make me feel. The confidence I had moments ago vanishes as I begin to shrink in on myself. What the hell am I doing here? Dressed like someone I’m not. I’m such an idiot.

Sebastien’s face falls as he watches me intensely, his dark brows pulled together. “Are you okay?” he asks softly.

“No. I need to get out of here. This was a bad idea. I can’t believe how stupid I was to come here.”

“Quinn, it’s okay,” he says as he goes to reach out to me but lets his hand fall.

“Look at me. I’m dressed like a hooker. It’s embarrassing, me trying to pretend to be something more than I am.”

“Come with me,” he says, grabbing my hand and pulling me through the crowd of eager onlookers.

I’m a mess. Having a meltdown in front of his customers probably isn’t good for business. No wonder he’s taking me somewhere else, I’m ruining everyone else’s night.

He opens the door to the private dining room and shuts it again. I take in my surroundings as I gaze around the luxurious dining room. I love its sleek modern look with its timber-featured wall that merges with the ceiling on all four sides. The dining room table is marble, and the place settings are white with gold cutlery. It’s not my style. I would have gone for something a little less glitzy for a table setting. In the middle of the table, falling from the ceiling is a sculpture-like chandelier made of golden bronze glass.

I wonder if this is what he likes in interior design.

“Sit,” he commands, pulling out one of the leather chairs for me.

I do as he says and take a seat, caught off-guard by his tone.

He then walks over to the gold and glass bar cart and pours me a straight vodka before turning and handing it to me.

"Drink," he commands, shaking the crystal tumbler in his hand at me.

I take the glass from him, our fingers touch for a couple of moments, and tiny sparks of electricity run up my hand as if he's given me an electric shock.

He felt it too and quickly pulls his hand away from me before heading back to the bar cart and pouring himself a whiskey. He throws back a large gulp, and I watch fascinated by the way his Adam's apple bobs against his olive skin. My eyes travel further down his thick neck, over the triangle of skin exposed on his hard chest where the top couple of buttons on his shirt are open. Lettie has got into my head. I will not find this man attractive.

Sebastien notices me looking at him and arches a dark brow at me.

Flustered, I look away and throw back my shot of vodka, the burn of the alcohol filling the holes my anxiety has given me.

"What happened just then?" he asks.

"I wasn't checking you out," I stutter.

Sebastien stills. "That's not what I was asking but good to know."

Will the ground please swallow me up right now?

"Before I mean, when I asked about the dress. You went straight to looking like a hooker? Did someone tell you that? You know you don't look like one, don't you?"

Oh, that. Yeah, I'm not about to spill about my relationship trauma to him.

"Lettie is running late. I thought you should know," I say, changing the subject.

Sebastien frowns at my comment. "Okay, but …"

"But nothing. I'm not going to talk about it."

"Not going to talk about it full stop or not going to talk to me about it?" He questions.

"Just you."

Sebastien nods, and we both fall silent for a couple of moments.

"How long were you with Chad then?" he asks, breaking the tense standoff.

"Since college."

"Explains it," he says with a huff.

"What does that mean?"

"Why you're struggling to be single."

"Why is that bad?"

"Never said it was."

"Your tone implied that it was."

"You're being sensitive, Quinn," he says.

"Sensitive? You're the one implying something's wrong with me because it's been years since I've been single," I argue with him.

"Don't think those words came out of my mouth."

This man is so frustrating. "We're talking around in circles, this is ridiculous."

"It's not really. Tonight, you decided to break the mold that people expected of you. And that's commendable."

He's complimenting me now after insulting me. This man is confusing.

"And I'm sorry I made you feel that it was wrong."

He's sorry?

"I don't understand the sudden personality change?"

"I'm not an asshole, Quinn."

He could have fooled me as a frown forms across my forehead.

"Look, you and Chad had this cutesy, Insta-worthy relationship. You were marketed as wholesome, all-American goodness. The public ate it up."

"What's wrong with that? It was the truth," I argue.

"It's unsustainable."

"What do you mean? Our show ran for five years. That's

hardly unsustainable."

"The façade of being perfect is."

"Who said I was perfect?"

"You were portrayed as #couplegoals. Like I said … unsustainable."

Is this supposed to be an apology? This man is getting on my last nerve—judgmental ass.

"We weren't perfect or sustainable, were we?" The tears well in my eyes as I raise my voice at him. "Chad was messing around on me for months. He stole my entire life and gave it to his new girlfriend. We're talking about our entire savings, the show, my home, my horses even. He took it all from me because I was so in love with him that I never questioned his motives. Never thought that the man I loved, who I would be spending the rest of my life with, would ever do the things that he did to me."

Sebastien is silent. His long, thick black lashes blink a couple of times.

An errant tear falls down my cheek, but before I get a chance to wipe it away, Sebastien is there doing it for me. It seems rather intimate to do something like that.

"I didn't mean to upset you, Quinn," he says.

"What did you expect to happen as you continuously push my buttons? Are you happy now that you have the entire sordid truth?" I ask him.

"Why would I be happy about that?"

"Because my life is a mess."

"I get it. I've been there before."

"You have?"

"You didn't Google me?" he asks, seemingly shocked that I haven't looked up his entire history.

"Wasn't that interested," I say, biting back.

Which pulls a smirk from Sebastien. "That would be a first," he says cockily.

I roll my eyes at him.

"I get it. I've been through it before, years ago. It's why I'm here in America, I needed to get away from my past. Even though we had broken up years before it still followed me around. It's why I have a wall up around me or as you like to say, I act like a dick," he explains.

"You act like that on purpose?"

He nods giving me a chuckle.

"Why?"

"To protect myself. No matter what Chad does or says, you can rise above it. The media loves nothing more than to rejoice in the drama."

"It's hard," I say softly, hating being vulnerable in front of this man.

"I know. But that's why you've got to wear the red dress and give Chad Bailey the finger."

I'm taken aback by his words. They are too nice.

"I'm going to let the kitchen know it's only the two of us for the moment. Don't know about you but I'm starved," he says, getting up and disappearing.

I let out an unsteady breath. This man has taken me on a rollercoaster this evening. One minute we are fighting and the next he's being nice. Hope it's not going to be like this all the time as I'm not sure how to take it.

Moments later, he returns to the room.

"Appetizers will be served in a moment," he tells me with a blinding smile showing off the dark, tanned features of his handsome face.

Why is he so good looking and why do I keep noticing it? Lettie, I hate whatever voodoo you have done to me.

"Would you like another drink?" he asks.

I nod and watch him head over to the bar cart.

"I've been admiring the design of your private dining room," I say, filling in the silence. "It's sleek and minimalist. Is that your preferred style?"

Sebastien shrugs as he pours us both a drink. "The network paid someone to design it. They were the best, and I had to trust their judgment."

"I'm surprised you would put such faith in someone like that. Aren't chefs known to be control freaks?"

He quirks a surprised brow at me as he picks up the crystal tumblers from the cart. "How many chefs do you know?"

"What does that have to do with anything?" I ask him.

"I'm trying to work out how you got to the notion that all chefs are control freaks." Those dark and stormy eyes flare at me as he stalks over to where I'm sitting.

"I, um …" His intense stare makes me flustered, and I can feel my cheeks burning with embarrassment.

He leans forward, handing me my glass of vodka. "The only places I want complete and utter control in are the kitchen and the bedroom," he says as his eyes dip down for the first time taking in my ample cleavage before slowly coming back up to my face. "Everything else … I will leave to the professionals." He doesn't break eye contact with me as he takes a sip of his whiskey.

Dick.

I lean forward, copying his actions, giving him a good look at my well-endowed cleavage. I watch his eyes dip again. Mr. Hotshot Chef, you're not as indifferent about me as you want me to believe.

"We are remarkably similar, then. I'm used to being in control of men in and out of the bedroom."

His lips quirk into a small smile, liking this new game we are playing. "One of us is going to have to convince the other to give up control if we work together, then." His accent swirls around the words adding a seductive layer to them. Those chocolatey eyes turn molten liquid as they take another glance over my cleavage.

"I'd like to see you try."

Oh, wow, Quinn. What on earth do you think you are doing? Am I flirting? Feels like I am, but I don't want anything to happen. So is that considered flirting?

"Game on, blondie," he says, giving me a dirty smirk that makes my body buzz with excitement … or that could be all the vodka I'm drinking. I'm going to blame it on the vodka.

Thankfully, we are rescued before I embarrass myself any further by two gorgeous waitresses who have brought in a couple of trays. They are covered, so I'm not sure what's underneath. They place them in the middle of the table and leave us to it.

"Have you had Spanish tapas before?" Sebastien asks.

I shake my head, indicating I haven't.

"Do you trust me?"

"Not really," I answer honestly.

He lets out a deep, timbered laugh. "Okay, I earned that. I want you to close your eyes while I feed you."

"Is this some kind of kink? Asking an unsuspecting young woman to open wide before stuffing your salami in her mouth?"

He gives me a what-the- fuck-are-you-on-about look. "I can assure you I don't think there's any salami on this plate."

"Salami is a euphemism for your dick."

Sebastien chokes on his breath at my comment. "Yes, I got that, Quinn." He chuckles. "I can promise you there are only pure intentions here. It's all about the food, nothing more."

I eye him suspiciously.

"Let me put your mind at rest … you're not my type."

Wow. Okay. Not that I am interested in him either.

I place my hand on the table as I push myself up from my extremely uncomfortable chair.

This was a mistake.

All of it.

I can't do this.

I can't do any of this.

I feel my throat closing as panic creeps over my skin.

"I've lost my appetite."

"Quinn?" He seems surprised by my reaction.

Shaking my head, I state, "This was a mistake." I try to turn on my heel to leave the room, but he reaches out and grabs my arm.

"I'm sorry if I offended you with my comment." His brows are pinched together.

"I don't give a crap if you are into me or not. You are the first man I've been alone with since …" throwing up my hands high in the air, "… college, other than Chad." I cringe as I say it out loud. "I don't know what I'm doing anymore.

"My entire life has been turned upside down. I feel like some kind of baby bird who's recently been kicked out of the nest, and I don't know what the hell this weird world is that I've been thrust into. I'm lost. Confused. Like the ground has fallen away, and I'm free-falling. Everyone tells me … screw him, you deserve better. You dodged a bullet, girl. And I know all this, but I can't stop my heart from wanting him."

Tears are falling down my cheeks.

"And now I'm having a breakdown in front of *you*, again."

Sebastien doesn't say a thing.

"You already think I'm some naïve country bumpkin. A stupid little girl, who probably deserved to have all her money taken from her because she trusted someone she loved *not* to fuck her over. You look down on me as some unsophisticated, pitiful girl, and maybe I am. Maybe I am that pathetic to try to flirt with Mr. Hotshot Chef himself … the sophisticated, worldly Sebastien Sanchez, just to make myself feel better. I'll blame it on the vodka for my misjudgment."

His face says it all—I'm a loser.

"Goodnight, Sebastien. Lettie will be here soon. You can have some sophisticated adult conversation, then." With that, I turn on my heel and walk out of his restaurant.

7

SEBASTIEN

"Hey, sorry I'm late, work stuff. How did it go tonight? Did you two hit it off? Where's Quinn?" Lettie asks, arriving hours later at the restaurant, just before closing.

What is she talking about? She isn't here. "Quinn left hours ago."

Lettie's brows pull together. "What do you mean she isn't here?"

"That girl is not ready to do the show. I think you need to rethink the two of us working together. She is not coping with the breakup," I tell her honestly.

"She was fine just before she arrived. She even seemed excited. What the hell did you do?" Lettie asks, raising her voice at me.

"Nothing."

"You have a reputation, Mr. Sanchez," Lettie says darkly.

"I would never touch her without her consent. What the hell, Lettie?"

"Then why the hell isn't she here? I thought I would give you guys some alone time to work out your shit without me there."

"We got talking about Chad and …" I'm not about to tell her we were flirting. I didn't realize my trying to reassure her that I wasn't going to take advantage of her with her eyes closed would trigger her. Thought we had turned the corner and we could joke with each other. I misjudged that. Obviously, her ex did a number on her, but from what I've read in the papers, and I of all people, should know that's not the truth. I thought they were all okay. That it was amicable. Also, I got a kick out of the bickering between us. Most women don't bite back like Quinn does, most find my company charming. And I can't deny that arguing with her and pushing her buttons lit a spark in me that had been dimmed for a while. But just because I found it fun didn't mean Quinn did, and I think I pushed her too far. And I do feel bad about that.

"Fuck," Lettie curses. "Where the hell could she be? I know she isn't at home otherwise I would have got a notification on my phone."

"I'm sorry, I didn't realize her breakup was that bad."

"Not your fault. I thought that maybe once you got out of the office the two of you would hit it off. I was wrong. It doesn't matter, I need to find her. She's not made for these wild, LA streets," Lettie states.

And I can see on her face how worried she is about Quinn. The normally put-together, in-control woman is now freaking out.

"You need to make this right. Because I'm going to be honest here … Quinn is your only chance of getting back to Spain. I've pitched the idea of the two of you working together to the higher-ups. They love it. They have given me carte blanche to give the two of you everything you want or need for this to work successfully. If not, they want season two of Hotshot Chef from you, like tomorrow," Lettie says, laying it all out for me.

"And what about Quinn?"

Lettie lets out a heavy sigh. "From what I've heard … they

might force her and Chad to work together. They don't know what else to put her in."

Shit. We're both screwed.

"Text me her number. I know some people who can help find her."

"You do? Thank you, that would be brilliant."

My phone dings a few seconds later, and it's Quinn's number.

"Okay, fingers crossed we find her." And with that, she's gone.

I try Quinn's number, and it goes to her voicemail. I forward her number to an old friend Jackson Connolly, who owns a security company. I met him through the Dirty Texas gang. He's done work for their record label, and his brother is the drummer in the band, Finn Connolly. Not five minutes later, he's found her. I grab my keys and step out the door.

I head on down to Santa Monica where her location is flashing. I find a park near the beach but can't see her anywhere.

Shit. This is not the place to be hanging out alone after dark. I follow the little flashing sign, and it says she's on the beach, but I can't see her.

"Quinn," I call out into the darkness. "Quinn, are you out there?"

Nothing but silence greets me. She has to be around here unless someone has stolen her bag and thrown it somewhere.

"Quinn," I call out again and again.

"Over here." I hear a faint voice.

My eyes try and adjust to the darkness. "Quinn?" I call out again.

"Here." I see movement with the help of the moonlight.

Oh, thank God, she's okay.

My feet move quickly through the sand until I collapse on my knees in front of her. She looks up at me with those damn doe eyes, all innocent, and shit it melts my jaded heart, or maybe it's the relief that now I've found her my ass is saved.

"Well, thank fuck. Lettie is worried sick about you," I tell her.

"My battery died. I'm lost, and I …" She sniffles her unshed tears. "I wanted to come to the beach to clear my head."

"Let me text Lettie and let her know you're okay."

"No." Quinn reaches out and grabs my arm.

"Quinn, I have to. She's worried sick."

Her hand falls away. "I know." She runs her finger through the sand making squiggly lines. "I just need some alone time to think."

"I'll text her to let her know you're safe and I'll bring you home when you are ready. How does that sound?"

She nods in agreement.

I type out a message to Lettie, letting her know Quinn's safe but needs a moment, that I've got her and will bring her home safely.

"Thanks for that." Quinn lays back in the sand and looks up at the sky. "I miss the stars," she mumbles into the darkness. A small shiver cascades over her as the cool night air hits her exposed skin.

"You're cold."

"Yeah, I know." But she doesn't move.

This girl is maddening. I lay down and pull her into me. She snuggles into my warmth.

"That better?" I ask. I can feel her cold skin through my thin shirt.

"Yeah, but don't think this means anything," she warns me.

I let out a defeated sigh. "Do you want to talk about what happened tonight?" I ask as I stare up into the inky dark sky. I miss the endless kaleidoscope of stars I can see back home in Spain, unlike LA, where there's so much light pollution.

"I guess I owe you an apology," she mumbles into my chest.

"No. Not really," I tell her because, in all honesty, she doesn't.

"Wasn't very professional of me."

"I wasn't very professional either," I confess.

She turns and looks up at me, a little surprised at my admission.

"I took my frustration over my contract with the network out on you." She's in the same predicament as me, if not actually worse.

"Thank you for saying that," she almost whispers as I absent-mindedly run my hand down her arm, which makes her shiver. "And I want to apologize for being on the hot-mess express." She chuckles.

"You've had your entire life taken away from you, and I should have been understanding," I say as my fingers run along her skin taking in the softness as I touch her.

"I don't know who I am anymore without Chad and the show," she confesses, which is understandable. Everything she owned—work and personal—was wrapped up together in a nice big bow.

"What do you want to do?" I ask.

"I'm not sure. That's why I thought I'd come to the beach. Perhaps the crisp night air would help me decide." She lets out a heavy sigh. "What do you want?" Quinn throws the question back to me.

"I want to go home to Spain. I miss my family and friends. I miss my old life. I thought running away to America would help me start afresh, but I feel like it has turned me into someone I don't know anymore."

"I think that's exactly what has happened to Chad. The bright lights. Beautiful women. The money. It has turned him into someone I don't even know. Someone I don't *want* to know. He was always about wanting more, whereas I was happy with what I had. I loved my job, and I loved the show. I didn't need to be world-famous. I didn't need to go to the Hollywood parties, but he did. I guess I could see it happening, but, in the end, I didn't want to recognize it." Her hand absently moves over my stomach sending tiny sparks of electricity to my dick.

No. Now is not the time. Think of peanut butter and jelly sandwiches to deflate any movement you might have down south.

"Greed can do crazy things to people."

Quinn nods in agreement. "Do you think we can work together?"

I pause. "I'm not sure," I answer honestly.

She nods. "Yeah, I'm not sure either."

We lay there in silence, both of us contemplating our future. The reality is if we both want out of our old life then we are going to have to work together.

"So, tell me about this vineyard you've bought in Spain," Quinn asks as her hand slowly moves over my abs. Is she trying to kill me?

Think about the vineyard, not how nice it is that her hands are on you. She must be drunk if she doesn't mind touching me like she is.

Focus, Sebastien.

"I purchased it from the internet sight unseen, from an elderly couple who wanted to retire. They have a little boutique winery selling Cava, which is Spanish champagne. There are a couple of rundown buildings on the land, but it's nestled atop a mountain. The view stretches over the vines as far as the eye can see. It's where the green of the vines meets the blue of the sky."

"Sounds magical." Her voice is soft, angelic.

"It is. I want to create a cellar door with a rustic, fine-dining restaurant. Maybe some boutique accommodations, too."

"Love it." She sighs, curling in closer to me. "You sound so happy when you talk about it."

"I do?" I'm surprised by her assessment.

"Yeah. I can see it … rustic stone buildings, maybe the walls are a little whitewashed. Inside … neutral, earthy tones. Nothing too over the top because you don't want to take away from the view. Woods. Linens. Leather even. Masculine and refined. Just like its owner."

Quinn looks up at me as I look down at her in amazement that she got what I was thinking just from my explanation. The cool sea breeze swirls around us, and with it, my hand slips from her arm and cups her ass, which brings her leg up over mine. Reaching down, I push away her blonde hair that the wind seems to have picked up and covered her face. Her tongue slides along her pouty lips. *Does she want me to kiss her?*

"I think we should do the show together," I tell her, and not because we had a moment or that I feel sorry for her, but because I feel like she gets the project.

"You do." Her eyebrows rise in surprise.

"Yeah, I think it might be good for us." Running my fingers down over her cheek, I watch as her eyes flutter shut at the action.

"Good, as in … we don't really have a choice," she says, giving me a small grin.

"Yeah. There's that, too," I agree.

"Might be fun." She moves and places her chin on my chest. "The only thing is ..." my brows pinch together at the but in her comment, "… we have to be professional. Like what we're doing now, that's not a good idea."

"We aren't doing anything?"

Her hand slips down and runs over my dick. What the hell? The action makes me jump.

"That seems like something," she says, arching a brow at me.

"I'm a male. You were rubbing yourself on me, it's human nature," I argue.

Next thing I know, she rolls over and is straddling me. "What now? Is it still hard because of human nature?"

Where the hell did this sex kitten come from. This was not at all what I was expecting from her. My hands come up and grab her G-string-clad ass, and my fingers sink into her smooth skin.

"I could ask you the same thing. How wet you are?" I ask, looking up at her as she grinds against my dick.

"Guess you're never going to know because I'm not your type," she says, rolling off me and getting up.

Fuck.

She shakes the sand from her body, and I watch in fascination the way her breasts jiggle.

Quinn Miller is a bombshell.

And I need to forget how she feels wrapped around me.

She is a complication I don't need in my life right now.

8

QUINN

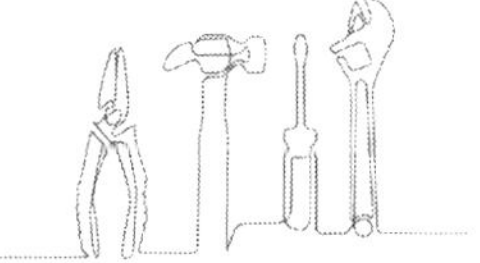

Tonight's the night of the network's fall show lineup, and the first time I'll see Chad since we split.

I'm a mess.

Over the past month, Sebastien and I finalized our show with the network and signed the contracts, both of us ensuring we have read every detail ten times and run it by our lawyers this time before signing. Once bitten, twice shy, and all that.

After that night at Sebastien's restaurant, the media were in a frenzy over the two of us hanging out, and they haven't stopped trying to catch us since. Thinking they can get an exclusive of the two of us together.

There is no us.

Contrary to the headlines being splashed across the gossip blogs like -

---

Quinn Miller Takes a Walk on the Wild Side.

Quinn Miller Not as Innocent as We Think.

Quinn Miller transforms from wholesome to ho-some.

And so on.

I have to laugh at the ridiculous stories they had concocted about the two of us, otherwise I'll cry. Lettie is frothing at the mouth over the coverage, and about how desperate people are to see Sebastien and me together. Since that night on the beach, I've only seen Sebastien a handful of times, and that is usually in a meeting with the network execs.

It's for the best. I remember the way he felt between my thighs. I guess what they say is true, he does have a big ego. I didn't tell Lettie about what happened on the beach that night after he dropped me home. Honestly, I want to forget it even happened because I can't believe I jumped him like a bitch in heat. He probably thinks I'm desperate or losing my mind from the hot and cold behavior I've been showing him. I'm not normally like this, and I hate that this breakup has changed how I am and turned me into someone that is overly emotional, that the mere mention of Chad's name triggers me, and I hate the self-doubt that has crept into my life. I don't want to be this woman I've become.

I'm really trying to let things go when it comes to Chad. Ignoring all his bullshit and letting him live whatever life he chooses because I want no part of it anymore. He was right when he said we are on two different paths. The funny thing was Chad called me the next day after he saw the photos of me online arriving at Sebastien's restaurant. Stupidly I picked up, it caught me off-guard and I didn't think, just answered. He had the audacity to give me an ear full for falling for the advances of a known womanizer like Sebastien Sanchez. He couldn't believe I would do this to him. Embarrass him like that. Parade around town like a harlot. How dare he. Chad has no say in who or what I do. To be fair, in the middle of his rant I burst out laughing, it was comical the things he was saying to me, and honestly, I can't believe I used to put up with it. It was satisfying telling him to get lost and then blocking him and Danika on all socials.

In retaliation for that phone call and media attention, he got engaged to Danika. Not going to lie, that stung. Eight years of dating and he never proposed. The kicker to the announcement was they got engaged in Mexico where they first met. That was the caption. I knew it. He met her on his boys' trip because that's when everything changed between us.

Lettie and I got drunk and may have thrown darts at a printout of their engagement notice from online. Petty and childish but oh so cathartic. The more things Chad does the more I see through his bullshit. He's left Lettie unblocked on his socials. She hasn't blocked him either so she can keep an eye on whatever bullshit he is sprouting in case it involves me. She told me the other day he scrubbed all traces of me from his socials. Eight years of memories wiped out. And he's uploaded an obscene number of photos of him and Danika.

I decided to rise above his pettiness and not delete images of him from my accounts. But I've made sure I post a lot more of my new life here in LA with Lettie, showing off how I'm living my best life.

"You look like a goddess," Lettie says, grinning at her handiwork.

I've spent the afternoon being prodded, poked, and buffed to within an inch of my life for tonight's event. Lettie suggested that I need to one hundred percent break the mold of my old life, no more All-American country girl. That tonight's event is where I step out as the new me, the new Quinn Miller.

She started off by cutting all my hair off. I had long blonde hair all the way down my back almost to the base of my spine. It's now shoulder length, in a choppy bob. I donated my hair to a company that makes wigs for cancer patients which made me feel better about the drastic length change.

Lettie hired a stylist for the show and my personal life, but I think that's a little much. The stylist dropped off some designer dresses for me for tonight to try. Each one worth a staggering amount of money. Lettie wanted to '*spice up my image*' but I put my foot down. I told her that it's cliché for someone like me to go from flannel to sexy overnight and I was worried that people would think I'm desperate since breaking up with Chad. I tried it Lettie's way once for dinner at Sebastien's and that didn't go so well.

"I love it," I say, twirling around in the most gorgeous evening dress I've ever seen, let alone worn. It's a black, long-sleeved sheer evening dress with beading all over, but the heavy beading ends just under my ass, and the rest is sheer beads to the floor. It covers all the right bits and shows some skin without being too exposing. It makes me feel all woman and sexy. My new shorter hair is pinned to one side, and I've been given the most gorgeous black diamonds to wear with the dress.

"Chad is going to choke on his coconut water when he sees you." Lettie grins.

I give her a look that tells her, *'I don't give a shit what Chad thinks,'* and *'that this is for me and no one else.'*

"You can still not give a shit and be petty at the same time," Lettie adds before turning on her heel and heading toward the car waiting outside for us.

Finally fighting through Friday night traffic, we arrive at the red carpet and wait for our turn in the line.

"It's going to be okay. Just take a deep breath," Lettie reassures me. "Show them the new Quinn Miller."

I can do this.

I *can* do this.

I try and pep myself up while we slowly move up in the traffic jam. Eventually, we make it to the front of the line, the door to the car opens, and a handsome usher holds out a hand for me to take to exit the vehicle.

Light flashes practically blind me.

The first things I hear are the screams of my name from the media.

I used to hate walking the red carpet, but Chad always held my hand and gave me the strength to strut with him. Shaking that thought from my mind, I straighten and take the first tentative steps on the carpet as a single woman. I stand in front of the large logoed network sign, pose, and do my thing, all while the photographers scream questions at me.

Blank it out.

Blank it *all* out.

"Sebastien," I hear Lettie call out. "Go … join Quinn," she says, pushing him toward me.

This is going to make everyone go crazy. He looks amazing, dressed in a black suit that fits to perfection with a black dress shirt underneath, leaving a couple of buttons undone, showing off tanned skin. He hasn't shaved, so there's a light five o'clock shadow across his chiseled jaw.

Sebastien turns and stops for a moment. Those molten chocolate eyes run up and down my body as if he's drinking me in. A small smirk falls across his plump lips, then he joins me in front of the photographers who go wild noticing him step up beside me. He places a large hand on my hip, pulling me into his side. Taking in a deep breath, I savor his cologne, all woodsy and male. *Damn, he smells good.*

The media screams questions about whether or not we are dating. We ignore all the questions.

"You look phenomenal," Sebastien whispers into my ear, his

lips touching my heated skin, sending prickling heat all over my body.

"You don't scrub up so bad yourself."

"How are you feeling?" he asks.

"Like I'm going to hurl."

He chuckles. "Don't think it would go well with your gorgeous dress," he jokes, trying to put me at ease. Then without notice, he takes my hand and walks me off the red carpet to the screams of questions from the media. He doesn't let go of my hand until we step inside.

"You both did so well," Lettie tells me as she joins us inside.

"Here." Sebastien grabs a couple of glasses of champagne from the waiter and hands one to Lettie and the other to me. "You're going to need it."

I take a sip of the bubbly liquid hoping the alcohol will ease the twisted knot in my stomach.

"You two looked so good on the red carpet together. They are all going to die when they hear the news about the two of you working together," Lettie says.

The network wanted the news of our show to be a surprise at tonight's event, and everyone had to sign NDAs to not tell anyone about what we have planned together. What happens if people hate it? What if people hate me as Sebastien's co-host?

"You both have done such great work drumming up interest in the two of you. This show is going to be a blockbuster," Lettie says excitedly.

"Only going to be one season," Sebastien warns.

"Yeah, yeah," Lettie says, waving her hand in his direction. "Oh, hang on, I'll be back. Just saw someone I need to talk to," Lettie tells us before disappearing into the crowd.

"I don't want this show to be a blockbuster," Sebastien confesses.

"Don't you want to be proud of it?"

"I want my life back. I don't want there to be a second season," he tells me as he throws back the rest of his champagne.

I nod in understanding.

"I also don't want to create a crap show," he adds, grabbing another glass of champagne from the waiter.

I reach out and lay my hand on his arm. "It won't be crap, but we will make sure it's not a blockbuster either."

Sebastien gives me a wide smile. "Thanks."

We stand in silence in the corner away from everyone. Neither one of us wanting to mingle with the other people but also not engaging in small talk between us either, but it's not awkward.

"I know I've said it before, but you do look gorgeous tonight," Sebastien says, breaking the silence.

I give him a smile as that was a nice thing to say.

"Has you-know-who arrived?" he asks, looking around the crowded room.

"I'm sure he will try and be the last person to arrive, so all eyes are on him," I explain, taking a sip of my champagne. I used to hate that. "I can't wait for this whole night to be over."

"You not excited about getting one over your ex?" he asks.

"Not really. I know announcing our show together is going to one-up his, but I don't want to deal with the nastiness that he's going to send my way when he finds out."

"What can he do?" Sebastien asks.

"Plenty," I say, finishing my glass and grabbing another.

"If you want, stick close to me tonight. I can help steer you away from any *uncomfortable* conversations," he adds.

He surprises me with his words and kindness. The glass of champagne must be going to my head because I can't seem to take my eyes off him as he surveys the crowded room.

Why is he so hot?

What the hell is happening to me? Pull it back, Quinn. Abort whatever crazy thoughts are going through your mind. You've been living with Lettie for way too long, and you need to get laid. And not laid by your co-host. I need to find someone else for some no-strings-attached fun. Chad cannot be the only person I've slept with, that's sad. There are plenty of available men at this event. *No. That's too close.* I need to find someone further afield.

"Thanks. Lettie promised me she would be my right-hand woman tonight but—"

"I've got you," Sebastien leans in and whispers.

The warmth of his breath along my skin sends it into flames. I need to stop drinking champagne before I do something I'll be ashamed of.

We spend the next hour milling around talking with guests and executives. Sebastien had to fight off numerous advances from women, which honestly, has been funny to watch him squirm as they practically shove their over-inflated chests into his eye line.

"Hey, we are going to be announcing the lineup soon. Head on over and stand next to the stage. I'll let you know when it's go-time. You've got this," Lettie tells me before disappearing into the sea of people again.

"Come on, like she said, we've got this." Sebastien smiles, helping me navigate through the crowd toward the stage.

We stand off to the side and wait for Lettie to come back and give us further instructions. The announcer begins calling out the fall lineup of shows, and each one goes up on stage, introduces themselves, and then sits down.

"Next, we would like to welcome to the fall lineup, the revamped *Farmhouse Reno* team and their new show, *Chad Bailey's Farmhouse Life*," the MC announces through the speaker.

Here is the moment.

The moment I've been dreading all night.

I feel Sebastien behind me. His hand reaches down and laces

his fingers with mine, silently giving me the strength to get through this traumatic time. The crowd cheers wildly as Chad and Danika walk onto the stage. She looks gorgeous in a white evening dress showing off her insane body, her silky, brunette hair pulled up into a high ponytail, and her skin is a perfect sun-kissed tan color. Then there's Chad showing off his megawatt smile to the crowd. He's dressed in a navy suit, a tighter cut than he'd normally go for, and he's lost his trademark cowboy boots. He's shaved and looks more city banker than a ranching reno king.

"Thanks, y'all, so much for that warm welcome. Danika and I are looking forward to letting you into our dream life," he says, looking over at Danika with a bright white smile, which is forced as if he's proving to the world, he's this stand-up guy. Danika is looking up at him as if he is the second coming.

I want to puke.

The announcer explains how their season will be about planning a wedding at a ranch while running a farm and building their dream home.

Sebastien's hand tightens in mine as we listen to them go *on and on* about how excited the network is for the launch of this new show. Thank goodness Sebastien is here beside me giving me strength because there's no way in hell I would have been able to listen to this bullshit by myself.

Half an hour later, it's our turn.

Lettie comes onto the stage, and everyone claps and hollers for her.

"I'm so excited for the fall lineup of shows, it's going to be a huge year for the network. But I have one more show to announce."

The crowd gasps and looks around excitedly.

"We are incredibly excited about this collaboration between the network's two favorite stars, and I think it is going to be a ratings goldmine. And one I don't think anyone saw coming,"

Lettie says, building up the suspense. "Please welcome to the stage, Sebastien Sanchez and Quinn Miller, in the new series *Under the Spanish Sun*."

The crowd goes wild as Sebastien takes my hand again, and we navigate our way onto the stage. He helps me up the stage stairs to join Lettie. He doesn't let go of my hand the entire time.

"Now it's a sad day that there won't be a second season of Hotshot Chef or a sixth season of Farmhouse Reno. But we will dive into something completely different when we follow Sebastien and Quinn on their new Mediterranean adventure in Spain. The series will be a mixture of Sebastien cooking and sampling Spanish food while Quinn helps him renovate his new vineyard and farmhouse. Sebastien will also get to show Quinn around his home country together. We are excited for this incredible mix of travel, food, and design. All while under the Spanish sun," Lettie explains.

The entire room erupts in applause, they are going wild for it.

Lettie then pushes Sebastien and me to the front to say a few words. I look out into the sea of unfamiliar faces, my legs begin to shake, and my throat is now parched. Then I feel Sebastien's hand squeeze mine again, and somehow, he's anchoring me.

We step up to the microphone together, neither one of us letting go of the other.

Sebastien starts with a chuckle. "What an introduction, Lettie. She's a hard act to follow." The crowd chuckles eating up his words. "I can't thank the network enough for allowing me to show my home to you all. But I can't thank Quinn enough for wanting to come on this journey with me. It's a huge ask to pack up your life and move halfway across the world so thank you for putting your trust in me, Quinn. I've got you," he says as he looks down at me with those molten brown eyes, giving me a wide smile. "We met for the first time not that long ago, and it already feels like I've known her a lifetime. I can't wait to see what we make together."

The crowd goes crazy, and I can't help but let myself smile at the lovely bullshit story he is weaving to the crowd as it's my turn to speak.

"I am so looking forward to this once-in-a-lifetime experience. I've always dreamed about traveling through Europe, but it was never the right time, until now. I can't wait to get out of my comfort zone, learn new things, and experience everything Spain has to offer."

"And who knows what might happen, Under the Spanish Sun," Sebastien adds with a wink before he pulls me into his side.

The crowd goes crazy at that action.

I'm going to kill him. I enjoy the moment until I look out into the crowd and catch Chad standing in the corner glaring, his arms crossed over his chest. His blue eyes look hard and are focused directly on me. Screw you, Chad.

Lettie ushers us to the back of the stage where she squeals excitedly. "Did you hear how crazy they were for you both? They're practically salivating when you added that little bit of flirtation at the end, Sebastien. Mama, proud. You have the entire network eating out of your hands. Keep up that sexual tension, and you will have ratings gold."

"We were messing around, it's not real," I remind my friend because I can see it in her eyes, she loves the supposed flirtation between us.

Lettie shakes her head as if she doesn't believe me. "Well, whatever it is, keep it up. The execs want more of that between you two." She gives us an exaggerated wink as if she's in on our little secret.

Then, she's gone again.

"Well, that didn't work out the way we thought, did it?" I spin around to Sebastien.

"We did our job," he says as he takes a sip of his fresh glass of champagne that he was given.

This is true. We fed off each other's energy up there and killed it.

"As long as they don't get the wrong idea. I'm all for what we did up there, but if we give the network too much you know they are going to push a different agenda onto us," I explain.

"Simmer the heat between us, got it," Sebastien states. "As long as you and I understand where we stand, then it doesn't matter what everyone else thinks now, does it?"

That sounds incredibly logical. Maybe he's right. And maybe I'm overthinking things again.

"Or is it because you saw the way Chad reacted?" Sebastien asks, raising a brow at me.

"What, no." My voice rises as I answer too quickly.

Sebastien doesn't look convinced.

"I couldn't care less about him."

Sebastien's eyes narrow on me.

"I mean it," I continue, trying to convince him. "It was weird seeing him up there with her, though. Not going to lie about that. It hurts, but I'll be all right," I say, giving him my biggest smile.

"Who are you trying to convince, blondie? Me or yourself?" Sebastien asks.

"I want my own life. But I also don't want my success to be because of a man," I confess.

"I get that. You were part of a power couple, and now people are pushing you into another one."

"Are you saying we could be a power couple?" I ask, raising my brow at him.

This makes him laugh. "They lapped up that little performance on stage earlier. We could be *the* power couple of the network if we wanted to be."

"Lucky we don't want to be, hey." My eyes narrow on him, but he just grins. "I need the restroom. All these nerves and champagne are playing havoc with my bladder."

Sebastien shakes his head at my TMI as he takes my hand again and ushers me toward the bathrooms.

"I'll be just out here," he tells me.

"You don't have to wait for me."

"Got nothing else to do," he says with a shrug.

I head into the bathroom, do my business, and then head toward the mirrors to check my makeup is still on. When I look up into the mirror as I'm washing my hands, I realize I don't recognize the image staring back at me. Flushed rosy cheeks, her back is a little straighter, and she has a wide smile on her face.

I've got this.

I leave the restroom area and step back out into the crowded ballroom, but notice Sebastien isn't there. *You did say he didn't have to wait.* True, but I'm slightly disappointed that he's not waiting for me. Which is silly.

"Like the hair."

That voice.

My stomach sinks upon hearing it.

Slowly, I turn around and see a smirking Chad. I thought being this close to him would be hard, that the love I once had for him would overwhelm me. And yet it doesn't. The last emotion I thought I would feel at this moment was nothing.

Not a thing!

I'm staring at someone I shared a large chunk of my adult life with, and it feels like I'm looking at a stranger.

"Thanks. Had to cut the dead weight," I add.

"It suits you."

Guess my comment went right over his head, typical.

"And that dress." He gives a low whistle as he takes me in.

Ew. I screw up my nose.

"Not something I ever thought I'd see you in. It's …" His

blue eyes run over my body hungrily, but all it does is make my stomach turn.

"It's what?" I wait for him to tell me how overdressed I look or that I'm trying too hard, some of the many comments he used to give me while we were together.

"Sexy." His eyes meet mine.

No.

Absolutely not!

He doesn't get to look at me like that and especially not after he destroyed my life.

"Which isn't really you, is it?"

Ah, and there it is.

The comment that in the past would have crippled my confidence, but I'm not his, and his words do not get to hurt me anymore.

"Or maybe you never really knew me," I say, standing straighter.

Chad bursts out laughing, which crumbles my newfound confidence.

"Or maybe you're trying too hard to be something you're not. It's obvious you need a man to keep you in line."

His words are like salt poured into an already open wound.

He's stunned me silent.

My throat closes over as I try not to give him the satisfaction of knowing he's just broken me.

Again.

9

SEBASTIEN

I watch Quinn walk out of the bathroom looking happy and confident, something that I've noticed has slowly started to appear each time we had a meeting at the network. Bit by bit she found her voice until tonight when she stood there in front of everyone and her dick of an ex and worked the crowd. I also wasn't expecting her to look like a fricken bombshell tonight. The girl is beautiful, I will not deny that, but she's moved from apple pie to spicy apple pie in that dress. It's sexy yet elegant in the same breath. Giving you glimpses of that insane body underneath. A body that was once pressed against mine and a body that I wouldn't mind having pressed against me again. But I've had to settle on holding her hand all night. I know she thinks it's because I was helping her get through a difficult night, but it's also so I have a reason to be able to touch her. I like being near here even though we bicker.

Her ex is a complete douche. Coming on stage with his new woman and rubbing Quinn's face in his infidelity was horrible to watch. I could tell that with every word he said about his new fiancée, it was a dagger to Quinn's heart. It was another reason I flirted with her on stage, to give the douche a taste of his own medicine. He thinks Quinn won't go out there and find someone better than him. Oh, she will, and when she does, he is going to realize what a mistake it was to let that woman go. I feel protective over her like she's a younger sister. *One you find hot.* I can find her hot but still think of her as a friend. *Friends, who flirt.* It's our job to create on-screen chemistry can't do that if you don't have it in real life. *I like to lie to myself.*

I knew once Chad saw the two of us flirt on stage, he would have to come over and find Quinn. He's been circling us all night since our show was announced. Like the coward I know he is, he's waited for her to be alone. He took the opportunity when I went to the bathroom to stalk her. Thankfully, women take a long time in there, and I was able to watch from the sidelines making sure this asshole didn't get out of line when he pounced on her as she exited the bathroom.

Not going to lie, I watched a couple of episodes of their show after meeting her. I wanted to see what she was about. She was the real brains behind their brand, and Chad just happened to look good on screen. You could see he hated it if Quinn was getting more airtime than him and he would come over and try and mansplain the design to her. She would smile and laugh at his dumb ass jokes because she was in love with him, you could see it, it radiated out from her. He was a dark cloud hiding Quinn's sunshine because he could see she was the *real star* of the show. He never appreciated what he had. If they didn't have the show, I'm not sure he would have stuck around. And I bet this wasn't the first time he ever cheated either.

The moment he whispers in Quinn's ear, she stills, and I move closer so I'm there if she needs me. Honestly, he has done Quinn the world's biggest favor by letting her go because, in the end, his true personality is going to shine through. You can only hide that shit for so long.

The longer he speaks to Quinn, the more I'm seconds away

from punching him in the face. I notice her shoulders deflate for every minute she spends with him.

Then I hear his words to her.

"Or maybe you're just trying too hard to be something you are not. It's obvious you need a man to keep you in line."

That fucker!

My legs are moving before my brain can catch up with what they're doing. Chad sees me barreling toward them, and he doesn't look happy.

"There you are," I say, reaching out for Quinn. I pull her hard against my chest as I look down into her doe-like eyes. "I've been looking for you."

"You have?" Quinn asks unsteadily.

"Yeah, I needed to give you something," I tell her as I cup her cheek with my hand. Then I give her one of my trademark smiles.

"You did?" she asks as her long lashes blink slowly as she stares up at me.

"Yeah, this." I pull her lips to mine. I know I said I wouldn't touch her, but I'm doing this for her not me. It was either kissing her or punching him, and I know which one I would rather do. I give her a slow kiss, putting on a show for Chad. His anger radiates behind us as I hear him huff.

Quinn seems surprised by my kiss that she hasn't kissed me back and I wonder if I've overstepped the mark with her. My thumb runs across her cheek, and that movement wakes her up, and then the next thing I know her fingers grab my suit as she pulls me in closer to her. As her mouth opens letting my tongue in, she kisses me back. She's all but forgotten about Chad as I feel the first swipe of her tongue against my own, she tastes like champagne and sunshine, and I want to drown in them both.

Then the next thing I know, she's putting distance between us.

What, no.

I need more.

I need …

A small smile falls across her swollen lips. "Thanks for that," she whispers, then taps my chest with her palm.

Spinning around to face Chad, he looks like he's seconds away from launching himself at me.

"I guess I've found a man who can keep me in line."

Chad's eyes narrow on Quinn. "Once the novelty has worn off, you will be just like all the other women before you. A notch on his well-worn belt."

I take a step toward him, but Quinn holds me back.

"And maybe, I don't care." She shrugs. "You don't have a say in my life anymore, *Chad*." She says his name with emphasis. "What or who I do is *none* of your business." She crosses her arms in front of herself as she stands up to the asshole.

"Good luck with your new show … you're going to need it. You'll soon realize you're nothing without me," he spits at us both.

"Maybe you're going to realize *I* don't give a shit," Quinn fires back.

And with that last barb, Chad turns on his heels and angrily stalks back into the crowd.

"Oh … my … god … I can't believe I just did that." Quinn jumps into my arms and squeals.

"I'm so proud of you, blondie," I say, twirling her around a couple of times before I place her back on the floor.

"Thank you. I couldn't have stood up to him if it weren't for you."

Shaking my head, I announce, "That was all you."

"Sorry for taking the kiss further than you would have wanted. I just …"

Now, it's me who's shaking my head as I reach out and run a thumb down her cheek. "You *never* have to apologize for kissing me. I didn't know how else to shut that fucker up."

She giggles at my words. "Well, it certainly did." She grins, now giddy with confidence.

"Did he always talk to you like that?"

Quinn's face falls at my question. "I thought it was because he was conservative, a traditional Southern boy, but now …" she looks up at me, "… I realize he was a controlling ass."

I let my thumb caress her cheek again. "You know you didn't deserve that. You can do whatever you want, and it's no one's choice but your own."

She nods slowly. "I'm understanding that more and more. Thank you."

"I didn't do a thing … this was all you." I lose myself in her doe eyes like I frequently do.

She pushes up on her tiptoes and places a kiss on my cheek. "You're a good man, Sebastien."

"You wouldn't be saying that if you could see the thoughts swirling around in my mind right now."

Quinn's eyes widen.

I shouldn't have said that out loud. *What the hell is wrong with me?*

"Like what?" she asks as her teeth sink into her bottom lip.

"Quinn," I warn.

"Tell me," she pushes.

"All I can think about is—"

"Am I interrupting something?" Lettie asks.

Both of us quickly break away from each other as if we've just been caught doing something we shouldn't be doing. What I shouldn't have been doing was nearly telling her how much I wanted to take her home and fuck her.

Lettie's dark brown eyes look between the two of us.

"Sebastien saved me from a horrid encounter with Chad," Quinn explains.

"Wait! What? Chad came over to you?" Lettie asks with

concern lacing her tone. Soon forgetting what she just saw between us.

"He's a dick. He said some shit to Quinn. I was going to step in, but she had it."

"We both had it," she adds.

"Wow! He's got some balls," Lettie mutters. "So, you ready to get out of here? My feet are killing me. I'm sick of smiling. I want to go home and get into my pajamas."

"Sounds good," Quinn agrees. "You going to be okay?"

"I'll be fine," I tell her. It's for the best anyway, things were starting to get out of control.

"Don't worry about him. I doubt he's going to be going home alone tonight." Lettie gives me an over exaggerated wink.

Quinn looks away.

I want to tell her that in all honesty, the only woman I want to take home tonight is her.

"Have fun, be safe," Lettie says, giving me a wave as she grabs Quinn's hand and pulls her from the party.

Quinn gives me a look over her shoulder before they disappear into the crowd.

10

QUINN

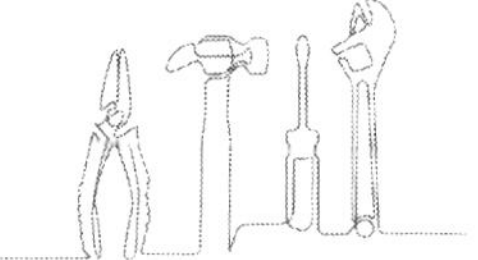

"I didn't interrupt anything between you and Sebastien tonight, did I?" Lettie asks as we get ready for bed.

"No. He was giving me a pep talk," I reply while grabbing a bottle of water from the fridge.

"It looked a little more intense than that," she pushes.

"Do you think Chad was emotionally controlling?"

Lettie is caught off-guard by my question. I can see in her eyes that she's confused.

"It was something he said that kind of triggered me. I'm starting to realize maybe what Chad and I had, wasn't a healthy relationship."

I can read her face, she agrees with me.

"It's easy to see from the outside, not so easy when you're on the inside," Lettie states.

"Tonight, sucked seeing him with her. However, what I've come to terms with is that I'm glad it's not me anymore."

Lettie pulls me into her arms as relief floods me. "I'm so proud of you," she says as she tightens her arms around me.

"I'm excited about my future," I mumble into her shoulder.

"Does that include an intense, hot Spanish chef?"

I pull myself out of Lettie's arms. "Stop it, will you? Nothing is going on."

She bursts out laughing as she holds up her hands in surrender. "Wouldn't care if there was."

"There isn't."

Lettie grins. "Okay then. Goodnight," she says as she sashays out of the kitchen, laughing.

I shake my head at my friend as I make my way to my bedroom.

Jumping into bed, I pick up my phone to scroll through my socials before I fall asleep, but I notice a message on my phone.

Sebastien: Hope you made it home safely.

Why is he messaging me? Thought he would be busy with someone else.

Quinn: Sure did. Just in bed now.

Sebastien: What are you wearing?

I stare at the blinking cursor on the screen.

Quinn: Nothing sexy that's for sure. Just a T-shirt.

Sebastien: Show me.

What?

Quinn: No.

Quinn: Where are you?

Sebastien: I'm at home.

Quinn: What are you wearing, then?

Sebastien: Nothing.

Is it getting a little hot in here?

Quinn: Of course, you are. Did you pick up?

He's naked all right, but not for me for some random girl.

Sebastien: Home alone. Unable to stop thinking about a certain blonde.

No. He's not talking about me, is he?

My phone vibrates, scaring me.

Shit!

I drop it.

The screen flashes Sebastien's name.

"Hey," I answer, a little breathless.

"I'm not interrupting anything, am I?" His accent adds a silky, sexual undertone to his question.

"Nope. Just surprised you called me, that's all."

"Thought it might be easier than text messaging." I can hear the grin in his tone.

"I don't do phone sex," I blurt out somewhat nervously.

Sebastien chuckles down the phone line. "Good to know."

"I mean, that's what you were calling for, isn't it?" My face feels like it's on fire with embarrassment. "I mean your text sort of … well, you know …"

"What?" he asks, and I can hear the laughter in his tone at my foot in mouth.

"They were flirty."

"I'm Spanish, everything sounds flirty." He chuckles.

Oh. Well, that deflated my ego rather quickly. I'm reading way too much into this.

"Good. That's what I thought." *An awesome recovery there, Quinn.*

"Quinn," he says my name pulling me from my thoughts. "I was flirting with you," he tells me honestly.

Oh.

"I like flirting with you. I can't seem to stop myself," he confesses.

Oh.

"Okay." I'm not too sure what else to say.

"But …" *Of course, there's a but.* "I don't want my flirting to get in the way of your new life."

Huh.

"I think you should try everything you can with this new beginning you have been given."

Okay, then.

"And that means dating people." I choke on my breath. "You've been stuck with someone for most of your adult life. Now is the time to explore what you really want."

"And you think that's sleeping around with a heap of men?"

Is he drunk?

"I said dating, but if it helps you work out what you want in life, then yes. I would never judge you for that. How do you know what you want when you have never experienced it?" Sebastien explains to me.

"You think I haven't experienced life?" My tone is a little defensive.

"Do *you* think you've explored it?" He throws the question right back at me.

"Have you?"

The line goes quiet for a bit.

"I like you, Quinn." He lets out a heavy sigh. "I didn't think I would from our first meeting, but you're growing on me."

"Gee, thanks."

Sebastien laughs throatily. "I also like flirting with you," he confesses, making my cheeks burn. "But I worry that due to your lack of, um … experience, you might misinterpret my flirtation as something *more.*"

Quickly my lust turns to anger. "Wow. You really do have tickets on yourself, don't you?" Anger bubbles through my veins, making me pull out my high-pitched Southern drawl. "Sebastien Sanchez kissed me. That must mean we are soul-mates. Be still my beating heart. Quick, Momma, call the priest. I found the man I'm going to marry. Is that how naïve you think I am?"

"No. I just didn't want to lead you on, that's all," he tries to explain himself.

"Please, I know exactly what kind of man you are. You have huge commitment issues from your past. Plus, you get distracted by any shiny thing who passes you by. That's not the kind of man I'm looking for. Maybe for a good time, but most certainly not for a long time," I tell him.

"Right, well, I'm glad we have that sorted, then," he adds gruffly.

"Me, too. Don't want to confuse the ditzy blonde, do we."

"Quinn, I didn't mean to offend you," he tries to apologize.

"One can only be offended if they cared in the first place. Goodnight, Sebastien." With that parting message, I hang up on him.

Urgh, he's so frustrating.

11

SEBASTIEN

The phone call with Quinn the other night did not go according to plan. For some stupid reason, I kept offending her. Maybe it's getting lost in translation? I thought I had a rather good grasp of the English language, but it appears maybe not.

What I was trying to explain to her, obviously not very well, was that whatever chemistry there is between us, and there does seem to be some, if we started anything, even if it was a fling, it could never go anywhere. She likes monogamy, and I don't like commitment. It would be a disaster if we overstepped that line. But I do like flirting with her, and that was what I was trying to say. I want to keep flirting with her, but I don't want her to think by me flirting that it's going to lead somewhere.

She's just gotten out of a controlling relationship maybe I shouldn't be offering her anything more than friendship. She deserves to see what is out there. She's young and needs to work out what she wants out of life since Chad destroyed her plans. But that isn't at all how the conversation went, and now we are back at square one again. *It's for the best.* Even if I can't stop thinking about the kiss. *I need to.* Nothing good can ever come from it.

I've finished my last meeting with the network before I head to Spain next week, and I can't wait to go home. Can't wait to smell the fresh air. Eat fantastic food. See my friends. My family.

"Hey, sexy," Derrick Jones greets me as we catch up for drinks. He's one of Hollywood's premium sought-after stylists. He's also an old friend I know through my sister, Yvette, who's a fashion designer in Paris.

"Hey." Standing up, I kiss his cheeks.

"You look a million miles away." He grins, sitting down.

"Just thinking about going home next week," I tell him.

Derrick gives me a pout.

"Boo. That sucks. Now, who the hell am I going to flirt with? Guess Christian is going to get all my attention again." Derrick waves his hand around in the air.

"I'm sure he will love having all your attention again," I joke with him.

Christian Taylor, from Dirty Texas, is his best friend and is married to his other best friend, Vanessa. He flirts with Christian all the time, but he loves it and gives it right back to him. I'm going to miss Derrick and the entire crazy Dirty Texas group. After hooking up with a couple of the band's girls, before they were together, I didn't think they would welcome me in when I was given the opportunity to live and work here. It took Finn Connolly a while to get used to me being around Isla again. She was my assistant in Barcelona for a while. We kind of had a mutual friends-with-benefits going on, and I may have helped her out when she found out she was pregnant with Finn's baby and didn't want anyone to know. And then there was Sienna, who used me to make Evan Wyld jealous. I wasn't complaining. I had always had a crush on her, but she was married, and when she wasn't any longer Evan got there first. It worked out for the best. She is happy and popping out babies, something I wasn't interested in doing.

Derrick squeals which makes me jump. "I've had the most fabulous idea," he says, slamming his hand down on the table, shaking the cutlery as a fork falls to the floor. "We need to organize a going-away party for you."

"No," I say, shaking my head because knowing Derrick, he will make it into something bigger than is required.

"Yes. We can't let you go back to Spain without a farewell. Why don't you bring that gorgeous new co-star with you? The girls and I are obsessed with Quinn Miller and *Farmhouse Reno*." He claps excitedly.

"Don't think that would be a good idea," I tell him, mainly because Quinn isn't talking to me.

"Oh, is it because she's upset about her breakup with Chad?" Derrick pushes. "I mean, Chad is hot, and he could get it anytime he wants, but we are all Team Quinn when it comes to the breakup. In my line of work, you hear the whispers and gossip, and word on the street is Chad was cheating on Quinn for a *really* long time, with multiple girls," Derrick states.

And that's probably a good reason for her not to come to my farewell party. Because I don't want Derrick to say something like that to her. She's been through enough as it is. Not sure if she would cope hearing this isn't the first time Chad has strayed.

Derrick's eyes narrow on me. "You and she aren't a thing, are you?"

"What? No," I argue back.

"But something's happened? I can see through your bullshit," he adds.

"It's not what you think," I answer before realizing what I've said.

Derrick smiles knowing he's got me. "Do tell, Mr. Sanchez."

"Nothing to tell."

"Don't believe you," he argues back.

"You don't even know her."

"I've seen every single episode of Farmhouse Reno. I've stalked her for years online. I love her. I need to meet her. I know as soon as we meet, we are going to be best friends."

Not sure if that is a selling point. "No."

"You know I have my ways and I'll go around you and invite her anyway. I was being courteous to you," he states.

As much as I am going to miss these guys, I'm not going to miss them all being in my business when I don't want them to.

"If she's going to be a part of our gang, we should really meet her," he states.

"Why would she be part of the gang? We're not dating," I argue, but I know it's futile.

"Yet!" he states as if it's a given.

"There's *no* yet," I try and convince him.

"I've seen the photos of the two of you." He eyes me suspiciously. "Walking the red carpet, hand in hand." He raises his brow at me.

"That's because she was freaking out about running into Chad," I explain.

He nods as if he's following, but I know he's not. "And what? You were just being chivalrous?"

"Yes."

"Have you kissed her?" His question catches me off-guard, and I slip up.

"Yes, but it wasn't like …"

Shit!

I see a huge smile form on his face. "It's not what you think," I try and assure him.

"I know it's hard being a gentleman sometimes." Derrick grins.

"She's a good girl," I tell him.

"I bet she is," he says, wiggling his brows at me.

"Quinn doesn't deserve this kind of gossip about her. I mean, I know I have a reputation, but she doesn't deserve one, too."

His eyes widen with surprise over my defending Quinn's honor.

"Now, we do have to meet her. Please," Derrick whines.

"She's busy. I doubt she'll be able to come."

Derrick waves my concern away. "Come on, who wouldn't want to meet Dirty Texas?"

He does have a point, I guess. My only saving grace is the band members are all happily married, so there isn't a chance she would run off with one of them.

"Fine, I'll ask," I say, giving in to him.

Derrick claps excitedly at my answer. "I promise we will all be on our bestest behavior."

Yeah, I highly doubt that.

I regret agreeing to this already.

Later that night, I send off a text message to Quinn and cross my fingers she answers.

Sebastien: How you doing?

Thirty minutes later, still no reply.

Sebastien: Dirty Texas wants to throw me a going-away party, and they want you to come.

The little dots appear under my message.

Quinn: You know Dirty Texas?

Okay, well, that's a start.

Sebastien: Yes. Known them for years.

The dots appear, then disappear, and then move again.

Quinn: So, you're telling me Dirty Texas knows who I am? And they invited me to your going-away party that they are throwing.

Sebastien: Their wives are huge fans. They want you to come. Begged me.

Quinn: Begged?

Sebastien: Yes. Begged.

Quinn: Anything for my fans. This is for them, not you.

I'd call that a semi-win for me.

Sebastien: I'll text you the details when I get them.

Sebastien: How have you been?

She never replies after that. Guess she is still upset.

12

QUINN

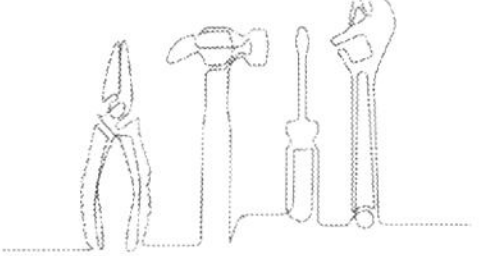

"Thanks for picking me up," I say as Sebastien holds his car door open for me. Lettie is away otherwise she would be my wing woman for the night. Plus, I hate driving in LA, so there was no other choice but to accept Sebastien's offer of a lift.

"No problem," he replies while closing the door. He then walks around the car and jumps in the other side.

It's been a while since our disaster of a phone call. Not sure why I am letting it bother me, still.

And he looks as good as my mind's memory, if not better. Damn him.

Sebastien's dressed in dark denim jeans and a white-collared shirt with the sleeves rolled up showing off his tanned forearms. The same ones that tense each time he shifts gears.

Hold it together, Quinn.

"How have you been?" Sebastien asks, being the first to break the silence.

"Good."

"Good?"

"Yep, good. Been busy too," I add.

"So good and busy. Right," he repeats as he changes gears and I try not to watch his arms tense. I need to do something about this. My hormones are out of control.

"How about you?" This conversation is awkward.

"Busy, good," he says, and I can see the tiniest of smiles pulling at his lips.

"Oh, busy, good," I answer as I nervously play with my skirt, then silence falls between us again.

He doesn't take his eyes off the road as he speaks. "I'm sorry, Quinn."

I know he is. I'm being stubborn and annoyed by his words and probably a little immature about the whole thing. Urgh. Being single sucks. I don't know how to act around men anymore.

He turns and looks over at me as we've stopped at a red light. "That phone call the other night didn't go the way I had planned."

I let out a heavy sigh. "I'm sorry for being a moody bitch. The problem is you made some interesting points."

"Did I?" He smiles.

Jerk.

"Like what?" He turns, looking at me with a grin.

"About figuring out what I want from life." His eyebrows rise. "I've never really thought about it before. Just followed the path I guess Chad had us on, and now …" I trail off as I look out the window, watching the traffic pass us by.

"Now, the world is your oyster," Sebastien finishes.

"As cliché as that sounds, yes," I answer, folding my arms in front of me with a sigh.

"It's not cliché. It's great. You have a clean slate," Sebastien states.

I pretend to pick some imaginary lint off my skirt so I have something to do with my hands. "I'm looking forward to the experience. I've never traveled to Europe before. Chad never wanted to. So, we never did."

I've been googling the hell out of what to do and see while I'm over there. Maybe I might stay on and explore a little more if I like it.

"I think you're going to fall in love with the place," he says, turning and giving me a panty-melting smile.

Maybe. Hopefully.

"Again, I'm sorry for that phone call. What I was trying to say was I like you. And I want the best for you, whatever that is."

"Whatever it is as long as I don't fall for you?" I say.

"Yes. I'm a selfish man, Quinn. Being a chef, you must be. I'm consumed by my passion for food, and that can be all-consuming."

"Like an artist?" I ask.

"Yes, very much like that," he says, giving me a smile.

"You don't have to worry. I promise to not fall for you. We have a job to do and sometimes that requires us to push the boundaries of our working relationship, and I get that. We both need to get through this show so we can both move on with our lives," I explain to him.

Sebastien is quiet for a while as we wind our way through the Hollywood Hills.

"I don't want to hurt you like Chad did," he tells me honestly.

I reach out and place my hand on his thigh. "You are nothing like Chad."

This makes Sebastien smile. "We good then?"

I nod. "We're good."

It doesn't take us long to arrive at the home of Dirty Texas guitarist, Evan Wyld, his wife, Sienna, and their family.

"I should warn you …" Sebastien parks the car but doesn't move to get out, "… my friends have no boundaries."

What does that mean?

"They are going to ask you inappropriate questions which you do not have to answer, okay?" I nod, becoming concerned by this warning. "They are good people, just nosey." He grins. "Ready?"

"Not so sure now after that glowing reference of your friends."

He chuckles, and we get out of the car. We don't even get to knock on the large door before it's yanked open, and a tall, gorgeous man rushes out toward me. He picks me up and swings me around. *What the hell?*

"Oh my god, I love you so much," he squeals, spinning me around. Eventually, he puts me down on my feet. "Love your hair. This length on you is stunning."

"This is Derrick Jones. Celebrity stylist, gossip queen, and personal-space invader," Sebastien says, introducing us.

"We only tolerate him for his looks, not his jokes," Derrick says as he places an arm around my shoulders.

This makes me laugh. I think I'm going to like this guy.

"Come on in, we are all so excited to meet you," Derrick says as he ushers me inside the home.

Stepping through the Hollywood home of rockstar royalty is not at all what I was expecting. Kids are running around everywhere. It's a circus. Then we pass a couple of members of Dirty Texas.

Oh. My. God!

"Welcome to my home," Evan Wyld says, introducing himself while kissing my cheeks.

Teenage me is totally fangirling.

"My wife loves you. She's made me sit through pretty much every single episode of your show," he groans happily.

Oh, wow, this is surreal.

"Go on through your super fans await," he jokes.

Derrick leads me outside, where a group of gorgeous women sit around a fire pit drinking cocktails.

"Look who it is," Derrick yells at the three women.

They all look up and squeal. Then they all jump up from where they're sitting and rush toward me. Each one of them talks a million miles a minute as they hug me and introduce themselves. *This is a little overwhelming.*

"Evening, girls," Sebastien greets them all.

"Hey, Seb," they say, ignoring him.

"The boys are in the man cave. Why don't you join them," states Evan's wife, Sienna.

"You going to be okay?" Sebastien asks me.

"Of course, she is," Derrick answers for me. "Now, run along." He dismisses Sebastien, which makes me laugh.

I've never seen this side of Sebastien before. I'm so used to people fawning over him. It's weird seeing his friends ignoring him for me.

"I'll be fine," I tell him.

He nods, pushing his hands into his pockets and walking toward a separate house, which I'm assuming is the man cave. I watch him for a couple more moments. It's unfair how good-looking he is.

"His ass looks amazing in those jeans, don't you think?" Derrick asks me, pulling me from that literal thought.

"I … well …" I'm totally flustered by his comment.

"Leave her alone, D," a blonde-haired woman tells him.

Vanessa, I think she said her name was. She's married to Christian Taylor, the other guitarist in the band. "You will have plenty of time to grill her about Sebastien later."

One by one the girls introduce themselves to me.

"Would you like a drink?" Isla, a gorgeous blonde asks me. She's married to Finn Connolly, the drummer in the band. She pours me a margarita from the pitcher.

"Thanks," I say, gladly taking the glass.

"Come, sit by the fire. We have food coming," Sienna states.

I follow their leads and sit with them.

"Stacey and Olivia are so upset they're missing this," Vanessa adds.

"Liv is in England, and Stace is in Australia for work," she explains. "They are obsessed with you also," she adds while giving me a friendly smile.

Felling a little overwhelmed, I take a sip of my cocktail. *Holy hell, that's strong, but I like it.*

"I can't hold it in any longer …" Derrick says, bouncing in his seat. "I just needed to tell you we are all Team Quinn in this house," he reassures me.

I choke on my drink at his comment, and it takes me a moment to recover. "You don't need to pick sides," I tell him diplomatically.

They all look at each other.

"Girl, please," Derrick starts. "I've heard some whispers around town that Chad Bailey is not the Southern gentleman he portrays on the television."

Oh.

I think I might look a little like a deer caught in headlights right now.

"You'll have to excuse him. He knows no boundaries," Sienna tells me. "Just so you know … most of us here have had our personal lives splashed across the tabloids for the critics to pick over. So, we get it," she says, giving me a reassuring smile.

"You don't need to tell us anything," Vanessa adds.

"The fact we get to hang out with you is awesome enough," Isla states with a smile.

Everyone is being nice and understanding.

"Okay, I won't ask about Chad. What about Seb then? What's happening between the two of you?" Derricks ask.

"Derrick," the girls all hiss at their boundary-jumping friend.

"Nothing. We are co-stars," I explain to them.

Derrick's eyes narrow in on me like he wants to say more but thinks better of it.

"Ignore him. Are you excited about going to Spain?" Isla asks.

"Yeah, I've never been to Europe before."

"Isla used to live there with Seb, she was his assistant, and they had a thing," Derrick explains.

"Derrick." Isla groans, shaking her head.

Isla is gorgeous. I can see why something happened between the two of them.

"It wasn't anything. Yes, we hooked up briefly, but at the time, I didn't know I was pregnant with my husband's child."

My eyes widen at that bit of news.

"Sebastien helped me through a dark time between Finn and me. He looked out for me like a big brother."

"I don't sleep with my big brother," Derrick teases.

"Would you stop it, D," Isla says through gritted teeth.

"Nothing is going on between Sebastien and me. Please, don't think there is," I try and explain again to them all.

"Why wouldn't you want to?" Derrick asks.

"D, leave it alone, babe," Sienna warns her friend.

"Sorry, you're right. Boundaries. I'm crossing them. I'm a work in progress. Please continue and ignore my questions," Derrick explains.

"Have you seen the vineyard yet?" Vanessa asks, changing the subject.

"Only online. It looks so charming. I'm excited to get there and see it up close."

"We are dying to see what you're going to do with it. It's going to be amazing whatever it is," Sienna adds, her words mumbling the further her glass empties.

"You're too kind," I tell her because really, they all are. "I have some ideas which are different from my old style. I want to branch out from being typecast in farmhouse style. I can do so much more," I tell the girls.

"Anything you do is brilliant," Vanessa adds.

As the night and the glasses of margarita go on, my lips become looser with each sip. These women and Derrick make me feel so safe and welcomed that I break down and tell them the truth.

"I can't believe he took everything," Isla growls.

"My ex did the same thing to me too, babe. He took everything I worked on. My savings. My homes. Not too dissimilar in our stories," Sienna explains to me.

If she can recover from that happening to her and fall for a rockstar then there's hope for me too, one day.

"And an influencer, too. How cliché," Vanessa adds.

"I had no idea," I say, shrugging my shoulders. "The bastard told me on the way to the meeting with the network. Where he then presented his new solo project right in front of me all while I was blindside and too stunned to say anything."

A whole pile of cusses comes from the girls.

"You're better off without him," Vanessa tells me.

"Seb is a better upgrade than him anyway," Derrick adds.

"Derrick," Sienna moans at her best friend.

"You have no idea how many hot guys there are in Barcelona. Forget, Seb. He has a younger brother who is just as hot," Isla says, giving me a slow wink.

Oh. I didn't know that.

"Wouldn't that be weird after she's already kissed Seb?" Derrick asks.

Everyone falls silent including me.

"Shit. I wasn't supposed to have said," Derrick says with a hiccup.

"You've already kissed, Seb?" Vanessa asks. Then waves her hands at me. "Sorry, you don't have to answer that."

"Yes. But he did it because Chad was putting me down,

telling me that no one would ever want me. That he was the best I would ever get. Sebastien heard this and came in and kissed me right in front of Chad."

Sebastien's friends clap at that.

"Was it good?" Derrick asks.

"Yes," I answer.

They all fall about laughing and teasing me, and honestly, it was the best time I've had in I can't remember. The rest of the night becomes a blur as more margaritas are consumed.

13

SEBASTIEN

After saying farewell to my friends, I get a very drunk Quinn into my car to take her home. What did they do to her?

"I love your friends," she tells me, resting her head back against the car seat.

"They loved you, too," I tell her as I buckle myself in.

"They're on Team Quinn," she says, waving her hand in the air. "They think Chad is a dick."

Her words make me smile.

"They also think I should sleep with you," Quinn confesses which nearly has me hitting the brakes in shock. "They said I needed a rebound, and that you're good at those."

Gee, who needs enemies when I have friends like that?

"But I told them we are just friends and I like being just friends. Sleeping together would ruin it."

I know we agreed to this, but now I'm second-guessing my stance on this.

"Derrick suggested one of The Sons of Brooklyn boys. They would make a good rebound. Lettie thinks I need to get under someone to get over Chad."

Maybe I should be offering my services because she sounds stressed about it.

"I'm thinking, oh no, I could never sleep with one of them …" she says on a hiccup. "I'm too … what did you say to me …?" She frowns as she tries to find the right words. "I'm too inexperienced," she whisper-yells the words to me.

"That's *not* what I said," I argue, then realize she's drunk, and I'm never going to win.

Quinn waves my comment away. "Just because Chad …" She scrunches up her nose at the mention of his name like she's smelling something off. "Just because Chad is the only man I've slept with doesn't mean I don't know things, you know." She pokes me in the arm with her pointer finger. "Oooh, you're hard." Her hand wraps around my arm, squeezing it. "How often do you work out? You're a chef. You're not meant to be this hard." She keeps poking my arm. "Chefs are supposed to have fat tummies." She tries to reach for my stomach.

When her hand touches me, I almost crash the car. "Maybe we should keep our hands to ourselves while in the car."

She lets out a huff. "I bet a gigolo would let me touch him while he was driving," she says.

What in the hell is she talking about?

"I should really book one in before I move to Spain. Do you have gigolos in Barcelona? Get that first rebound sex over and done with. Maybe that way I won't have to finish myself off with my vibrator when he's done like I had to do with Chad."

"You don't need to pay for sex, Quinn."

"Um … yes, I do. It's easier than picking up some random, and then he goes and sells his story to the press."

Well, she certainly has a point there.

"What about a male friend … no-strings-attached sex."

She shakes her head. "Not sure if I'm a *friends-with-benefits* kind of girl," she states beside me.

"But you're a *pay-someone* kind of girl."

"Hey." She sits up and turns her attention to me. "Don't be a Mr. Judgey McJudgeyson. I think it's more respectable than picking up some random at a nightclub." Her eyes narrow in on me. "That might be your MO, but it's not mine." She sits back in a huff and crosses her arms in front of her.

"It might surprise you, Miss Judgey McJudgeyson, that I don't pick up women in nightclubs. That's not my MO either," I say, setting her straight.

"You don't need a nightclub. You have a private dining room."

I don't reply because that's exactly my MO.

"Oh … burgers! Stop," she screams while pointing to a burger joint on the opposite side of the road.

Turning the car around, we head on over and order up a feast. As soon as she gets the meal, she starts shoving fries into her mouth like a starving person. We aren't far from Lettie's house where she's staying, so it doesn't take long until I pull into her driveway and stop.

"You want to come in and eat your takeout?" she asks. Those doe eyes flutter at me.

I should say no.

"Lettie's away for the weekend," she adds.

Even more reason why I should be getting home.

"Okay," I reply.

I'm an Idiot.

Parking my car, I grab my bag of American heart attack food and follow her inside. Lettie has a gorgeous home. It's a typical Hollywood Hills bachelorette pad, all sleek and modern with views over the city.

Quinn pulls up a seat outside on the large daybed by the pool, and I take a seat beside her. She kicks off her heels and crawls up, laying back, shoving some fries into her mouth. Then she unwraps her burger and takes a humungous bite.

"Oh, my goodness, this *is* good." She moans around her mouthful.

I take a bite of my burger and curse every single bite. I notice she's watching me, then bursts out laughing. "You hate it, right?" she asks.

"It hurts my soul."

"Snob." She giggles, popping a few more fries in her mouth.

"You do realize who you're sitting with, don't you?" I jokingly ask her.

"Chef extraordinaire, Mr. Sebastien Sanchez," she mocks. "The bad-boy chef of Spain." She wiggles her eyebrows, making me roll my eyes. "How many women have you slept with?" she asks.

The question catches me totally off-guard, and I choke on my burger. "What kind of question is that?" I ask, trying to breathe.

"A genuine one." She gives me those doe eyes again, looking all innocent and sweet, yet all I can think about is lying her back against this daybed and making her forget her ex.

"I don't know … I don't keep count. A lot." Shrugging my answer, I stuff some fries in my mouth to hopefully get out of answering any more of her questions, but she's relentless.

"Is a lot like over fifty, over a hundred, over a thousand?" she pushes.

"Do you really want to know?" Frowning at her, she thinks this over for a couple of beats.

"No," she says, shaking her head. "I'm guessing it's a lot because of the nickname."

"I'm not *that* guy anymore," I tell her.

"Doesn't bother me if you are." She takes another bite of her burger.

Why does that comment bother me?

"Men and women look at sex differently," I add.

"If you give me the whole *Men Are from Mars, Women Are from Venus* spiel, I'm going to throw this burger at you."

I shut my mouth and don't say anything more. We lay back against the daybed and look out over the twinkling lights of LA.

"Are you going to miss anything about this place?" she asks sleepily.

"My friends."

"That's all? Not your restaurant?" She turns to look at me.

"Don't get me wrong, I love my restaurant, but the network had a lot more say over it than I wanted."

"Oh . . ." She lays her head back but still looks at me.

"Yeah. I kind of signed away everything on this deal, thinking it was what I wanted," I explain.

"But you didn't have any control," she adds.

I nod in agreement. "It felt like a sellout. I never thought I'd be that guy, and there I was becoming everything I said I never wanted to be." I haven't told anyone that before.

"I get that." She gives me a genuine smile. "That's why going back to Spain is such a big deal, right?"

"Yeah."

"Looks like we are both going to Spain to find ourselves, then."

Hadn't thought about it like that. "Guess we are," I say in agreement.

14

QUINN

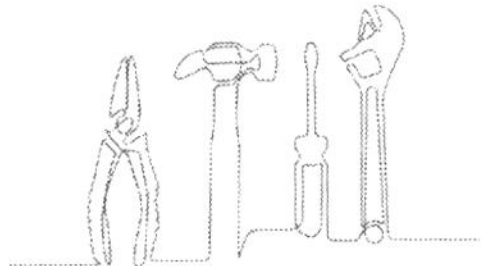

My head feels like it's been hit by a truck.

Why is it so cold and warm at the same time?

Did I leave a fan on high last night?

Why is it so breezy?

Opening my eyes, I notice a tanned arm wrapped around me.

What the hell? Sebastien!

"Wake up," I say. Pushing his arm off me, he rolls over with a groan.

"Where the hell am I?" Sebastien sits up and tries to orient himself.

"Looks like we fell asleep on the daybed last night."

He looks around with a very confused look on his face. "Oh." Then he looks me up and down, then himself.

"No, we did *not* sleep with each other," I tell him, shaking my head.

"I should go," he says, jumping off the bed eagerly.

"This doesn't have to be awkward. Nothing happened."

He nods his head.

"You're more than welcome to stay or go. It's up to you," I ask him, putting the ball firmly in his court.

"You want me to stay?"

"The network sent through some promotion stuff yesterday for us to use, and I thought maybe we could run through it together. Seeing as you are here."

"Oh, okay."

"I'm going to go freshen up and make myself feel human again. The guest bedroom is down the hall to the left. There are fresh towels and a shower if you want to use it."

"Thanks. That would be great." Sebastien turns and heads to the guest room.

Thankfully, I'm in the opposite direction.

After having the best shower of my life, I walk out to the most delicious-smelling food, and my stomach instantly rumbles. Turning the corner, the last thing I expect to see is Sebastien in the kitchen, half-naked.

He hasn't noticed me yet, so I take in the pure pornographic scene before me. I watch in fascination as his muscles ripple across his tanned back while he works. His jeans are slung low on his hips, showing off the male dimples that sit right above his perfect ass.

Sebastien Sanchez in clothes is hot, but out of them, he's totally combustible.

"Hope you're hungry?" Sebastien calls out, surprising me.

How the hell did he know I was there?

He turns around with a spatula in his hand and a devilish grin.

I make my way over to the breakfast bar and take a seat, then he slides a perfect omelet onto my plate.

"Did you enjoy the view?" He grins, resting his elbows on the counter.

"Don't know what you're talking about?"

"The backsplash is mirrored, so I could see you standing there watching me." His left eyebrow twitches up and down.

"I don't think you need me to stroke your ego," I bite back.

"It wouldn't mind a little stroking every now and again." He grins.

I pick up the dishcloth on the counter and throw it at him, which just makes him laugh.

Not wasting any more time, I grab a fork and dig in. "Oh my god." I'm drooling over the most amazing omelet I have ever tasted.

"Good, huh?" Sebastien gives me a knowing grin.

"You know it is." Shoving another delicious bite into my mouth, I keep going until I'm completely full. "Okay, so that was amazing."

Picking up the plates, he takes them to the sink. "I aim to please," he tells me as he places the eggs back into the refrigerator, which makes me roll my eyes at his joke.

Sebastien helps me clean the kitchen before we head into the dining room and run through what the producers have sent through to me.

I open the computer, and he sits beside me a little too close.

"These are some of the sponsors' products," I state while opening a million and one PDFs filled with product endorsements.

"Oh, wow, okay," he says, looking very overwhelmed which makes me laugh.

"I have some storyboard ideas instead. They might be easier to see the concept than looking at individual products," I explain.

Clicking on the files, I open my digital storyboards. "These might change because I've only seen photos of the buildings, but I want to make sure we are on the same page. After the show and I have left, I want you to love what's there."

Sebastien nods in agreement.

So, for the next couple of hours, we talk about his vision until we are exhausted.

"I think that's a great start," I state while closing down my computer.

"And you think you can match our ideas with the sponsors' products?" he asks.

"Of course. Also, you can always change it if you don't like it once we have all left," I remind him.

"I trust you," he tells me.

Aw, I felt that compliment all the way to my toes.

"I should probably go. I'm leaving in a couple of days, still have a heap of packing to do."

That's right, he's going over earlier than me. We get up and head toward the door.

"Thanks for today," he says, turning as he reaches the front door. "And for last night." He grins.

"I had fun on both occasions," I tell him truthfully.

He nods but hesitates to leave, his hand staying on the door handle for a couple of moments before he shakes his head and opens the door.

"Hey …" I run after him. "I'm not going to see you for a couple of weeks." So, I hold my arms open for him. "Let me say goodbye."

He smiles, moving toward me.

I wrap my arms around his neck as he wraps himself around me, holding me tightly against his chest.

His lips press against the crook of my neck, sending tiny shockwaves over my body.

I swallow hard.

The hug continues a little longer than one might deem appropriate. Eventually, we pull away from each other.

"Have a safe flight," I say. My legs are shaky after our hug. Who knew a hug could feel that sexy?

"I'll see you soon," he says.

I watch as he slides into his car, then I wave him goodbye.

It's for the best nothing happened.

It would only complicate things once I arrive in Spain.

I need to get some new batteries if I'm going to survive the next three months with that man.

15

SEBASTIEN

"You're home." My mama rushes up and pulls me into her arms.

It's been a long time since we've seen each other.

"I've missed you so much," she says, squishing my face.

"Sweetheart, leave him alone. He's a grown man," my father chastises, but she simply waves him off. "Welcome home, son." He pulls me into a bear hug.

"I've cooked all your favorite things," she tells me. "You look so skinny." She rubs my taut stomach. "You haven't been looking after yourself in America."

"Mama," I groan.

I don't think it matters how old you are, you will still be a child in your mother's eyes.

"I'm fine. Just been working out, that's all."

She tuts and tells me to follow her into the living room, where all my favorite foods are laid out for me. My mouth waters at the aromas circling the room, so I close my eyes and inhale the homely scent. A sense of calm washes over me, and I realize now where I'm supposed to be.

Here.

Home.

Spain.

"Where is he?" My brother's voice echoes through my family's villa. "Hey, dickhead." Joaquin, my brother, enters the room.

"Language," my father chastises my younger brother.

"Sorry, Papi." He grins.

It's been ages since I've seen my brother.

"Hey, you." Standing, I embrace him. "It's been too long."

My brother is a celebrity in his own right. He's a Spanish soap star in *Ama a tu Vecino,* which translates to, *Love Thy Neighbor*, and he's a singer. If you think I'm the bad-boy playboy of the family, then you're totally wrong. My youngest brother has me beat.

"I'm surprised you've been able to take the time out of your busy day to say hello to your brother."

"I was kind of hoping your hot co-star would be with you," he says as he looks over my shoulder, and I punch him playfully in the stomach.

"Don't you dare," I warn him.

Quinn would probably like him. All women do.

He frowns, then smiles, unsure if I'm joking or not.

I'm not sure if I am either. I mean, if Quinn is interested in Joaquin, then I guess I can't really stand in her way. However, I know my younger brother, and he's worse than me when it comes to no-strings-attached fun.

"Stop fighting, you two, and come sit down," Mama yells.

We spend the rest of the day catching up on lost time.

"It's strange being back," I say while walking into my old apartment in one of the hip suburbs of Barcelona named Gràcia. It's bohemian and casual, with loads of culture, and a great little neighborhood full of restaurants. No one cares who you are here.

"You've been gone a long time, Seb," my brother tells me.

"I know." Letting out a heavy sigh, I drop my bags by the front door and look around at my old life. In the last two years, I've changed, it seems, and I didn't even realize it.

"It's good to have you back." My brother slaps me on the back.

He opens the refrigerator and pulls out a couple of beers, and before I can say anything, Joaquin fills me in, "Mama filled it up."

Of course, she did.

I take the cool bottle from my brother's hand, and we head to the rooftop terrace. The sun is setting over the city, and you can see all the way to the ocean. It's perfect. We clink our bottles together and drink in relative silence for a couple of moments.

"So, you going to tell me about your co-star?" He turns and gives me a knowing smile.

"Nothing to tell."

"Nothing's happened?" my brother pushes.

"Nothing has happened nor will happen. She's had a bad breakup, and we are just friends. Neither one of us has time to complicate what we have," I tell him, enjoying the sights, sounds, and smells of my home.

"But you want something to happen?" he pushes as his dark green eyes glare at me, but I don't answer him. "I've seen photos of her. She's hot." He grins. "And I saw photos of you two together at your network thing, too," he adds.

"So."

"So?" His voice raises in a question. "Come on, Seb, I know you."

"She's a nice girl."

My brother chuckles. "Too nice for you. Is that what you're saying?"

"Maybe." This is what I remember. It's all flooding back. My family likes to stick their noses into my business.

"So, you've thought about more, then?"

My brother is becoming annoying as fuck, so I switch it up. "How about we delve into your sex life, hey, Joaquin?" Anger laces my tone, but this only makes him burst out laughing.

"Oooh … I've touched a nerve." He grins. "My sex life is fine. Great actually," he boasts.

"You know there's more to life than fucking groupies and extras," I warn him.

"Maybe when I'm an old man like you, that will be true, but at the moment, I'm enjoying fucking groupies and extras."

The smug bastard. I'm only ten years older than him, and at thirty-four, I don't think I'm that old.

"Maybe your co-star would be more interested in someone closer to her age."

I'm ready to throw my beer bottle at him. The annoying little shit, but somehow, I ignore him.

"Have you called Yvette?" he asks.

"I texted her when I got in," I tell him.

"Well, it's good to have you home, brother." He sits there with a giant smirk on his face as he lays back on the daybed, making himself at home. We spend the night drinking way too many beers and talking shit.

It's been a perfect homecoming.

I hear ringing beside me as I try and force my eyes open. It's dark outside. The twinkling of the Barcelona skyline is my only source of light.

"Hola, Seb's phone," I hear my brother answering it. "He's asleep at the moment. Can I take a message?" Then there's silence. "You have the cutest accent." Joaquin's voice dips low. "Keep talking, I love it."

Who's he flirting with? Shaking my head, trying to wipe the

cobwebs of my jetlag away, I continue to listen. "We should catch up when you get here. I can show you the sights."

Wait! Shit! Jumping up and swiping my cell from my brother's hand, he bursts out laughing.

"Hello," I answer, sounding breathless as I walk away from Joaquin, who's clutching his belly as he's bent over laughing.

"Oh, hey, Sebastien," Quinn answers happily. "Sorry if I woke you. I just wanted to check in to see if you had arrived safely."

"Thanks. Sorry, I forgot to text. I kind of lost track of time with my family around and had one too many beers with my brother."

"No need to apologize at all. Your brother sounds nice," she adds.

"He's not," I answer quickly, making Joaquin laugh harder.

"Oh, really?" she questions.

"No. I mean, he is nice. But you know … he likes women. A lot of women." Feeling like a dick for warning her off him, she shoots back with a chuckle.

"Just like his older brother, then?"

"He's worse," I reply, smiling as I say it.

"Well, I won't take up much of your time. Just wanted to say hi, and um … you know? Actually, I don't know why I called. I just …" She becomes flustered all of a sudden.

"You can call me anytime," I tell her. It's great hearing her voice. I'm surprised at how much I've missed hearing it, and it's only been a couple of days. It feels like a bridge between my two worlds.

"Okay, well, I'll let you go. Have fun and see you soon." And with that, she hangs up and is gone.

"So, you still going with the lie that nothing's going on?" my brother grills me.

My answer is to flip him off.

16

SEBASTIEN

"Thanks for bringing me today." My mama smiles at me as our car makes its way through the Barcelona traffic. "I still can't believe you bought this without seeing it."

"I know. It's a little crazy, but I have a good feeling that it's going to work out," I tell her.

"Of course, it will. We have faith in you, Sebastien. You've always worked hard and achieved any dream you set your mind to." Mama takes my hand in hers and gives it a little squeeze. "I know the divorce from Maria was hard, but it was for the best." She gives me a sad smile.

Maria Gomez.

My first love, my only love.

Spanish superstar and socialite.

She swept me off my feet when I was twenty-three years old. A struggling chef in a town overrun with the world's best chefs. We met through my sister—she wore one of her creations for her end-of-year design school graduation. It was young love at first sight. Next thing I know, she's investing in my dream of owning my own restaurant, and my star begins to rise as Maria and her friends hang out at my bar.

Her influence catapulted me into the Spanish social scene, and we were Spain's 'it' couple. Our photographs were plastered all over the magazines. And then the pictures of her and her co-star naked on the beach, where they were filming in Mexico came out. She tried to play it off as scenes from the movie, but thanks to the gossip magazines, her explanation turned out to be all lies.

Apparently, he was not the first co-star she had a fling with, just the first one she got caught with.

I filed for divorce straightaway—I'd been humiliated.

Maria flew into a rage when she got the papers, telling me that I was embarrassing her, and that I should forgive her for what she had done.

But I couldn't.

Then she turned nasty.

She started to threaten me, saying she would take everything I had away because I wouldn't be Sebastien Sanchez if it weren't for her.

Problem was—she was right.

It was the truth.

She may have financed the first restaurant, but all my talent in the kitchen kept it running.

Unfortunately, the courts didn't see it that way. She had expensive lawyers who were able to argue that I was just an employee and that she owned everything, including the money behind it all.

I lost everything.

I had five restaurants at that time, one had even earned a Michelin star. I was at the top of my career, and through no fault of my own, I lost it all.

After the divorce, I lost my mind for a couple of years. I

wanted to make her pay for what she had done to me. I'm not proud of the way I acted. I slept with all her friends, making sure that a beautiful woman was seen on my arm everywhere I went. I did everything in my power to seek my revenge, but in the end, it hurt me more.

Maria didn't really care. She knew she had lost her toy but had others to keep her company. Instead, I painted myself in the media as a bad-boy chef, a womanizer, and a party boy.

Problem with that? Investors won't put their money into that kind of public display. No one would hire me. No one wanted to invest in my ideas.

That was when my amazing family came to the rescue and helped me. It wasn't long until I was the talk of the town again, but this time it was through my own hard work.

That's why I took the offer in the states.

I owed my family.

With the advance I was given for Hotshot Chef, I paid them back. I was also able to start a mentorship program at my restaurant to help other struggling young chefs. I wanted to change the narrative that was out in the public domain. It worked for my profile in Spain, but then I kind of lost myself a little in LA. Found myself resorting to my old ways filling a lonely void that had opened inside me. Hence, the crazy decision to buy a vineyard from internet photographs.

We travel the hour to the famous winemaking region, Penedès, just south of Barcelona.

"It's so beautiful here, Sebastien," Mama remarks as we pull up along the old dirt road to the ancient vineyard. It really is with its dusty pink dirt, to the expanse of green valleys filled with vines, to the impressive mountains and the endless blue sky. "It's peaceful," she adds, stepping out of the car.

The only sound you can hear is the noise of cows and chickens. There's no traffic, no helicopters, and no bullshit.

"You must be Sebastien." A crinkly old man shuffles out of a dilapidated old building.

"You must be Gorge." I shake the older man's hand. "This is my mama, Alma." They greet each other kindly.

"It is a little unconventional buying something you haven't seen," Gorge muses. "But I can assure you, you will be happy here." He grins. "Sixty years I have been working this land. It's as close to paradise as you can get," he tells me as we make our way around the hundred-acre farm.

Gorge shows us the acres of well-looked-after vines. He tells me he stopped production of their wine when it became too much, so instead, they sell their grapes to a local co-op. He speaks about how not all of the land was used for making wine and that there are paddocks that are now empty which were once filled with goats, chickens, and cows. They used to make their own cheese too.

There are a lot more buildings on the land than I was expecting—an old dairy, abattoir, machinery sheds, cottages, and then there's the main house that he and his wife live in, which is small yet comfortable. It doesn't need much work, but probably should be brought into the twenty-first century. Also, there are rows and rows of old vegetable gardens which can be put to good use.

"Oh, there is one more building I forgot to show you. It's down the very back of the property." My mother and I look at each other and shrug. "I completely forgot about it as I haven't been down there in who knows how long." The old man chuckles. "It was too big and expensive for my wife and me to look after anymore." The old truck bumps us along the rocky road until the vines open up, and the most magnificent building comes into view.

"Oh my, Seb." My mother reaches out and grabs my leg. Standing before us is a run-down villa, something that would have been grand in its heyday.

"I remember the day my wife and I moved into the villa her parents left her. We were so excited to start our life together," he tells us sadly. "Alas, we were not able to have children of our own, so all this space seemed … pointless in the end. So, we moved to the worker's cottage at the top of the farm and left the villa the way it was." I had no idea I had bought this home too. "I'll leave you to explore." The old man gets back into his truck and waits for us there.

I take my mother's hand as we walk down the old cobblestone stairs. I rip away some old vines that have grown over the front entrance. Turning the handle on the old wooden door, it takes a couple of tries for the rusty mechanisms to work. With a squeaky groan, the door opens, and we are transported back decades to a time long forgotten.

"Oh, my … this is so beautiful." Mama gasps as she takes in the villa filled with antiques under a thick layer of dust. We continue to explore the two-story villa, where we see thick wooden beams run along the ceiling with a million spider webs. Oversized windows that were once clean now sit under decades of grime, but still look out to what appears to be a courtyard or garden. Mosaic tiles line the floors as you walk further through the villa. Exposed stone walls with flaked-off paint surround us.

I pull my cell out of my pocket and look at the time in LA—Quinn needs to see this. It's early in the morning, but I think she will be okay with me waking her. I press her number and wait for the line to connect while I continue walking through the rustic villa waiting for her to pick up.

"Urgh, hello," she grumbles.

"Quinn, wake up. Wake the hell up. I have something amazing to show you." The excitement in my voice gains her attention. "You're on FaceTime," I warn her. The phone stills, then she moves it so her face comes into view. Her blonde hair is a mess, and those blue eyes squint as the glare from her cell flashes in her eyes.

"This better not be some kind of joke, and the amazing surprise is your dick," she says then covers her mouth when she realizes what she's said.

Mama gasps then bursts out laughing behind me.

"Quinn, you're on speaker."

Her doe eyes widen, and a small flush appears across her cheeks. "I was in the middle of a good dream. It's 4:38 a.m. I'm allowed to be not quite with it. Tell whoever heard me I'm sorry." She moans.

She was thinking about my dick, hey?

"I'll tell my mother you're sorry."

"Sebastien, your mother heard me," she squeals. Then she jumps out of bed, looking more awake now.

My mother is smiling as she continues walking through the villa.

"She thought it was funny," I reassure her.

"Well, I don't, okay. That is not the first impression I want your momma to see of me," Quinn chastises me.

My mother sends me a thumbs up at Quinn's comment. She has a large grin on her face.

"I promise she doesn't think any less of you," I tell her.

Quinn glares at me.

"And I'm going to call you later to enquire about that dream that made you think of my …"

"Don't you say it. I want to die from embarrassment," she says, shaking her head.

"Can I please show you what I called about?"

She nods, and I turn it around so she can see what I'm seeing.

"Oh my …" Quinn covers her mouth, "… are you at a museum?"

Her question makes me laugh. "No … apparently I own it," I explain to her.

"What?" She raises her voice.

"It's rather sad actually. The older man was showing us around the farm, which is so freaking amazing, Quinn. You are going to die when you get here."

Her eyes widen with excitement, and a small smile falls across her plump lips.

"This was the original home, but they weren't able to have a family, so they decided to live in the worker's cottage, which I thought was the original home, instead. He hasn't been to this villa in decades."

"Show me more," she says excitedly.

So, I do. I give her a live tour of the home. She sprouts off ideas and suggestions as we walk through each room.

"I have to go … the owner is waiting in the car for us. But we can talk about it more when I get back to Barcelona," I tell her.

Her excitement for the project radiates through the phone. "My mind is buzzing with so many ideas. Okay … we'll chat later."

We say our goodbyes. I hang up, and we head back with the owner.

A short time later, we are on the road home to Barcelona.

"You and this Quinn girl seem to get along well," my mother questions me.

"We work together. That is all, we're good friends," I explain to her, but she eyes me suspiciously.

"You both seem at ease with each other," she adds.

"That's because she isn't high maintenance." Unlike Maria, but I don't add those two words into the sentence.

"You had a smile on your face the entire time you were chatting with her." My mother raises a questioning brow in my direction.

"Because I was excited about the project … that is all."

"Okay, my boy." She grins.

"Mama … do not think there is anything more to us than co-stars," I warn her.

"I look forward to meeting her when she comes out." She grins.

17

QUINN

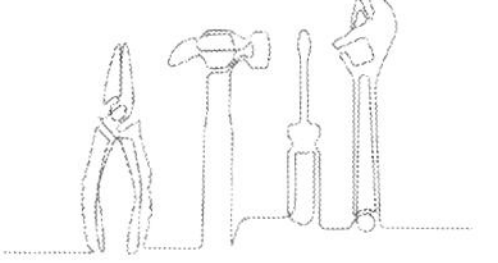

My mind is buzzing after I get off the phone with Sebastien. I've grabbed my computer, a cup of coffee, and all my design folders and have everything spread out all over Lettie's dining room table.

"You're up early." Lettie yawns as she grabs herself a cup of coffee from the machine.

"Yeah. Sebastien called me this morning as he was walking around the property."

Lettie raises her brow as she sips her coffee.

"The sellers showed him this old villa that he didn't even know was part of the property," I explain to her excitedly. "He video-called me because he was so excited by this new find. He did the walk around with me. The place hasn't been touched in maybe fifty years. It's beautiful."

Lettie grins.

"So, you were the first person he called upon discovering this time capsule?" Lettie asks.

"Yeah, why?" I question her.

"Wouldn't he call production or something? They probably would like to go through it with him, especially if there's an added building to renovate. You know it might mess up their timelines and things," she explains to me.

"Maybe he doesn't want them to know about it. I guess we both got caught up in the excitement of it all."

Lettie bursts out laughing. "I'm kidding, Quinn. I think it's sweet that he called you first, that's all."

I frown at her. "You know it's not like that," I remind her.

"I know." As she takes a seat beside me at the dinner table, she looks at the scatterings of paperwork all over it.

I've sketched a couple of ideas down as well.

"It nice seeing you excited about work again."

Flicking through a design magazine, I stop. "You think I wasn't excited about work before?"

"Not like this," she adds. "I think working on *Farmhouse Reno* you were a well-oiled machine. You knew what you had to do and just did it." Her words make me frown. "But you were expected to stay within a certain box."

"Yeah, Chad's box," I grumble.

"Exactly. Not to say all those years on *Farmhouse Reno* that you didn't do beautiful work because you did. You're so talented. What I'm trying to say really badly is … I like seeing you having freedom with your designs."

Freedom with my designs? I hadn't thought about it like that. I always thought I was the one running the design portion of the show on Farmhouse Reno, but the more freedom I've been given on this new project, the more I realize how much creative control Chad really did have over me.

"I'm starting to realize now that the old life I thought was so perfect really wasn't," I say. Running my finger over the pages of my notebook and the scribbles of ideas for Sebastien's villa, I smile.

"You were happy. I didn't want to rock the boat," Lettie states.

"I feel stupid, Lettie. Like the world could see that my life wasn't as perfect as I thought it was." I let out a defeated sigh.

"Hey, I'm sorry. I didn't mean to bum you out this morning." She reaches out and grabs my hand. "I'm just excited to see you like this." She waves her hand across the table at the paperwork. "That you and Sebastien are getting along so well." I give her a what-do-you-mean look. "Not like that." She grins. "Even though my inky black heart does think you two would be great together as a couple …" she gives me a pointed look, "… I actually mean that Sebastien is including you in his dream, that he trusts you. From the network's point of view, I'm excited to see how all this translates on screen."

"He's not at all what I thought he would be," I confess to her. "He's easy to get along with, and we kind of just click."

"That's what I mean … the chemistry is there. Sexual and non-sexual. The viewers are going to eat that up," she says excitedly. "I think you two should play up on that will-they-won't-they chemistry."

"What? No," I tell her. "This is a renovation program, not a dating show."

Her dark brown eyes narrow on me. "I think you two should play up the natural chemistry you both share. I know the network approves." I frown. "Just think about it, okay?" she asks me as she gets up from the table. "I've got to head to work. Have fun."

A couple of hours later, my cell begins to ring, and I can see it's Sebastien calling me. I take a quick look in the mirror to check if I'm okay before answering the call. "Hey," I say after pressing the answer button. His handsome face fills the screen.

"Hey, yourself." He grins.

Seriously, his smile should be utterly illegal.

"I'm exhausted after today." I see him lay back against a chair as he raises a beer to his lips. I watch in fascination as his mouth wraps around the end of the bottle and takes a sip.

Why did that give my body tingles all of a sudden? No. No. No.

I try and clear my head from whatever brain fog has just occurred.

Work. Talk about work.

"How amazing was that villa? It has totally inspired me. Look ..." I say. Switching my phone around, I show him all my work that's in progress.

"Oh, wow. You have been busy."

"I've been sketching, too, but it's hard to remember everything because I was too excited at the time."

"Don't worry, I took photos. I'll email them through to you," he adds.

"So, where are you now?"

"At my apartment in Barcelona. Want to see it?"

Oh hell, yeah, I want to glimpse into the secret Spanish life of Sebastien Sanchez. He flips the camera around and shows me the view from where he is sitting. It's so stunningly beautiful with all the different rooftops scattered across the screen. The architecture here is completely different from America, so much so it looks like I'm in a fairy tale.

"There are beaches in Barcelona … in the city?" I question.

His throaty laugh echoes through the phone. "Si. Of course."

I think I need to read up a little more on Barcelona before I arrive. "It looks beautiful." Looking at the long stretch of blue on the horizon, I take it all in.

"Hey, Sebastien, you home?" a male voice calls out from behind him in Spanish. He turns the phone around, and there's a couple of gorgeous guys standing in a living room with some women who look like they belong on the cover of Vogue. They appear sophisticated, chic, and the complete opposite to me. As I look down at my coffee-stained tee, he turns the phone back to me.

"Sorry, that's my brother and his friends," he says, rolling his eyes. "Looks like he wants to hang out."

"Is that the hot girl from America?" his brother shouts out in Spanish.

"Has nothing to do with you," Sebastien grumbles back in his native tongue.

Little do they both know I'm fluent in Spanish. There's no way I'm telling them, I want to know what they are saying when they think I can't understand them.

"I think I'd find it hard being friends with her. Especially when she's supporting such a fantastic rack," his brother adds.

Sebastien curses at him and moves away from the group.

"Sorry about that. I better go. I'll call you tomorrow, okay? I can't wait to see what ideas you come up with," he says quickly, rushing to get me off the line.

"Make sure you send those photos before you go so I can work on them for you."

"Will do. Bye," he says before hanging up quickly. Unfortunately for him he accidentally turns the video off only and not the audio, which is still on, so I can hear everything. I know I should end the call, but I want to listen in to their conversation.

"Now we can party," someone screams in the background.

"So that was your American friend on the phone?" a deep voice asks Sebastien.

"Yes," Sebastien answers.

"And there isn't a part of you that doesn't want to screw her? She's fucking hot. And now single," the male voice asks.

"She's not my type, Joaquin," Sebastien tells him.

"What? A blonde with great tits isn't your type?" another voice asks.

"She's a little young. I like my women with more experience," Sebastien states.

Oh.

My stomach sinks upon hearing Sebastien's words. They

always say nothing good comes from eavesdropping on someone else's conversation, but maybe it's for the best, to quash any stupid feelings I might have started to develop toward Sebastien.

"Sabine is here, and she has a ton of experience."

They both chuckle at the guy's statement.

"You know Sabine is more than happy to hook up with you again."

"It's been a while since I got laid. Maybe I should," Sebastien adds, then there's more chuckling.

I press the end call button on my cell, feeling my ultimate high deflate into a bottom-dwelling low.

18

QUINN

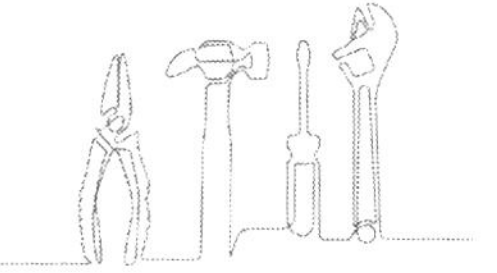

"Let's go out!" I ask Lettie as soon as she walks through the door after work.

"Okay." She looks at me strangely as if I've sprouted a second head.

"I'm free and single. I should be out there enjoying myself not inside working," I explain to her.

"Are you drunk already?" she asks while giving me the once over.

"No, but I want to be."

Lettie frowns. "Look, I'm all for going out and having fun, but—"

"I know, I've been a killjoy for too long. Screw Chad. Screw men," I state while waving my hands in the air.

"Did something happen?" Lettie asks.

"No. Nothing happened," I answer quickly, maybe too quickly because she isn't convinced.

"I've just spent all day working, just like the day before that and the day before that," I explain. "This is the first time I've been single as an adult. I'm twenty-seven years old. I'm in the prime of my life. I should be out exploring my options."

"Now, I'm all for girl power and all that jazz …" she gives me a look, "… but you, Miss Quinn, are not this girl who goes out and goes crazy."

"Maybe I should be. I'm sick of being a boring person, Lettie."

She frowns again at me. "You're not boring."

"I've been with one person my entire life. I've never had a one-night stand. I've never dated. I'm practically a virgin. This isn't right for my age," I explain to her.

"You were in a long-term relationship, Quinn. And that's okay. But if you seriously want to go out and have fun and be someone else for the night then fine, I'm all in," She says with a smile.

I knew Lettie would understand.

"I warn you though, if we're doing this, we are doing it right, okay?"

I shouldn't have agreed to Lettie's demands because hours later, I don't recognize myself anymore.

"I'm so thankful you called me, Lettie." Derrick grins. "I've wanted to work my magic on Quinn for years."

"I knew I had to bring her to the best," Lettie tells him.

Seriously, LA is a small world. I had no idea Lettie knew Derrick Jones, who I met the other night along with Dirty Texas.

"I'm so proud of my work." He gives me an appreciative look over like he's a proud father or something. "She has a banging body and hides it away." Lettie nods in agreement. "And those legs …." He gives me a whistle. "I have to take a photo. Pose, sweetie." He pulls out his cell and starts snapping away. I give him my best red-carpet poses—I think the champagne is going to my head.

"Thank you so much," I say. Running my hand down the sheer fabric. "This is too much, really." Admiring myself in the floor-length mirror, in all honesty, the woman staring back at me I don't even recognize.

"It is my pleasure." He leans in and kisses my cheek. "You girls should come out tonight with me. There's a party at the Sons of Brooklyn house. Why not come?" Derrick asks.

Oh my god, Sons of Brooklyn, I love that band, and they're so hot.

"Hell, yeah, we'll be there," Lettie tells Derrick.

They talk amongst themselves organizing tonight. I take the solitary moment to really take myself in. Looking at the revealing white dress that hugs every inch of my body, the low-cut neckline that exposes a little too much cleavage, and then the hem that only just covers my ass, I feel like a different person. Maybe this is what I need to be a different person. This woman in the mirror looks like someone who's experienced, who knows how to use her feminine wiles and how to flirt and pick up men.

Maybe I can be her for tonight? It's only one night. What harm could it do to be someone else?

Hours later, we are pulling up in front of a Hollywood Hills home with Derrick by our side. The valet greets us and parks the car. We walk a couple of steps to where a large man is standing. Derrick gives him our names, and we are let in through the matte black steel gate. We follow the polished concrete walkway toward a home entirely made of glass.

I wouldn't want to be in charge of washing those windows.

Music is pumping loudly throughout the entire home. I think there might even be speakers in the garden because it feels like it's all around you. Can't imagine the neighbors will be happy, but since when do rock stars care what people think?

"Welcome, ladies, to the fun house." Derrick grins.

We step into the entry foyer where waitstaff greets us with a tray of cocktails. We each take one and follow Derrick through the extravagant home.

"So, they all live here?" Lettie asks.

"Yep, when they are in LA. It's easier to keep an eye on them." He smirks.

The foyer leads through to the living area which melds into the garden and pool area. The entire side of the home looks like one giant piece of glass that has been slid open to merge the inside and the outside.

Beautiful women are draped haphazardly across the furniture like exotic throws.

"Derrick, you made it." A gorgeous blond guy races over, pulling him into a tight hug. He's covered in tattoos, intricate drawings up his arms and legs. He's wearing a holey gray T-shirt, which probably is designed that way, black jeans with strategic rips, black Chucks, and a wide-brim hat. Once he's greeted Derrick, his attention is turned toward us, and oh boy, he's gorgeous. He looks like he's stepped right out of Scandinavia with his tan skin, piercing blue eyes, and square jaw which he's left unshaven for a couple of days. He's scruffy chic. I think it might be Tyler from Sons of Brooklyn.

"Ladies." His face lights up when he sees us. "Who do we have here, Derrick?" He looks to his friend for an explanation.

"Tyler, this is Lettie and Quinn," Derrick introduces us. "Lettie runs the Lifestyle section for a TV network, and Quinn is one of their stars," he adds.

"Pleasure to meet you, ladies." Tyler kisses our hands.

What a gentleman.

He then turns his attention to me. "Would I have seen you on anything? You look familiar?"

"Do you watch home renovation programs?" I ask him, even though I'm sure rock stars don't have time for that.

"I have five sisters. I've probably watched them all." He grins, which makes his dimples pop.

"I was on a show called *Farmhouse Reno*." Internally, for some reason, I cringe when I say the name of my old show.

"No, shit!" His blue eyes widen. "I thought you looked really familiar. My mom adores you," he tells me. "Can I get a picture to send to her? There is no way in the world my mom will believe I met you."

"Sure."

Well, this is a little bit surreal. Tyler, from Sons of Brooklyn, wants my photograph and not the other way around.

"Lettie and I are just going to go outside. Come join us when you're finished," Derrick whispers to me.

No, don't leave me with the hot rock star, I think as I watch my lifelines disappear from me.

"Don't worry, you're safe with me." Tyler grins, and somehow, I highly doubt that. He places a muscular arm around my waist as he takes a couple of selfies of us together. "What's your number? I'll send them through to you," he asks.

I give him my number, he enters it into his cell, and my phone vibrates moments later.

"Hey, I'm sorry about you and that Chad dude breaking up."

Even at a rock star's house, I can't escape my past, and my face pales.

"Sorry, you're probably sick of people doing that at parties."

"It's fine. I understand the fascination."

Tyler shakes his head. "I'm sorry. I shouldn't have said that. Me, of all people, should know not to read the gossip mags. It's just my mom told me she was super upset over the news because you know … she loves you both," he tells me. "But then, she found out about the other woman and the ring he gave her over you, and she was angry for you."

Those blue eyes look down at me, and he gives me another lopsided grin. "Shit! I did it again. Look, I'm sorry, I'm not normally this weird around a hot chick."

He thinks I'm hot. My insides do a giddy dance.

"Just that … shit." He rubs the back of his neck nervously. "You're really pretty, and I'm fanboying, and …."

I reach out and touch his muscular arm. "It's totally fine. In all honesty, your reaction kind of makes me feel utterly normal. It's something I would do," I reassure him.

"Yeah?" He doesn't sound convinced.

"Yeah. I'm not used to talking to attractive rock stars."

Nice flirtation.

"Well, tonight seems to be looking up for us, then." He places an arm around my shoulder and leads me into the party.

19

SEBASTIEN

Things got a little wild after I hung up with Quinn. The night became a bit of a blur. And I wake up to a slew of messages from Derrick who's probably drunk dialed me again.

Opening the first message, I freeze. There is a picture of Quinn dressed as if she's going to a party. Various poses in a white dress that leaves extraordinarily little to the imagination.

She looks stunning.

Who is she looking good for?

Derrick: Do you like my latest creation? I think it's my best work yet.

He can say that again because Quinn looks gorgeous. The pit in my stomach opens like a gaping chasm.

No. I'm not thinking about it.

I'm not going to think about what she's up to and who she is with. She needs to live her life, and I need to live mine.

Dammit! I scroll through the photographs again.

Derrick: Just arrived at the Sons of Brooklyn guys' house for a party. Think Quinn's made a new friend.

There's an image of Tyler with his arm wrapped firmly around her while they sit on his couch. They look like they're in the middle of an intense conversation. My eyes run over every inch of the picture, and I try to figure out what's happening. Deep down, I know what is happening, but Derrick could just be fucking with me. Her entire body is leaning into Tyler's, and her hand is on his leg.

I rake my fingers through my hair.

Derrick: It's great seeing her laugh again.

He then sends through an image of Quinn laughing while Tyler is practically wrapped around her.

Dammit.

No.

You shouldn't care.

You don't care.

She is free to do whatever she wants just like you did last night with Sabine. I open the next message from him, and it's a photograph of him and Lettie.

Derrick: Alas, then there were two.

And that was it.

No more messages.

Did Quinn stay the night with Tyler?

No. I shake my head. She's a good girl. She told me she doesn't do one-night stands. *And yet?*

It doesn't matter at all. We are friends. Colleagues. Nothing more.

I throw my cell onto the bed and stumble into the shower. I'm just hungover, and that's why I'm in this mood.

Stepping out of the shower, I walk into the kitchen, where my brother is sipping a coffee, flicking through his cell.

"Morning," I say as I pour myself one too.

"Morning." He looks up from his cell, his eyes narrowing in on me.

Frowning at him, I ask, "What?"

"I'm assessing your mood?" He looks me up and down.

What does that mean?

"And?" I question, taking a sip of my coffee which is exactly what I need.

"I'm guessing you haven't seen the news." He gives me a weird look.

"What news?" Panic begins to race up and over my skin.

What's happened?

He turns his cell around and shows me a link on Instagram.

Quinn Miller's Rebound with a Rock Star

Then there are grainy images of Quinn and Tyler making out in his home. What the hell? It's early morning there. Someone messaged this to a blogger as soon as it happened.

That's not right.

Quinn is going to die when she sees these pictures.

"You seem pretty cool about it," my brother tells me.

"Actually, I'm really upset about this."

"I knew it." He slaps the table. "I knew you had a thing for her, and now you're upset because she's hooked up with this rock star instead of you," Joaquin tells me.

"It's not that at all. I'm fucking upset because this is the first person she's been with since her breakup, and I know she will be mortified that the world has seen her in this moment."

My brother's eyes narrow on me. "So, you're more upset that her privacy has been breached than her sleeping with some rock star?" he questions.

"You don't know if they have," I add.

Joaquin's lip curls up on one side. "Ha." He points at me. "This has affected you." He grins like he's unlocked some magical secret.

"Quinn's private, especially after everything with her ex. She is trying to reinvent herself out of the shadow of her past relationship. I know what that's like."

Joaquin's face softens at that comment. He knows exactly what hell I went through with Maria.

"Now, people are going to paint her in whatever light they want to suit their narrative, and it could damage everything she's trying to build for herself."

"You're protective over her, I get it." My brother slaps me on the back. "I'll stop giving you crap over her," he says as he walks out of the kitchen.

I grab my cell, copy the link, and send it to Lettie and Derrick. Hopefully, they will be able to get on top of it before Quinn wakes.

20

QUINN

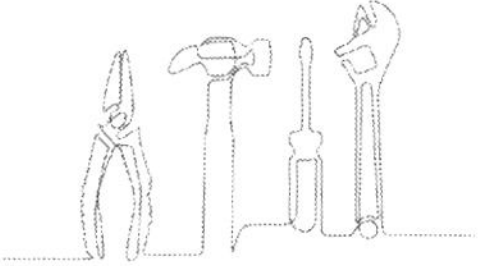

What is that ringing sound?

Rolling over in the darkness, I reach out and grab my cell phone.

"Hello," I answer groggily.

"Okay, so don't freak out," Lettie tells me.

These few words sober me up quickly.

Sitting up in bed, I'm wide awake. Why do I have a sheet wrapped around me? Then I look down and see a nipple poking out the top of the sheet. Pulling the sheet away from my body, I notice I'm naked.

"Quinn?" Lettie's voice filters through my freak-out.

I'm naked in bed.

"Quinn?" Lettie repeats my name again.

"Um … yeah." Feeling a little confused, the night's coming back, but it's fuzzy.

Movement beside me pulls me from my thoughts. Turning my head, I spot the naked torso of a heavily tattooed man, who is sound asleep beside me. I lift the sheet and am greeted by tanned buns of steel.

What on earth! I internally scream.

"So, we have it all under control." Lettie's voice pulls me back to the conversation I completely just blanked out of.

"I'm sorry, can you please repeat what you just said? I got distracted by the naked man in my bed," I tell her slowly.

"You're in *his* bed, not *yours*?" Lettie asks.

Looking around, I search the room for anything that screams Lettie's spare bedroom, but there isn't anything, especially when I spot a myriad of guitars in the corner.

Shit.

Shit.

Shit.

"Okay." I don't know what else to say because I think I'm having a heart attack as I grab my chest.

"Someone at the party took a photo of you and Tyler kissing, and it's gone viral," Lettie tells me slowly.

No. No. No.

"Fuck," I scream loudly, which wakes the snoring rock star beside me. For damn real, I'm having a heart attack.

"You all right, babe." Tyler rolls over and puts his hands behind his head showing off his insane biceps.

I think I might have licked them last night.

"I've sent you the link to the story," Lettie tells me.

My cell vibrates with her message, and I pull it away from my ear and open the link. The article's headline reads …

Quinn Miller's Rebound with a Rock Star

"Shit," I groan as I see the headline.

"What?" Tyler asks. He's sitting up now that I have his full attention. Turning the phone around, I show him the article.

"Oh." He runs his hand through his hair.

"They're saying nice things about it, Quinn," Lettie calls out through the phone. "Most of the women are giving you high-fives."

I can't hear this, not while I'm still naked in Tyler's bed.

"I'll call you back," I tell Lettie as I hang up on her. "Fuck, fuck, fuck, fuck, fuck!" I curse as I cover my face. I can feel the tears prick my eyes and then begin to fall down my cheeks.

My heart is racing out of control.

I just wanted one night of not being Quinn Miller.

"Hey, it's all right." Tyler places a reassuring hand on my naked shoulder. "I have an awesome PR team. We can spin this any way you want." He gives me a sideways grin.

"What do you mean?"

"Oh, babe, no tears. I hope the thought of spending the night with me doesn't make you want to cry." He wipes my tears away with his thumb.

Awe, he's so sweet.

"I had fun," I tell him as heat races over my body.

"I had fun, too." He gives me a wink. "I wouldn't mind having some more fun, but we need to sort this out first." He points to the phone. "Because I don't think you're going to be *in the mood* if we don't." He gives me a Cheshire cat grin. "The photo's grainy, and we can spin this," he explains. "I understand why you would be upset. I have five sisters, remember?" he tells me.

"Men and women are treated differently on social media. They could be high-fiving me and calling you names." He shrugs his shoulders in understanding. "I don't think it's fair or right. So, I'm happy to play it whichever way you want."

Leaning over, I press a kiss to his cheek. "Thank you." I smile. "Thank you for being so kind and understanding, and so cool about my mini freak-out."

"I get it. Not to sound like a fanboy, but …" he smiles, "… you were with Chad for a really long time. Finally, you've decided to dip your toes back into the singles' market, and it's gone viral. Now, I'm honored that you chose me for your rebound, and I'm happy to provide that service again for you."

I laugh.

"Whatever you do, don't feel ashamed about having fun." He reaches out and takes my hand in his, then leans over and kisses my knuckles. "You are a gorgeous, smart, funny, caring, talented, kick-ass woman." He continues kissing my knuckles. "Don't you ever forget it."

I couldn't have picked a better guy to jump back into bed with.

"Thank you. That was exactly what I needed to hear."

"My services are at your disposal anytime." He kisses my knuckles again.

"What about now?" I raise a brow at him.

"Now seems like a great time to me," he says.

After another couple of rounds of rebound sex and some kick-ass pancakes, I eventually make it home, and never have I been so thankful for Lettie's gated community.

Tyler dropped me off. Thankfully, he had an underground garage and blacked-out windows on the car he borrowed. He decided to take one of the other guy's cars, so it wouldn't tip off the paparazzi that were hanging around outside his gates. He was able to lose them in the LA traffic and was able to get me home with the paparazzi none the wiser. He asked if he could take me out again. I told him I was leaving in two weeks for Barcelona, to which he replied that is two weeks' worth of rebounding we could have. I might have agreed. I like Tyler, but in all honesty, I don't see anything more happening than having some fun with him.

"Oh my god, are you okay?" Lettie frantically greets me as I make my way in from the downstairs garage.

"I'm fine," I reply while grinning at her.

Lettie looks me over with a frown on her face. "Who are you, and what have you done with Quinn Miller?"

"It's me. Just not as highly strung as I once was."

"Multiple orgasms will do that to a girl," Lettie tells me.

"Damn right, they do."

We high-five each other.

"So, it was a good night, then?" Lettie asks.

"I've never had sex like that before. You know the type where you rip each other's clothes off up against the wall or whatever surface you can find? Down and dirty sex …." My body buzzes, remembering the crazy night I've just had.

"Good sex will do that," Lettie tells me.

"I think I've been missing out all these years," I confess.

"So, you and Chad weren't like that?" Lettie asks.

"No. Never. I mean, it was always good, and I didn't know any different, so I assumed that was it." Shrugging my shoulders at her, she lets out a low whistle.

"And now … it's 'A Whole New World,'" she sing-songs while I nod excitedly. "By the way, and not to rain on your orgasm parade or anything, just so you know … it was Sebastien who alerted us to the post."

Everything stills.

"Sebastien?" *Did I hear her correctly?*

"Yeah, he wanted to warn you. He was worried about you," Lettie explains.

"He was worried about me?" I point to myself.

"Yep." She smiles smugly.

"I think I'm just going to go grab a shower, and you know …" Waving my hand in front of me, Lettie nods and lets me be.

I rush into my room and close the door behind me. I pull out my cell and stare at it for a couple of moments.

Sebastien knows about Tyler and me. I wonder what he thinks about the whole situation. Is he jealous? Does he care? Probably not. Did he hook up with that Sabine girl? Shaking my head, I thought he wouldn't care. Still, it was nice of him to warn Lettie, though.

I'll just send him a quick thank you, and that will be it.

Quinn: Thanks for giving Lettie the heads up.
Much appreciated.

A perfect response, and moments later, my cell beeps with a message.

Sebastien: It's what friends do.

I stare at the message.

Friends.

He's friend-zoned me.

It's probably for the best.

21

SEBASTIEN

"Morning, Derrick," I answer his phone call.

"Evening, Sebastien. I hope you're doing well on this fine day," he carries on.

"Been pretty good. Production is here setting up on-site while I've spent most of my days riding a tractor and cleaning up the weeds," I tell him.

"Sounds like fun," he says, but it's entirely sarcastic.

"To what do I owe the pleasure of your phone call?"

"Just thought I'd check in on my favorite chef, that's all."

He's fishing for gossip.

"I'm good. How's LA?"

"Fine. Fine. Things are going good here, but ..." *I knew it.* "Have you spoken to Quinn recently?" he asks.

It's been a week since the whole Tyler situation, and I haven't heard from her other than a thank you for the warning. But I have seen that she's been spending time with Tyler, according to the blogs.

"Nope. I've been busy," I tell him.

"Right. Yeah. Well, if you get a chance, check in with her."

What is he getting at?

"Spit it out, Derrick?" I ask him.

"Chad has sent her a slew of abusive text messages after the whole Tyler incident."

Oh, that fucker.

"He's gone to the blogs and spoken some shit about her, trying to ruin her reputation."

My hands ball into fists—that weaselly little shit.

"I think it's shaken her newfound confidence," he adds.

"What can I do?"

"Ask her to come over earlier," he suggests.

"What is that going to achieve?"

"The paparazzi attention is getting a little much for her from what I've heard from Lettie," he adds. "You of all people know what it's like when the paparazzi turn on you," Derrick reminds me.

"I can't force her to come if she doesn't want to," I reply.

"But you can ask?"

He's right, I could. "I'll do it. If things are as bad as you say they are, I don't want her to go through that."

"I knew you'd understand. Well, my work here is done. Have a great day," he says before hanging up on me.

I type out a message to Quinn.

Sebastien: Hey, heard things are a little crazy there at the moment. You wanna come over earlier? I have a spare room you can crash in, away from it all.

There, that's my good deed for the day done.

Moments later, my phone buzzes.

Quinn: Let me guess, Lettie told you.

Sebastien: No, Derrick. The offer is there.

Quinn: Are you sure?

Things must be bad if she's contemplating the offer.

Quinn: I mean me staying. I can stay in a hotel.

Sebastien: No. You are more than welcome to stay with me. Come over, let me show you Barcelona. Have a break before we have to work nonstop for the next three months.

Quinn: Ok.

That was a little easier than I thought.

Quinn: I'll text you when I know the details. And thanks.

Sebastien: Anytime. See you soon.

Looking around my apartment, why does it feel awfully small knowing Quinn is coming over and staying with me?

22

QUINN

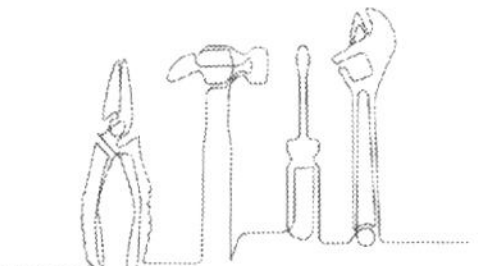

Picking up my cell, I call my sister, Aspen, and let her know I'm heading to Spain sooner than anticipated.

"Hey, how are you going?" she asks, answering straight away.

"I'm over Chad and his bullshit. I can't be in this town anymore." I moan.

"Chad's a dick. The bullshit stories of you being boring in bed and that just isn't true. If you were boring in bed, I don't think Tyler from Sons of Brooklyn would keep coming back for more," my sister says with a laugh.

"He's definitely not boring in bed."

"I hate you so much. You know how much I love Sons of Brooklyn." She chuckles.

"Sebastien invited me to come to Barcelona earlier, and I'm going to go. It's too much."

"That's a good idea. Bummed that I'm not going to see you before you go," she says.

"I'll be gone for three months. It's not that long. You're just as busy as I am."

Aspen works for one of the best events companies in New

York City, Starr & Skye events. Our cousin Meadow, who is COO of The Rose Agency a PR and Influencer agency, knows the owners and put her forward a couple of years ago as an intern, and she hasn't looked back. She loves it and is good at her job too. All those years growing up with a socialite mother hosting parties have paid off.

"It's crazy, but I still miss you."

"And I miss you too."

"Maybe I need to come over and visit you in Barcelona. Does Sebastien have any hot brothers?" Aspen asks.

"Apparently he has one, but I haven't met him yet."

"How are things going with the Hotshot Chef?" Aspen asks.

"Fine."

"You sound fine."

"My life is complicated enough without everyone speculating about Sebastien and me," I tell her.

"I'll stop pestering you. I think everyone can see the chemistry between the two of you and they automatically jump to conclusions."

"We do get one well, but all we are focused on is making the best show we can to topple Chad in the ratings."

"You are going to smash that cheating asshole with your show. No one cares about him and his side piece and whatever bullshit they are trying to peddle. It's a stale show idea. Yours is going to be epic."

"Sure as hell hope so. I have so much riding on this."

"Take all the network bullshit out and have fun. What an epic trip to Spain, changing out in vineyards, and eating delicious food. You're winning, Quinn," Aspen explains to me.

I love my sister. She always knows what to say to make me feel better.

"What about Tyler? Will you keep in touch?" she asks.

"I have to message him that I'm going to Spain earlier, but

I'm assuming we will go our separate ways or maybe we will keep in touch, I'm not sure. I've never done this before."

Aspen chuckles. "You've got this. Now go let that rock star down gently and get your ass on the next flight to Spain." And with that, we say our goodbyes.

I send Tyler a quick message explaining what is happening and that I've decided to head to Spain earlier than I thought. He sends one right back and tells me it's understandable, wishes me good luck, and to message him whenever I am back in town.

That seemed simple.

I've got this.

Now I need to pack my things and hightail it to Spain without anyone noticing. This should be fun.

23

SEBASTIEN

Forty-eight hours later, Quinn is touching down in Barcelona. I'm at the airport waiting at arrivals for her with a baseball cap on, hiding my identity.

The doors finally open, and a planeload of passengers come through. I scan all the faces until I see a familiar one. She looks pale, almost fragile as those bright blue doe eyes look around the waiting area for me.

"Quinn," I call out her name and wave my hand so she can see it's me. Her face lights up, and she rushes toward me. The last thing I expected was for her to rush and jump into my arms, but I catch and swing her around when she does. She holds me tightly. It's nice having her in my arms, feeling her warm, soft skin against mine. We stay wrapped around each other for a little longer than would be considered normal.

"I'm so happy to see you." Quinn sniffles into my neck.

"Hey." Pulling her face away from mine, her blue eyes are now red-rimmed. "It's going to be okay now." She nods slowly. "I've got you," I tell her.

Her body relaxes almost instantly at my comment.

"Thank you." She gives me a sad smile before wrapping herself around me again.

"Come on, let's get you home. You must be exhausted from your flight." Letting go of her to grab her bag, she links her arm with my free one, and we walk arm in arm out of the bustling airport. We head over to the parking garage, and I place her bag in the trunk of the car as she slides in.

Quinn lets out a heavy sigh as her head hits the headrest. "I'm so happy to be out of LA." She stares out the front window as I reverse out of the parking space.

"I've heard about what's been happening," I say. Looking over at her, I am gauging how she might take that news.

"Of course you have." She groans. "I feel like the entire world knows about my indiscretions."

"It's hardly an indiscretion. You're single," I remind her as we head out of the airport and onto the freeway that leads back into town.

"Urgh, I was trying to have 'new experiences,'" she says, her fingers making air quotes. "And now, instead, I look like a slut."

I turn my head to look over at her. "One man does not make you a slut. When my divorce came through, I lost track of how many women I had in that first month. Now that's a slut."

Quinn just shakes her head. "You're a man. Everyone probably high-fived you," she says, sinking further into the car seat.

"Not when most of those women were my ex-wife's best friends."

Quinn's head slowly turns, her blue eyes now wide open with shock.

"Sebastien," she says my name on a gasp. "That was—"

"Yeah, I know … pretty bad form. But I was angry and upset that I wanted her to hurt as much as I was. She took so much from me like Chad did to you, and I needed to get some kind of control back over my life. It worked, and I felt better after it, but

I wouldn't suggest my methods of revenge," I say with a chuckle.

"I understand that level of revenge. But the thought of sleeping with Chad's friends, ew," she says, shivering at the thought which makes me smile.

Quinn turns and looks out the window and sees Barcelona for the first time as we drive into town, her eyes widen as she takes it all in. "Oh, wow!" she says as she moves forward in the car. "Look at all these buildings. They're so gorgeous … and old. Look at all the history." She gasps.

"We aren't far," I tell her as she continues to ooh and aah at the architecture, which makes me smile seeing her enthusiasm for my city.

Eventually, we pull into the underground parking garage of my apartment building, one of the only ones in the area. I grab her things, and she follows after me. I press the button on the elevator. Soon after, it arrives, and we get in. It takes me straight up to my apartment on the top floor, and I usher her into my home.

"Sebastien …" She gasps as she bypasses everything and heads toward the balcony. She slides open the glass door and rushes to the balcony's edge. "What a view." As she soaks in the hustle and bustle of Barcelona beneath her, the sunlight hits her at the right angle and bathes her in streams of light. She looks like she's glowing, like she's an angel that has fallen from the sky.

Shaking my head, I think, *where the hell did that come from? When did you get poetic and shit? Get it together, Sebastien.*

Quinn turns around to face me. Her face is lit with a huge smile.

"I'm in love with Barcelona." She grins. "Can we go exploring," she asks excitedly.

"Of course. Don't you want to rest up after your flight?"

She shakes her head. “Nope, I feel invigorated. I might have a shower and get changed, but then I need to see everything!”

I nod and show her to her room, where she will stay for the next week, so she can freshen up. Then I sit and check my cell while I wait.

“Okay, I’m ready to explore.” She walks out, and I nearly swallow my tongue. She’s wearing very short denim cut-offs, a simple white T-shirt that looks like it’s straining against her large chest, and a pair of light pink chucks. I swallow hard. She has a wide-brim hat in one hand, and a small black backpack and glasses in the other. Her blonde hair is freshly washed, and it looks like she’s air-drying it. “I want the full local Barcelona experience.” She smiles at me.

“Of course,” I say, jumping up off my sofa. I guide her by the back to the door. “Barcelona awaits,” I state, and she follows me out of the apartment.

It takes us a little longer to wander down to the Plaça de la Vila de Gràcia as Quinn stops and admires everything. It’s awesome seeing your hometown through fresh eyes. You forget how beautiful everything is because you see it daily. You tend to gloss over areas while you’re rushing around doing your errands.

“This place is charming. History is written all over every single building,” Quinn muses. “I think the oldest thing on my old farm in Texas was a barn that was built in 1910.” She shrugs her shoulders. “I can’t imagine having a building that is like three hundred years old in my city.”

We continue along the little streets until we make it to Plaça de la Vila de Gràcia.

“Oh my god …” Quinn turns to me. “This is the cutest little square and look at that clock tower.” She points up at the tower. The square is filled with people enjoying their day, and the cafés and shops are filled with patrons around the outskirts.

We continue to the Casa Mila or La Pedrera, one of Gaudi’s masterpieces.

She stares at the stone apartment building with its waves and pointy towers on top. "I've never seen anything like this before."

"Gaudi was a distinguished architect here in Barcelona, and he has created some of Barcelona's famous landmarks," I explain to her. "We can check out more of them during your stay."

She excitedly claps her hands together.

We continue wandering the streets, stopping at local stores so Quinn can have a look. We walk past one of the most famous of Gaudi's works, the stunning Casa Batlló.

"It's so beautiful." Quinn stares in marvel at it. This gorgeous building's façade looks like an ancient gingerbread house, and the roof looks like it's made from mermaid scales. Crazy-shaped balconies line the wall, and there are little twisty towers. The walls have a ceramic glaze with glass fragments stuck to the outside, and when the sun catches it, the entire building sparkles.

"They wouldn't build something like this in Texas," Quinn whispers to me, which makes me smile.

We check out the other famous buildings that surround Casa Batlló.

Eventually, we make it to the famous La Rambla, which is touristy, but I don't think Quinn is going to care. We follow the streets stopping for ice cream, coffee, and maybe some retail therapy too. We make it all the way down to the harbor, where we take a seat, resting our weary feet and looking out at the expensive yachts bobbing in the water.

Quinn sucks in a deep breath and lets out a heavy sigh. "I love this place. I feel comfortable here. It's so different to LA."

"What do you mean?" I ask while trying not to drip ice cream everywhere.

"I can see why you wanted to come back home. There's something magical about this city. I can feel it seeping into my bones," Quinn says, turning to look at me. "I used to feel at home in Dallas, then Waco …" she lets out a heavy sigh, "… but now I feel like I don't belong anywhere. Texas will always have my heart, but it doesn't feel like home anymore. Do you know what I mean?"

I reach out and place my hand over hers on the park bench. "Give yourself some time, Quinn. You'll find what you're looking for when the time is right."

"That's the thing. I don't know what I want anymore."

"It's okay to not have a plan," I reassure her.

"I always have a plan. I've always known where I'll be in five years. To be fair, I didn't foresee Chad and I breaking up, and me losing everything we had built or me sitting on a park bench in Barcelona with the Hotshot Chef," she says with a chuckle.

"Look what happens when you don't have a plan," I say, nudging her with my shoulder.

"Are you telling me I need to release the reins on my life and just roll with it?"

I nod as I continue licking my ice cream.

"Things could be worse than rolling with it in Barcelona."

24

QUINN

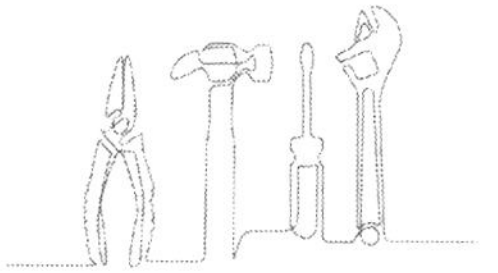

I must have slept through my alarm after getting back from our day traipsing around Barcelona because it's dark by the time I get up. I can hear voices as I walk out into the living room, and other than Sebastien, there's a hot guy as well.

"You're awake," Sebastien says, greeting me warmly.

"I feel like I've slept all day. What time is it?" I ask, rubbing my eyes.

"It's early, nearly nine in the evening," the hot guy answers.

That doesn't seem early to me, and my brows pull together as I stare at him.

"Quinn, this is my younger brother, Joaquin," Sebastien says, introducing us.

Oh. That's his brother. What the hell is in the Spanish water? The man is stunning.

"It's a pleasure to meet you," I say, holding out my hand to him.

"The pleasure is all mine," he says, taking my hand, but instead of shaking it he pulls it to his lips and kisses it.

I turn and raise a brow at Sebastien, but he isn't looking at me, he is solely focused on his brother. He doesn't look happy. I pull my hand away, and Joaquin turns and gives Sebastien a wide smile. He was pushing his brother's buttons.

"If you're up for it, you are more than welcome to join us for dinner," Joaquin asks.

"We're meeting friends at our local which isn't far," Sebastien adds.

I wonder if these friends include the woman I overheard them talking about on the phone.

"Great food, wine, and music." Joaquin turns on the charm.

I'm not sure if Sebastien wants me there or not, but seeing as I've slept through most of the evening, I'm now not that tired.

"Why not? Sounds like fun. Can you give me a moment to get ready? I won't be long."

Sebastien nods in agreement.

Turning on my heel, I rush back into the bedroom, then pull out all my clothes searching for something that doesn't scream country. Because I can guarantee these people are going to look hip and sophisticated, which, let's be honest, isn't really me. *Where's Derrick when I need him?* I decide on my cute boyfriend-style jeans, a black slouchy blouse with some heels, pull my hair up into a high ponytail, and add a chunky necklace and some earrings.

"Okay, I'm ready," I say, walking back out into the living room after taking a quick selfie to send to Lettie for her approval. Sebastien turns, and I notice him give me a full sweep before he realizes he's done it.

"Great." He clears his throat while his brother laughs.

We head down to the street level and begin to walk along the gorgeous ancient streets.

"So, how have you enjoyed Barcelona so far?" Joaquin asks me.

"I love it," I answer enthusiastically which makes him chuckle.

"I see someone has fallen under Barcelona's spell already." He gives me a sly grin.

"Don't get me wrong, I love Texas. But I don't know, there's something to be said about starting afresh halfway across the world where nobody knows you," I say as we continue to walk along the crowded streets.

"It worked for my brother, so it will work for you," Joaquin adds.

I look over at Sebastien, who appears lost in his thoughts.

Suddenly, out of nowhere, a group of teenage girls rush at Joaquin and start screaming at him. They practically push Sebastien and me out of the way to get to him. He poses for photographs and chats with them like it's normal behavior.

"Joaquin is a bit of a heartthrob here in Spain," Sebastien whispers in my ear.

"Well, well, well … I see the playboy gene runs in the family," I joke, elbowing him in the side.

"Difference is … Joaquin loves it." He looks over and shakes his head as his brother gives the teenagers what they're after.

Eventually, Joaquin disentangles himself from them and rejoins us as we lazily walk to wherever we are heading.

"You made their night," I tell him.

"Of course," he states humbly. He reaches over and puts his arm around my shoulder, pulling me into his hard side. "They just had a Joaquin Sanchez experience."

"And you thought my ego was big, his is bigger," Sebastien adds.

"Not just my ego." Joaquin gives me a wink while his brother chastises him. He skips off before laughing to himself.

"Healthy egos run in the family, too, then?"

"Apparently," Sebastien grumbles.

We stop in front of a gorgeous bright blue bar with gold lettering above the door. People are spilling out onto the street.

There's a buzz going on inside just like all the other little places we passed along the way.

Joaquin leads us through the bustle of busy diners, saying *'Hola'* to the numerous people that call out his name, as does Sebastien.

An older man greets us, then leads us down a long corridor and out to the back courtyard, which has one long wooden table down the center. Fairy lights twinkle in the palm trees surrounding the edges of the white picket fence that cordons off the courtyard.

Joaquin and Sebastien's names are called out from the group already sitting down. The guys hug and kiss their way around the table, chatting with the various hipsters and gorgeous people already there.

"Everyone, I would love you all to meet Quinn Miller, from America, who thought it would be a great idea to be my co-star on this crazy journey," Sebastien explains to everyone.

They all raise their glasses in my direction shouting greetings to me.

"I don't think either of us had much of a choice," I say to the group, which makes the table burst out laughing. The group urges us to sit. A beautiful brunette shuffles down as I sit beside her.

"It is so nice to meet you." She greets me with a double-cheek kiss. "We have heard so much about you."

That's nice, seeing as I'm not sure who she is.

Sebastien sits across from me at the table.

"I'm Lucia, those idiots' cousin." She points to Sebastien and Joaquin.

Well, I never thought I'd be meeting some of the family already.

"It's so nice to meet you, too."

"Would you like some sangria?" Sebastien asks.

Not sure what that is, but why not.

He pours me a large glass and hands it to me. It has chunks of fruit floating in red liquid. I take a sip—okay, that contains alcohol for sure.

"It's red wine, brandy, and fruit." Sebastien grins.

The concoction tastes delicious—I can see it's probably going to give me a hangover.

"Have you tried tapas before, Quinn?" Lucia asks.

"No. Never." Looking at the tiny plates of food laid out down the middle of the table, Lucia's face lights up.

"You're not allergic to anything, are you?"

I shake my head.

"Good." Lucia turns to Sebastien and tells him in Spanish, *"Hotshot Chef, fix Quinn some tapas for her to try. Oh, and she's cute,"* she adds at the end.

Sebastien looks over at me, then shakes his head, turning back to glare at his cousin.

"I asked Sebastien to put a plate together for you, seeing as he is the chef of the group," she explains.

Then she gets up and takes Sebastien's seat. By the time he returns from grabbing me some goodies, the only spot left is right beside me. Sebastien stares at the seat, then over to his cousin and back again. He lets out a frustrated huff and sits. Then he places the plate between us.

"This is Chorizo in red wine." He places a bite-sized morsel on the fork and feeds me. A little random and intimate. I look around the table to see if anyone has noticed, but they are all happily chatting away.

"Mmm … that was nice. What's Chorizo?" I ask.

"Spanish sausage," he explains.

"See, I knew you had a feeding kink," I whisper.

Sebastien stills.

"That first night at your restaurant, just before I had my meltdown, you wanted to feed me your food. Just like you did then."

His eyes crinkle at the memory. "Didn't think I had a feeding kink, but maybe I do. The sounds you made while enjoying that Chorizo were sinful."

I bite my lip as I wasn't expecting him to flirt with me so openly.

"Next, salt cod fritter," he says, placing the bite in my mouth.

It looks like a golden tater tot, and it's just as delicious. I'm not the biggest seafood eater, but these taste amazing. My head is fuzzy. It might be the sangria or the fact that Sebastien is sitting so close and feeding me.

Sebastien then offers me another golden fried little ball. This time it's a croquette made of ham and cheese. Bite after bite, he talks to me about the food, explaining that Spanish cuisine is defined by where you are in Spain. Barcelona is in the Catalonia district of Spain, so it's heavy on seafood because it runs along the Mediterranean coast. There are a lot of farms, so fresh vegetables like tomatoes, garlic, mushrooms, and eggplant are used a lot in their food as well as olives. Pork is the main meat in the area. He then explains some of the other areas of Spain and what's local to those regions.

"We have a lot of TexMex food in our area which is quite different from traditional Spanish food."

"You do realize Spain and Mexico are two completely different countries," he asks me seriously.

"Of course I do." I punch him in the arm, offended that he thinks I'm some ignorant tourist. "I know that the Spanish settled in Mexico, but I didn't know how much influence they had over Mexican cuisine," I tell him.

"So, you're used to eating Mexican food, then?" he asks.

"Not really. Mexican food is super spicy for me," I tell him as I pop an olive into my mouth.

"And you don't do spice?"

I shake my head.

He thinks this over before he gets pulled away into a conversation with one of his friends.

I happily sip my sangria as I listen to the conversations around me.

"What is she doing here? I thought they weren't working together till later." I hear a female voice behind me say in Spanish. I turn around and see a tall, tanned brunette kissing Lucia while throwing daggers my way. I pretend I don't understand and smile at her, then sip on my sangria and look away.

"Sabine, be nice," Lucia warns the woman. *"She's Sebastien's colleague."*

"I don't see what the fuss is all about. She's very American. Very ... simple," she adds with a chuckle.

"Behave," Lucia hisses at her.

"I always behave," Sabine tells her. *"Sebastien,"* she calls out.

He spins around and stills for a moment, then gives her a smile through gritted teeth.

Why is he not happy to see her? He seemed happy to see her the other night on the phone. He shouldn't feel awkward in front of me.

She walks over to Sebastien, leans over, and bumps my hand, sending sangria all over me.

Shit.

I'm drenched in sangria. Thank goodness I'm not wearing a white shirt tonight, otherwise, this stuff would be hard to get out.

"Sabine," Lucia calls out, cursing her friend.

As I jump up, I feel the cool liquid run down my chest and pool inside my bra. *Ew.*

"Sorry, I did not see you there. It was an accident," she says in perfect English, giving me a fake smile.

25

QUINN

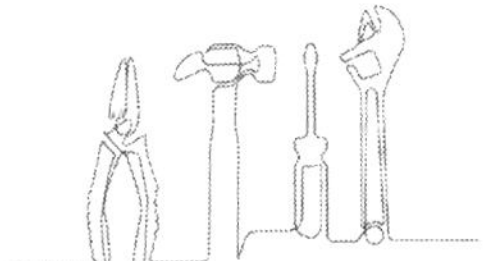

"Quinn, are you okay?" Sebastien looks over at me.

"I'm fine. It was an accident." I wave his concern away. Clearly, it wasn't, and it was a bitch move by Sabine. "I might head back to your place and get cleaned up. Sangria is sticky," I say with a chuckle. I've noticed the tension around the table at the incident, and I don't want to ruin their night because of this.

Sebastien gets up and stands beside me. "I'll take you home, then."

"What? No. You stay with your friends," I tell him. I'm not going to let a jealous woman like Sabine ruin my first night in Barcelona for me.

"No. It's your first night, and I'm not sure you know how to get back to my place, anyway."

Oh yeah, he's right. I wasn't paying much attention on the walk here.

"She's staying with you?" Sabine asks him in Spanish, her tone sounds surprised.

Ha. Take that, you Spanish bitch.

"Of course, she is. I wouldn't want her anywhere else," Sebastien answers her.

Oooh, burn.

Sebastien makes his way around the table, saying his goodbyes to everyone while Sabine huffs beside me.

"Guess you didn't think that through very well, did you?" I whisper to her in perfect Spanish. Her mouth falls open as she stares at me. Lucia's eyes widen as she realizes I speak Spanish and tries to hide her giggle. Turning my back on bitchy Sabine, I say my goodbyes to Lucia, who has been so welcoming tonight.

"We need to catch up again soon. How about I take you shopping?" Lucia questions in English.

"Oooh, that sounds great. Might have to be this week as we start production work next week and then filming the week after and once that starts there isn't a spare moment," I explain to her.

"I'll be in touch," she says in English to the table. *"Your Spanish is perfect. Why are you hiding it?"* she whispers in Spanish as she kisses my cheek.

"People like to underestimate me, so I let them. You find out a lot more about someone's true character when you do," I reply in Spanish.

Lucia smiles and nods.

Sebastien holds out his hand for me and escorts me out of the restaurant.

"I'm so sorry about Sabine," he apologizes as he places his hands in his pockets.

"Not your fault."

"Well …." He makes a face. "Kind of is. Sabine and I had a thing a long time ago."

"Oh, really?" I fake my surprise a little too obviously which makes him laugh.

"She's a jealous woman. I thought she might have gotten over me since I've been away, but …" He focuses his eyes on the ground before him, "… maybe seeing me again has brought up old feelings."

"Was it serious between the two of you?" Must have been if she's still jealous. A broken heart can do that to someone.

"How do I say this without looking like a jerk? She was a long-standing booty call." He cringes as he says it.

"Sebastien …" I playfully hit his arm. "That's terrible." He holds his hands up to defend himself.

"I was in a bad place after my divorce, and she was there, and …" He keeps digging himself a bigger hole, and I give him a look. "I know, I'm the worst."

"Have you hooked up with her recently? She could think your old relationship might be back on if you have." Remembering the conversation I eavesdropped on the other week, I await his reply.

"No." He shakes his head fervently. "No. She has tried, but no." The horrified look on his face tells me he's telling the truth.

"Not even a kiss?" I ask.

"No. I don't want to lead her on," he explains.

"You might need to have a chat with her then. Otherwise, she's going to keep spilling drinks on people … namely, me." I laugh.

"Urgh, I'm sorry. I'll sort her out, don't worry," he says again as we turn the corner to his apartment complex. "I heard Lucia invited you out shopping this week. That's great."

"I like her. She's so nice."

"Lucia is a tough one, but she seems to have taken a shine to you," Sebastien tells me.

"She's lovely, and I'm excited to hang out again."

We head into his building, he presses the brass button for the elevator, and then we ride up in silence.

As we enter his apartment, I shake my shirt and say, "I'm just going to have a quick shower."

"Do you want to have a drink on the terrace?" Sebastien asks. "The view at nighttime is quite nice."

"That sounds great."

I quickly refresh myself and jump into my pajamas, which consist of shorts and a T-shirt, but I also put my bra back on. No one wants to be high beaming their co-star.

Walking out onto the terrace, the cool breeze runs over my freshly showered skin, instantly giving me goosebumps.

"Here." He hands me some bubbles. "This is Cava," he explains. "I grabbed a bottle earlier today while you were resting. It's the type of grapes growing on the vines at the property."

I take a tentative sip, and it tastes divine. "Might need a couple more bottles for … you know … research purposes," I tell him, which makes him burst out laughing.

"Maybe we should ask production for a trip to France to their champagne region to research the competition," he adds, then takes a sip of his wine.

"Do you think they would?" My eyes widen with the possibility. "Because I would love to go to France."

"Let's email them and see." He takes out his phone and furiously types, then sends.

"Oh, I wonder what else we could ask for in the name of research?"

Sitting back against the oversized chair on the terrace, we fall silent for a couple of moments, thinking about things.

"Maybe test chocolates in Switzerland."

"Or truffle hunt in Italy." Sebastien grins.

Not sure about that, but sure, let's add Italy to the list.

"Hunt for antiques in Marrakesh," I throw out.

"Good one." Sebastien nods. "Shop for linens in Ireland."

We go back and forth adding more and more ridiculous things to our list until we have finished the bottle of Cava and are a little too giggly than we should be. I stifle a yawn as my eyes become heavier and heavier.

"I think I might be ready for bed," I say. Stretching out in the chair, Sebastien raises a brow. "Alone." I give him a pointed glare, and we both burst out laughing again.

"Night, Quinn," Sebastien calls from his chair.

"Night, Sebastien. And thanks for a brilliant first day."

"Anytime." He gives me a salute and continues drinking his wine.

I leave him on the terrace in the darkness and collapse into the most comfortable bed known to man.

26

QUINN

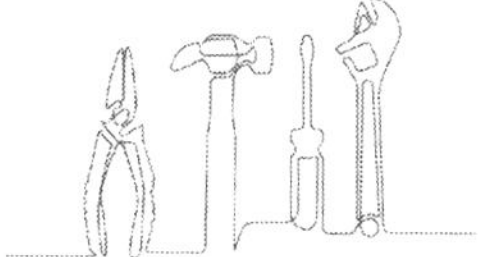

A couple of days after the restaurant, Lucia organized for us to catch up and go shopping. Her only request was to bring my passport. Random. But I've done as I am told.

"You ready for an adventure?" she asks, greeting me at Sebastien's apartment.

"Of course." Excitement and trepidation fill me.

"Please bring her back in one piece." Sebastien walks out of his room and greets his cousin in the usual manner.

"Don't wait up. I have the best day planned." Lucia smiles.

Oooh, I can't wait to hear what we will be doing.

Sebastien's eyes narrow on his cousin. "Please don't do anything stupid," he warns her. "The network won't be happy if it makes front-page headlines."

"I promise, Seb." Lucia playfully hits his chest. "I will look after Quinn." Lucia turns her attention to me. "Are you ready?"

I nod eagerly.

"Have fun," Sebastien tells me as he kisses my cheek goodbye.

As we disappear out of his apartment, I give him a small wave.

"Ignore my cousin, he likes to worry. I promise you are going to love my surprise," Lucia explains.

A black town car is waiting for us on the street as we emerge from the apartment complex. We slide in and drive off through the ancient streets of Barcelona. We happily chat about nothing exciting until I look out the window and realize we're at the airport. I look over at Lucia and give her a questioning glance which she ignores.

The next thing I know, we are turning away from the main terminal area and down a side street, where there's a heap of smaller aircraft, and we pull up next to one of them. A man dressed in a pilot's uniform greets Lucia, and they start talking about today's route. *Is she taking me on a scenic flight?* The pilot then asks to see my passport which he double-checks, then signs off on some paperwork and tells me we're going to Paris.

Paris? As in France?

"Lucia?" I turn and question her.

"Surprise." She gives me a wide smile.

"I thought you said we were going shopping?" I ask as I follow her up the private plane's small steps.

"We are … in Paris." She grins. *What on earth?*

The private plane is lush with cream leather seats and mahogany wood paneling.

"We will be landing in Paris in a couple of hours," the pilot tells us before disappearing into the cockpit. I take a seat against the buttery-soft leather seats and do up my seat belt with a sense of shock still fluttering over my body.

"You okay?" Lucia asks, taking me in.

I nod slowly. "I just never thought I would be going to Paris today."

"You're okay that I did this?" she asks.

"Yes, of course." Realizing my shock makes her think this

may not have been such a great idea, I continue, "Thank you. Thank you so much. I've dreamed about going to Paris since I was a child. I never in my wildest dreams thought I would ever get there." To reassure her, I smile widely.

Lucia nods and smiles back at me.

"Um … who's plane is this?" Looking around at the extravagant mode of transport, I wait for her to answer.

"Mine."

Wait! What? *Hers?* As in, *she* owns this plane.

"I got it as part of my divorce settlement."

She's divorced?

"I'm sorry," I reply, not really knowing what else to say.

Lucia waves my concern away. "Don't be. I was young and didn't know any better. I'm so much happier now. Plus, I deserved it." She pulls out a bottle of champagne from the mini-fridge and pours us each a glass.

"May I ask what happened?" Taking a sip of my drink, the bubbles tickle my nose as the plane makes its way up the runway.

"My ex played for FC Barcelona. He was a footballer. I think you say soccer player." I nod in understanding. "We had been dating since high school." This story sounds familiar. "His star started to rise. His bank balance began to grow. The groupies went from normal people to models and celebrities, and well, that adoration from beautiful women is sometimes hard to resist." She shrugs her shoulders. "Thankfully, I listened to my mama who told me I should invest my money separately for a rainy day and not spend it as if it will never end. Because you never know what might be around the corner."

Wise words. Wish I had done the same. The only difference is that I thought it was my money as I earned it.

"Alas, he screwed around on me one too many times, and I'd had enough. We never had a pre-nuptial agreement. His management didn't want our divorce, but with it, all his indiscretions came to light. They were in the middle of negotiating his new deal with FC Barcelona, so he gave me half of everything and some assets, so it could be amicable." This girl is kick-ass. "I heard from Sebastien that things were not so great for yours?"

Yeah, that's putting it mildly.

"Nope. He blindsided me. Took everything we had built and put it all in his name." Lucia gasps. "My fault entirely. I didn't read the fine print on the documents he asked me to sign."

"Oh, Quinn," she says, feeling my pain. I can see it by the look in her eyes. "Were you *not* able to fight it?"

I shake my head. "Legally, my lawyers said because the document was signed by me, there was no way to prove that I didn't know what I was signing. It was a huge learning curve for me."

"What an asshole," Lucia curses.

"Yep. Also, he told me we should breakup moments before going into a meeting with the network executives where he talked about his solo ideas, etc., and I stupidly let him because at the time, I hadn't had a chance to process what had just happened," I explain. "I was completely and utterly blindsided."

"That man is despicable." Then Lucia adds a long list of Spanish curse words.

"I was able to get *some* money out of our separation. Plus, the network is paying me well to do this show with Sebastien, so I have to be thankful for that."

"But still, your life's work gone because he's a greedy fucker," she states.

"I know, and maybe I'm stupid for not fighting it more." I shrug my shoulders. "But I just … I felt so alone at the time." The emotion of saying it out loud tightens around my throat.

"Well, screw him!" Lucia tells me. "Here …" She takes out her cell. "Let's take a selfie together. Show him that he chose the wrong girl." We take the picture which makes me laugh, then she tags me in it. #livingmybestlife

I burst out laughing at her post.

"Darling, you are." She says, reminding me I am living my best life. We raise our champagne glasses and cheers.

It feels like we have just left when we are touching down in Paris.

The captain holds out his hand for us as we descend the plane's steps, and there's a luxury car waiting for us on the tarmac. We jump in and head into the center of Paris.

My nose is glued to the car's tinted windows as I watch the famous monuments pass by in wonderment.

Eventually, we pull up in front of a gorgeous stone building with the name Yvette Sanchez written in gold on the front.

"It's Sebastien's sister." Lucia smirks, and I raise an eyebrow. "Come on, she's waiting for us."

And with that, Lucia links her arm with mine and walks me into the gorgeous boutique.

"You made it," Yvette greets her cousin in Spanish, kissing her cheeks, then switches to English to greet me. "It's so lovely to meet you, Quinn." She gives me a wide smile then kisses me on each cheek.

Yvette's beautiful with her long brunette hair, dark cocoa eyes, and tanned olive skin. She looks like she should be modeling the clothes, not making them.

"Thank you so much for having me. It's such a surprise to be here."

Yvette looks over at her cousin.

"I kind of highjacked her." Lucia shrugs her shoulders unapologetically.

We're interrupted by one of the staff members coming out and handing us a fluted glass.

"Champagne and shopping go hand in hand." Yvette grins.

We take a couple of selfies for our socials before we start the fun.

"Family and friends discount is available for you today," Yvette whispers in my ear.

"I don't know where to start," I whisper back to her. "Everything is gorgeous."

"Would you mind if I picked a couple of items for you?" she asks.

"Of course not, I'd be honored," I tell her.

"Take a seat by the dressing rooms, and I'll be back." I do as I'm told and take a seat on one of the beautiful blush velvet chairs outside the dressing room, which is covered in cream silk curtains. Everything about the boutique screams sophistication, class, and Europe. Honestly, I feel a little out of place.

A little while later, Yvette arrives back with a handful of dresses her assistants are carrying for her.

"Let's get you set up, shall we?" As they pull back one of the silk curtains and hang the multitude of dresses for me, I feel like I'm in some kind of fairy tale or rom-com montage.

I've just gotten dressed into one of the most gorgeous evening gowns when my cell starts ringing. Reaching down into my bag, I pull it out.

Sebastien's name flashes across the screen. I wonder what he wants. So, I answer his FaceTime call.

"Hey."

"Are you okay?" He looks panicked.

"Yeah, why?" Worry starts to creep into my mind.

"Because you're in Paris!" His voice raises. "I can't believe she did this. I knew my cousin was crazy, but this ..." He's pacing around his living room, then a slew of curse words follows.

"Sebastien," I call out to him. "Sebastien," I say his name again a little more clearly and precisely. "Look at me." Finally gaining his attention, I give him my biggest smile. "I'm. In. Paris." I start to jump up and down giddily on the spot.

Sebastien's eyes dip down, then back up again to my face. I

still and see my reflection on the cell's screen. The dress Yvette gave me has a plunging neckline, and I'm large-breasted, so when I jumped up, my girls did their own little dance as well.

"And you're okay?" he questions me again.

"Yes, I am. I mean, everything's amazing … well, the tiniest bit I've seen so far, anyway." The tension in his face subsides. "Now, what do you think of this dress?" I tilt my cell to show him and then give him a little bit of a wiggle for added measure to tease him. I notice he closes his eyes, shakes his head, and bites his bottom lip. Not sure what that means.

"It's nice," he replies unenthusiastically.

"Just nice? Not sure your sister would like to hear you say that. We're at her shop." As I look in the mirror, my self-confidence begins to take a nosedive. Sebastien must see the disappointment on my face because he decides to be honest.

"You look beautiful, Quinn," he tells me softly.

Oh, I can see it written on his face now that he's telling the truth.

"It's the first dress I have tried, but thanks." Giving him a curtsy that he can't see, he clears his throat, breaking whatever awkward spell had just fallen between us.

"Well, I'll let you go then." He gives me a small smile.

"Okay, I'll see you when I get back home tonight."

"Enjoy Paris, Quinn."

And with that, he's gone.

27

QUINN

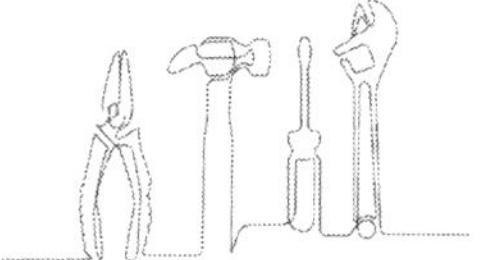

After spending some time at Yvette's gorgeous showroom, where I snagged a couple of evening and cocktail dresses, Lucia then took me to the Rue du Faubourg Saint-Honoré, where we strolled along the enchanting street, browsing the designer boutiques. We continued on around the corner to the Rue Cambon, so we could see where Coco Chanel lived. Then we continued our shopping tour to the prestigious tree-lined street Avenue Montaigne, one of the most beautiful streets in Paris, where we browsed more luxury shops.

We stopped for baguettes and pastries, where I fell in love with buttery croissants and an array of decadent desserts I had never seen before. We stopped for arbitrary Paris selfies along the Champs Elysée, under the Arc de Triomphe, and eventually on top of the Eiffel Tower.

We checked out the Louvre, where I saw the Mona Lisa, which was not as big as I thought it would be.

Lucia explained the different artists like Picasso, Renoir, and Van Gough. I purchased a beret to wear, which had Lucia shaking her head at me while I posed with it in front of a tower of baguettes.

We climbed the steps to Montmartre, Lucia refusing to get the tram all the way to the top. She told me to think of it 'as a French Stairmaster.' The view from the top of the stairs once I had caught my breath was amazing, looking out over the rooftops of Paris, which looked exactly like it does in the movies. We moved on and explored the Sacré-Cœur Basilica. Honestly, it felt like I was living someone else's life.

"Oh my god, you bitch. You're in Paris," Lettie squeals down the phone when she wakes to my messages.

"Isn't it amazing?" I reply while sipping my champagne in one of the many picture-perfect cafés that line the Parisian streets.

"Are you there with Sebastien?" Lettie questions.

"Nope. His cousin kidnapped me, put me on a private jet, and whisked me away to Paris," I wistfully tell her.

"Private jet? Who the hell are you?" Lettie laughs.

"I have no idea, Lettie." Staring at the locals walking past, I continue, "This is *so* not me."

"It's the new jet-setting Quinn Miller. Watch out, world, she is coming …" Lettie screams down the phone, which has me in fits of laughter.

"Europe feels so right, Lettie," I confess. "I thought Barcelona was amazing, but Paris …" I let out a long sigh. "It's stolen my heart, too."

"I can hear it in your voice, Quinn. You sound *happy*."

"For the first time in months, I'm looking forward to my future," I confess to her.

"Grab it by the balls, Quinn." Lettie has always had a colorful vocabulary.

"I promise I will," I tell her. "I miss you so much. When do you think you will be over?" I ask because I want Lettie to experience this new world like I am.

"Not sure … I'm swamped here at work."

"Boo," I moan, which makes her laugh.

"Go grab yourself a hot French man and kiss his face off," Lettie demands.

"I'll do my best. Love you."

"Love you, too." Lettie signs off just as Lucia comes back from the bathroom.

"Looks like our time in Paris has come to an end. I have to get you back to Barcelona before Sebastien kills me." She grins.

I finish the last of my champagne, stand, and give Lucia the biggest hug. "Thank you."

She's surprised at first, but eventually, she hugs me back.

"You have no idea how much this day has meant to me." Getting a little emotional now, we pull apart, and Lucia gives me a look.

"You better not start crying. Otherwise, I will, too." She grins. "I've had so much fun, Quinn. It's just what I needed, too."

We link arms and walk over to where our car is waiting. We jump in and head to the airport, the car's trunk filled to the brim with designer outfits. Never in my life have I spent so much money on clothes or shoes. I decided to throw caution to the wind because maybe European Quinn Miller wears designer clothes. Maybe I should embrace the sophisticated woman I'm trying to be. It's time to reinvent Quinn Miller.

Champagne and altitude don't mix, which I am finding out the hard way as I'm unable to stop laughing on the return flight.

The captain helps us down the stairs and into the waiting car while the chauffeur collects our multitude of bags and deposits them into the trunk.

"I've had so much fun, Quinn." Lucia sags against the leather interior of the car.

"Me, too."

"I hope we stay in touch when you and Sebastien finish filming," Lucia tells me.

"Of course, I would love that. Maybe you can visit me in America, and I can show you around."

She nods in agreement. "Hey …" she turns to look at me, "… just so you know … Sebastien *is* a good guy. Under all that …" She waves her hands in the air, trying to find the right word.

"Womanizing?" I finish for her.

"There is that." She rolls her eyes at the comment. "He's been hurt. He has a wall up, and no one has been able to climb over it. But I see when he is with you, he's relaxed, more natural," she muses.

"That's because we are friends," I explain to her.

She gives me a look that says otherwise.

"I'm not interested in him," I reiterate my stance on Sebastien.

"Why not?" she questions.

"Because we work together?" I tell her the obvious.

"And after that?" she asks.

"I go back to America, and he continues his life here in Spain."

Honestly, it's not rocket science.

Lucia just shrugs, and her eyes begin to flutter shut.

We arrive at Sebastien's home a short time later. I buzz the apartment, the door opens, and the chauffeur passes over all my bags.

"Thank you." I go to tip him, and he shakes his head.

Lucia is sleeping peacefully in the back of the car. The chauffeur closes the door, and the car disappears back into the Barcelona traffic. I wait patiently for the elevator, and I'm surprised to see Sebastien stepping out to greet me.

"Hey." I'm happy to see him, and he looks so hot dressed casually like he is in a pair of jeans and a t-shirt.

"Oh, wow." He eyes all my bags. "Lucia has taught you well." He grins.

"It's all part of the new aesthetic I'm creating," I tell him as he takes all my bags from me and steps back into the elevator.

"New aesthetic?" he repeats.

"Yes. Me being here is a chance to reinvent myself."

"Reinvent yourself?" he repeats more words again.

"Yes, to leave the old Texan Quinn Miller behind and hopefully discover the new Quinn Miller here in Barcelona." Explaining my grand plan to him, I have to admit it sounded a lot better when I was sitting on a private jet drinking really ridiculously expensive champagne.

The doors open, and we step back into his apartment.

"Why do you think you need to change, Quinn?" Sebastien asks. He places my bags beside the sofa.

His question stops me. I turn around and run back into him which sends me off-balance, but his hands reach out and steady me.

He seems awfully close suddenly.

Those intense chocolate eyes are staring down at me.

Thud. Thud. Thud.

I can hear the echo of my heart in my ears, the buzz of the champagne tingling all over my body.

"Because I …" I'm trying to find the right words to answer him, but they are not coming easily. "I don't know if anyone will want the old Quinn."

Sebastien stills as tears begin to well in my eyes.

I was not expecting to become emotional tonight. I blame the damn champagne.

"Because Chad didn't think I was enough," I say the last bit on the tiniest of whispers.

Sebastien lets go of my arms, and I feel his loss instantly. He rakes his hand through his hair, then those intense eyes narrow on me again. "Why do you care what Chad thinks?" He sounds angry. "Do you still love him?" There is slight irritation to his question.

"No." Wrapping my arms around myself for protection, I stare at him.

"Then why do you think you need to change?" Sebastien raises his voice slightly.

"I don't know …" I raise mine back, and his softens a little as he sees my eyes well up with tears. "I worry that no one is going to want me ever again."

There I have said it out loud—it's out in the open now, my biggest fear.

"Oh, Quinn." He gives me a pitying look that I am not too keen on.

"No …" I point at his face. "Don't you dare look at me like that," I warn. He raises his brows in surprise at my stern voice. "Don't you dare feel pity for me."

"Pity?" he states. "I don't feel pity for you, Quinn," he tells me. "I feel anger toward your ex. I'm furious actually that he's made you feel less than perfect." He shakes his head angrily.

Sebastien takes a couple of purposeful steps toward me. "You are an amazing woman, Quinn Miller," he tells me, but his kind words make me look away from him. "You're funny, smart, and beautiful," he continues.

No, I can't hear this. The first tear falls. I simply can't keep them in.

Sebastien reaches out, and his thumb grazes the tear and wipes it away. "A man needs to earn you, not the other way around."

With his kind words, he's melted me into a puddle on the floor. It's probably the accent which has made them feel like so much more.

"Thank you." The two words fall from my lips as I meet his stare. Those chocolate eyes are almost black as he intensely holds my look. His hand cups my cheek, which sends shivers over my skin. Time seems to have stopped in this moment between us. As his hand tightens, I feel his fingers sink into my skin. My tongue slips out and wets my lips, and his eyes follow the movement.

Is he going to kiss me? I feel like he's going to.

Thud, goes my heart in my chest.

"Oh, fuck it," he says just before his lips descend onto mine.

28

SEBASTIEN

I've had a weird feeling all day since finding out Lucia took Quinn to Paris, and I'm not sure what that feeling is. Then Quinn answers the phone looking like a goddess. I may have continued to stalk her Instagram all day just to see what she was up to.

Eventually, although it felt like a lifetime, they came back home with Quinn a little tipsy. She had the brightest smile on her face, and she practically glowed as she excitedly told me about her time in Paris.

What I didn't like hearing was her thinking she needed to change, to be someone other than herself. Watching the tears fall down her cheeks because Chad has made her feel less than worthy makes my blood boil. That someone as amazing as Quinn could be made to feel anything other than the magnificent woman she is. So, when she began to break down, I just couldn't stop myself.

"Oh, fuck it," I curse as I pull her lips to mine.

This is probably the stupidest, most ridiculous thing I've ever done. But to be fair, it makes total sense.

Her hand reaches out and pulls me to her as our lips tangle. The kiss starts off heated before turning molten.

The next thing I realize, I've picked her up and placed her on the kitchen counter. Her strong legs wrap around my hips, pulling me closer to the holy grail. Her hand explores under my shirt, and warm, eager fingers run along my heated skin. It feels so good while our lips continue to collide with each other. She tastes like champagne and sunshine, the two things I love. Tiny mewls fall from her lips as her fingers dig into me.

Reluctantly, I pull myself away from the kiss, both of us needing a minute to catch our breath.

"Wow. Um …." Quinn bites her bottom lip. "That was unexpected."

"I … I'm …" I try to find the right words, but my blood is still sitting further south, so it's going to take me a little while to collect myself.

"If you say to me that you're sorry, that whatever just happened was a mistake, then I'm going to punch you in the dick," she warns. Those blue eyes narrow in on me, her cheeks are flushed, and her pink, pouty lips are swollen from our kiss.

Her reaction makes me smile.

"It wasn't a mistake, Quinn," I reply. Quinn's legs are still wrapped around my waist, and I can still feel the heat between us.

"Good." She grins at me. Then a frown forms across her forehead. "So, while that kiss was hot and all," she states awkwardly. "I'm not sure why you did it?" Those doe blue eyes widen as she looks up at me, waiting for my explanation.

Reaching out, I cup her face again, my thumb running along her flushed cheek. "I wanted you to know I like you the way you are. I don't want you to change, and especially not for a man."

Her mouth forms an O-shape as she listens to my explanation. "So, you like *me*, just the way I am?" she questions, her eyes tracing over my face to find a crack of untruth.

"Yeah, I kind of do." Giving her a wide smile, I continue, "Just the way you are." Leaning forward again, I kiss her lips, and she hums her approval.

"So, um …" her face screws up a little bit, "… not that I'm complaining about anything, but why do you keep kissing me?"

My hand falls away from her face as I contemplate her question. "I don't know. I just want to."

"So, what you're telling me is I should expect random make-out sessions with you?" she pushes the subject.

"Well, no … because um … I …." Dammit! She is confusing the hell out of me. "We are friends," I add.

"Oh …" Her eyes widen. "So, that's how you kiss your friends?" She chuckles. "No wonder Sabine is confused as hell about where you stand if you kiss your friends like that."

"Quinn …." I give her a look, which she ignores and simply smiles.

"I think I might go and have a shower."

As she tries to move away from me, I declare, "I think we should talk about what just happened?" This woman is confusing me.

"I thought we just did." She shrugs her shoulders nonchalantly.

Did we? She has me all tangled up.

"You said that you kissed me because we are friends, and you wanted to make me happy," she explains.

Is that what I said? I don't even know anymore.

"Yeah. That seems about right."

"Great." She taps me on my chest with her palm. "I'm glad we have that sorted. I need to go shower. I feel icky from all that travel."

I move to the side for her to jump off the counter. "Have you eaten?" I ask.

She turns and looks back at me. "Nope, and I'm starved."

And with those few words, she turns back and disappears into her bedroom.

Shaking my head in confusion, I walk into my kitchen.

What on earth just happened?

I stare into the pantry, trying to figure out what I should cook for dinner.

A little while later, Quinn steps back into the living room freshly showered. She's dressed in some black leggings and a red slouchy top that falls off the shoulder exposing her black lacy bra underneath.

Is this woman trying to kill me?

"Whatever that is, it smells delicious." She floats toward the kitchen with her nose in the air. "What is it?" she asks while watching me plate in the kitchen.

"It's Esqueixada de bacallà. Salted cod, shredded, then I've added chopped tomatoes, red peppers, and onions. I've also added some wilted spinach and olives with a splash of olive oil," I explain.

"Smells great. Do you need me to do anything?" she asks, and I shake my head.

"I've set up a table outside for us to eat," I tell her. "There's some wine if you want to grab yourself a glass." She smiles at me and makes her way out to the terrace. I finish plating the food and then take the dishes out to where she's sitting.

"Que aproveche or bon appétit," I tell her as I take my seat.

"This looks amazing, Sebastien." She studies her meal. "Cheers." She lifts her red wine glass toward me.

"Salud." I raise my own, and we clink our glasses together and start on our meal.

"This is delicious." Quinn moans as she savour the mouthful she takes from her fork.

"You sound surprised?"

Quinn rolls her eyes exaggeratedly. "Sorry, I didn't mean to offend the chef." She chuckles as she takes another mouthful of food.

"You've tasted my food before, in LA," I remind her.

"That was breakfast. Who knew you could kill for dinner too?" She laughs.

"The three-month waiting list at my LA restaurant would indicate I kill it at dinner, too."

Quinn bursts out laughing. "I didn't realize chefs were so needy. Yes, Sebastien, your food is amazing. I now understand why millions of women fangirl over the Hotshot Chef."

"All I care about is the one sitting in front of me."

"Yes, you have a new fangirl here, too," she says with a smile.

We continue eating our dinner, and the conversation flows easily. She talks about her family in Dallas, how she grew up under the shadow of her socialite mother who runs Dallas society, and the pressures of always being perfect. It makes a whole lot of sense now why she is finding it hard to work out who she is. Her family is so prominent in Dallas thanks to her father's family's company that she had to be the perfect daughter and never step out of line and embarrass them. She explained how she grew up surrounded by wealth and money, which is why she's never coveted it, like Chad did, who didn't have the same upbringing as her. This really explains so much, especially why Chad is so obsessed with being better than Quinn. He felt emasculated because she was rich, and he wasn't. I understand that feeling as I felt it for a time when I first dated Maria, then being thrust into this new world I knew nothing about. It's hard, but also, I grew up and realized it's not my partner's fault that they were born into that family. They can't change who their parents are no more than you can change the color of the sky to purple. I got over my own insecurities and stopped blaming my partner. Chad never grew that far. Quinn then tells me about her sister Aspen who lives in New York and her crazy cousins who are scattered around the country and the wild times they had growing up together.

Then it was my turn to fill her in on my own family. It isn't quite as big as hers. My parents only had another sibling each, so my list of cousins is not that extensive. She asks me questions about growing up, and I share childhood stories about my family. It's nice, easy. We are both enjoying each other's company, and if I'm honest, it's one of the best dinner dates I've ever had. I know it's not a date but … it's good either way.

Quinn insisted on cleaning away the dishes because I cooked. She told me not to worry, that she would pop them in the dishwasher and join me for more wine out on the terrace. I've commandeered one of the daybeds and laid back against the cushions while looking out at the twinkling lights of Barcelona, feeling content.

Quinn's cell starts ringing on the table beside me. Looking over at it, UNKNOWN NUMBER flashes across the screen. Standing, I pick up her phone and walk it inside to her, but it stops before I have a chance to tell her.

"Someone just called but it was an unknown number."

Quinn places the last plate into the dishwasher, then turns around to look at me.

"Weird."

"Maybe it was someone from the network calling."

"They'll call back if it's urgent."

The phone vibrates in my hand again. "Answer it," she says.

"You sure?"

"My hands are dirty from the dishes. Put it on speaker."

I quickly tap the answer button and put it on speaker. "Hello, Quinn's phone, Sebastien speaking." Putting on my best customer-service voice, the phone is silent for a couple of moments.

"Put Quinn on," a male's voice echoes angrily down the phone.

Quinn's eyes widen, and her face pales as she mouths the word Chad to me.

What the fuck. Why the hell is he calling? What could he possibly want from Quinn? Isn't he supposed to be happy and in love?

"She's busy at the moment. Can I take a message?"

A smile falls across Quinn's lips at my reply, but she still looks nervous.

"Didn't think it would take her long to fall into your bed. Taking advantage of a poor heartbroken woman like that. Pretty disgusting to take advantage like that, but I guess with your reputation, it makes sense." Chad slurs down the phone. He's drunk.

Explains the phone call. Probably got in a fight with the fiancée too. So, he thought he would call Quinn and get his fix that way.

"She didn't seem too heartbroken when she was screaming my name earlier. But you tell yourself whatever you need to."

'Sorry' I mouth to Quinn. It wasn't the nicest thing to say, but the man has my blood boiling.

She shakes her head, indicating she's okay.

"Nice story, bro, but it didn't happen. Quinn's like a limp fish in bed."

My hand balls into a fist. I've never wanted to reach down the phone and strangle someone more than I do right now.

"Or maybe you were doing it wrong." I bite back angrily. Turning, I see Quinn wiping away tears.

"She's a notch on your belt. You don't give a fuck about her. Quinn and I have a long history together. Whatever is going on between the two of you can't compete. Her #livingmybestlife all over her socials is proof that she isn't over me. I can see through her pathetic attempt to make me jealous." He slurs down the phone.

"And yet here you are supposedly happily engaged and drunk calling your ex."

"Fuck you. I could get Quinn back anytime I want," he spits.

"Highly doubt that. I'll make it my mission that you will be the furthest thing from her mind every single night." And with that, I hang up the phone call over listening to his venom.

"Quinn, I'm so sorry you had to hear all that," I say. Placing the phone down on the kitchen counter, tears are welling in her eyes, her hands are shaking, and I can physically see anger bubbling to the surface as a red mark forms across her chest.

Walking around the island counter, I reach out and pull her into my arms, which she takes gladly, and I hold her tightly.

"You never have to listen to that man's words ever again. You hear me? If he ever calls you again hang out and let me deal with you."

29

QUINN

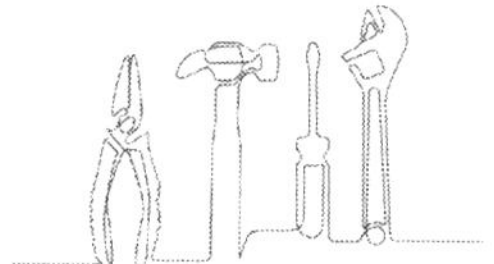

That person on the other end of that phone call, I don't know who he is anymore. I never thought he could be like that and treat someone who he supposedly loved with that much disrespect. Why am I still surprised by anything Chad does anymore?

The way that Sebastien handled him was brilliant. Was I happy that he insinuated that we were sleeping together? No. Do I care? I don't think I do. Chad can suck a dick for all I care. He's supposed to have met the love of his life and yet here he is calling me, drunk, after seeing photos of me online going to Paris.

Jealousy is a curse, Chad Bailey.

I'm glad Chad is still watching me. I hope he sees just how much I don't care about him anymore. I'm living my life for me and no one else.

Being wrapped in Sebastien's arms feels nice, and I don't want to let him go, not yet anyway.

"You never have to listen to that man's words ever again. You hear me? If he ever calls you again hang up and let me deal with him," he says, placing a kiss against my temple.

I nod against his hard chest. His words are a soothing balm against Chad's tirade.

Is there a full moon or something?

Because tonight has been crazy. No, the entire day has been crazy.

First Paris.

Then Sebastien kissing me.

Chad calling.

Now, I'm back in Sebastien's arms. And I don't want to leave.

Will he kiss me again? Do I want him to kiss me again?

What a stupid question. Of course, I want his lips on mine again. I also want them on other parts too.

Think about work. You are about to embark on three months' worth of intense work in front of a heap of cameras that will catch every little thing, and the last thing I need is for the producers to turn a renovation show into a romance.

The man is hot. *No.*

But it feels nice being in his arms. *No, just no.*

He's all warm and hard. *Nope.*

He smells so good. *Stop it!*

No, no, no, I try and remind myself.

You're a good girl.

Or are you a bad girl disguised as a good girl? *No.*

I think I'm going mad with the way I am talking to myself. Reluctantly, I pull myself out of Sebastien's arms.

"Thanks for that." I let out a long sigh.

"Anytime," he tells me.

"Think I might go to bed. Today's been quite eventful." As I step out of Sebastien's space, I smile back at him.

"Oh," Sebastien says.

Oh? Does he not want me to go to bed?

"You're right of course. What a day it's been," he adds.

"Did you not want me to go to bed?" I question him.

He stands there and stares down at me, and I can see him trying to work out what to say. “I think it’s for the best.”

He’s right. And I hate that I’m disappointed by it.

“See you in the morning.”

Hours later, I still haven’t fallen asleep. As I roll over and punch my pillow for the hundredth time trying to get comfortable, my brain doesn’t seem to want to shut off. I sit there and stare at the ceiling for five minutes before I give up. I jump up out of bed and grab my laptop from the armchair beside my bed. Might as well do some prep work for next week seeing as I can’t sleep. I creep out into the hallway not wanting to disturb Sebastien. Just because I can’t sleep doesn’t mean he can’t. I stroll through the darkened living room and head toward the terrace. Sliding open the glass door, I step outside, and the sound of the city fills my ears. There’s a slight chill to the air because of the time, so I head back inside, grab a throw from the living room, and wrap it around me before I set myself up on the daybed and begin working.

“What are you doing out here?”

I scream at Sebastien’s voice, and it echoes through the neighborhood setting off the neighbors’ dogs.

“You scared the hell out of me.” Pressing my hand to my chest, trying to still my heart which is traveling a million miles a minute, I ask, “What are you doing up?”

“I was getting a drink of water and noticed movement outside. Came to investigate and saw you out here working. What are you doing up at this time?”

“I couldn’t sleep,” I confess.

Sebastien takes a seat beside me.

“My mind doesn’t seem to want to shut off.”

He nods in understanding.

“I thought I would catch up on some work.”

“Want some company?” He doesn’t wait for my answer, he decides that he’s joining me anyway. He takes a seat on the daybed opposite mine. Sebastien then lays back against the fabric and closes his eyes.

"What are you doing?"

"Shh … I'm sleeping," he tells me.

"Sebastien … come on. This is ridiculous. You can't sleep out here because of me."

"I can sleep anywhere. It's all good. Promise." He cracks an eye at me.

"Sebastien." I shake his arm. "Please …" I plead with him. "It doesn't make me feel right you are out here when I'm the one with insomnia."

"I told you, I'm fine. I don't like you being out here alone," he tells me.

I guess we are at a stalemate.

"Unless …"

"Unless what?" I repeat.

"What I'm about to say might sound weird, but I promise you I'm not being weird." Sebastien swings his legs over the daybed and sits up to face me. "Come sleep in my bed." I choke on my surprise at his words. "In a platonic kind of way."

Yeah, right. Isn't that what all men say?

"Lucia said that some nights she suffered insomnia, but when she had someone else in her bed, she was able to relax and fall asleep."

My eyes narrow on him. This is not cool if he's using his cousin's misfortune to get laid.

"She said it was like when your partner would go away, and you don't seem to have the best night's sleep because they're no longer there," he explains.

That does sound plausible, and I used to hate being in my bed by myself when Chad was away.

"I think so much has happened today my brain can't process it," I explain.

"Well, the offer is there. No strings attached. No funny business. Nothing." He lays back on the daybed and closes his eyes as if he doesn't have a care in the world.

"Urgh. You're so annoying." I hastily pack up all my stuff. "Fine! Take me to bed, Sebastien."

His eyes fly open at my comment.

It's late.

I'm tired.

I didn't mean for it to sound so flirtatious, or did I? No. Maybe. I don't know.

We make our way back inside. I drop my stuff onto the sofa and tentatively follow him. He opens the door to his inner sanctum, and I'm surprised at how clean his room is. There's no crusty underwear on the floor, which is a bonus. It's decorated in various shades of gray—simple masculinity. The bed is huge and looks comfortable. I slide into the opposite side to where the sheets are pulled back as I assume that's his side of the bed, and he follows after me.

"Night, Quinn."

"Night, Sebastien."

And moments later, I'm passed out.

That was the best night's sleep I have had since arriving in Spain. I feel rested, relaxed, and refreshed. I try to roll onto my back, but something's in my way. That's when I feel the warm breath against my skin.

My body tenses as I feel the hardness against me.

What the hell happened? Did we? No. I don't think so. I would know, wouldn't I?

"Would you stop freaking out?" Sebastien groans beside me.

"I would if something wasn't poking me in the back."

"I can't control that," he grumbles.

"Um … yeah, you can," I tell him, making him chuckle.

"Aah, so you want to watch me take care of it, then? Because I can. I won't mind the visual of you dressed in next to nothing in my bed to relive it."

My thighs clench together as I try and ease the throb that's started as the images of watching Sebastien servicing himself filter through my mind.

"Looks like you might need some relief too," he whispers against my neck, his warm breath lacing my skin with goosebumps.

Yes. I do feel like I need him to relieve what is happening between my thighs, but I'm not sure if it is a good idea.

Sebastien chuckles as if he can read my mind. "How did you sleep?" he asks.

Taking in a deep breath, I turn over and face Sebastien directly. He looks all soft and messy in the mornings. His dark brown hair has fallen haphazardly over his face. His five o'clock shadow on his jaw is in full effect. I probably look a mess, like someone has dragged me through a bush backward.

"Your crazy theory seemed to have worked."

"I've been known to be right a couple of times," he jokes.

"Thanks for dealing with the hot mess my life seems to be. Not exactly what you signed up for when you signed on to do the show."

"Pretty sure you didn't think you would be here in bed with a handsome chef in Spain, either," he adds playfully. "Yet, here we are."

"Your ego knows no bounds."

"It's nice lying here with you," he muses. "Surprisingly."

"What does that mean?" I raise a brow at him.

"I meant to say … surprisingly normal. Not weird," he reassures me.

I kind of agree with him. I should be freaking out more, but I'm not.

"After my initial freak-out brought on by your hard-on in my back, which, let's be honest, most women *would* freak out over, it feels relatively normal lying in here with you. But don't get used to it," I warn which makes him laugh out loud.

"I promise I won't." He grins. "I was thinking of traveling up to the site today while no one was there to do a walkthrough if you're up for it," he asks me.

"Yes. Give me twenty, and I'll be ready to go," I say excitedly, sitting up in bed. I've wanted to go up to the site since I arrived. Getting there before anyone else will be fantastic. I want to walk the site and see if the plans I have created work.

"Didn't realize you would be *that* excited. Right, let's get freshened up and hit the road."

He doesn't have to tell me twice. I jump out of bed and rush back to my room.

30

SEBASTIEN

I should be stressing out.

Did I cross the line yesterday with Quinn? Absolutely. Do I want to do it again? Hell yes. Each time we cross that line it feels natural, not that we are doing something wrong. The woman is insanely hot, funny, smart, and optimistic. Who wouldn't want to blur the lines with a woman like that? I like this easy friendship we've developed. The way we can be honest with each other. The way we can just sit in silence and not have to fill it with awkward conversation. The way she leans on me for strength when she needs it. The fact I don't mind her being in my space says a lot too. I don't like sharing my personal space with anyone, ask my brother and sister.

Yvette called me after Quinn's surprise Paris trip and spoke about how nice she was and of course, asked the question if I was interested in her. I kept the party line of we are colleagues but I'm not so sure if we are just that anymore. Things feel like they changed last night and I'm okay with it.

She has the approval of Lucia who never likes any of the women I'm interested in. She especially isn't fond of Sabine. Then there's my brother who thinks Quinn's amazing, but that's because he wants to bang her. That's never going to happen. I'm going to make sure that Joaquin keeps his hands to himself, and that Quinn is off-limits to him and to any of my friends. Like I said, I don't share.

Quinn and I have a natural chemistry, but I do worry if we will have on-screen chemistry. I'm so worried about something happening in our personal lives together that I haven't even thought about what happens if we don't gel on camera. They are two different things. You can have the greatest of chemistry off-screen, but on-screen, it's a disaster and vice versa. This is the first time working together, and we have a lot riding on this project that we can't mess it up. There would be nothing worse if we had no chemistry. The three months would drag, and the viewers would notice, which means the show would bomb, and as much as I don't want to do this show, I also don't want to do a shit job of it, either.

"A penny for your thoughts?" Quinn asks, noticing my brain working in overdrive.

We've been traveling for a little while, and I hadn't realized I'd zoned out in my thoughts.

"I was wondering how we're going to work on screen together," I tell her.

"You think we might not get on?" she asks.

"Yeah, I mean between the two of us, we get on well in normal life, but add in a crew, deadlines, renovations … is it going to be as natural as we feel now when it's just the two of us?" I confess my concerns to her.

"Your worries are valid. I know neither one of us really wanted to do this show." She turns and looks over at me, and I nod in agreement. "But that doesn't mean I don't want it to succeed. Also, I want our show to kick Chad's show in the ass."

"Agreed," I tell her. "Are you worried?"

"Yeah, of course. It's like the first day of school, day one of shooting, but Lettie assures me we have a dynamite team around us, and I trust her," Quinn explains. "I haven't seen the call sheet yet, but we may not have that many scenes together. You will be cooking and doing whatever it is on your end, and I'll be exploring and creating on my end."

I hadn't thought about that, but Quinn might be right.

"The team will let us know if what we are doing doesn't translate on screen. As long as you and I are on the same page and communicate if we think things are not working then it will all work out."

Seems fair.

"I'm overthinking it?" I ask, turning and smiling at her.

"I'm happy it's not me this time overthinking things," she says with a grin.

It's not long till I turn the car down a dusty dirt road that winds up the hill. On either side of the road are the vines, and you make your way past them until you reach the top. We park on the gravel driveway at the first building, a gorgeous old wood and stone barn that has seen better days but has good bones, so they say.

Quinn gets out, and her mouth is already hanging wide open. She leaves me behind and rushes toward the barn. "I love it," she squeals with delight. Her hands run over the old wooden barn doors, then over the stone walls. "This is …" she trails off, letting out a contented sigh.

"Come on, let's check out inside," I say. As I pull open the creaky barn doors, the smell of hay and farm hits you instantly, but that can be easily erased, I hope. "I was thinking this will be the cellar door and restaurant. Thanks to the view and the easy access from the road."

"I love it." Quinn squeals again, giddy with excitement. "Look at those beams. They don't make them like that anymore." She points to the thick wood beams above us.

I walk her step by step through every bit of the barn and how I envision the restaurant. I know we have already done this with an architect and also with Quinn's input, but it's different once you're physically in the space.

"It's so much bigger than I expected. It's so tall," she says, scanning the entire room.

I'd forgotten how tall the barn is. It's practically two stories, and the area is vast but a blank canvas.

She has a frown on her face as she looks over the space—I can see the wheels ticking over.

"Now that I'm here …" she starts, then turns and looks at me. "Do you think it's too late to change things up?"

"I did write into the contract that I have creative control over the project and can veto any plans the network may want if it does not fit in with my branding. So, if we need to change something because it might be a better fit for my business, then it's fine. What are you thinking?"

"With the height of this barn, you could build a mezzanine level. Maybe make it for private dining or an event space, something like that." She points out the area she means which is above the current dining room. "By going up another level, you have increased the number of people you're allowed to have in here."

That is an extremely good point.

"We could even cut into the roof and replace a portion with glass above this section, and the guests could enjoy dinner under the stars." She shrugs as if she's worried I will hate the idea.

"I love it," I tell her, which makes her smile. "Let's go outside and see if you have any other fresh ideas."

Excitement laces my veins as we head out the other end of the barn to the overgrown gardens surrounding it. Once you step outside, as far as the eye can see, there are hills of old vines with mountains showcased behind them.

"Wow." Quinn stands and stares at the majestic view. "This is spectacular."

We both stand in silence taking it all in. We then do a walkthrough of where we decided to build the outdoor terrace area, so people could sit outside and look at the vineyard and over the mountains.

"If we can add that upper level, you could build an upstairs terrace, too. I mean, we would be building the patio area, so the square footage is already there. We would just need to change the strength of the beams, so it can hold the terrace above," she explains.

I've taken out my cell, and I'm furiously typing notes into it.

"Imagine fairy lights with maybe grape vines entwined out here along the terrace. We could even make some outdoor tables out of old wine barrels. Upcycle them, the DIY crowd loves that."

These are all brilliant ideas.

We continue walking through the barn area, talking about colors, furniture, and décor.

After the barn, we explore a couple of the other old working buildings.

Then we continue on a little further where I show her the building that will be housing the Cava, the wine the grapes will produce.

I've hired a vintner who specializes in Cava to set it all up because I know nothing about wine other than how to drink it and what food to pair it with. He arrives next week. We won't be filming that building being refurbished, so I've given him carte blanche to do what he needs to get everything up to industry standard and running by next summer.

We also discuss turning the old cottage and some of the unique buildings into accommodations. People can stay, explore the region, eat, and drink the wine right at their doorstep.

I walk Quinn through where we will be building the market gardens. I want to use fresh ingredients, and now I have the space to grow everything I could possibly desire for the restaurant's kitchen. I explain how I want to use some of the back paddocks for chickens, ducks, geese, pigs, cows, and goats. I'm also interested in making my own cheeses where possible and even having fresh milk for dairy products. I explain to her how I would like it to be farm-to-plate as much as possible. So, I might have to build an abattoir in one of the outbuildings on the property.

Quinn's not as keen on killing the animals for food as I am. I talk to her about even having a couple of beehives, so I can use the honey and the comb for cooking.

Quinn and I talk back and forth about what to do with turning this run-down, dilapidated old farm into a thriving business once again.

"Are you ready to go check out the secret villa?" I ask as we make our way back to the car.

"Hell, yes," she states excitedly.

We get back into the car and head down one of the dirt tracks away from the main building. I can feel Quinn's excitement building beside me. We turn the corner, and the old building comes into view.

"Oh … wow," she whispers. Her hand reaches out and squeezes my leg while she can't take her eyes away from the awe right in front of her.

"I know." Loving her reaction and remembering my own just the other week, I park the car, and we get out. Quinn follows behind me as we walk down the old stone path through the overgrown garden, and I push open the door.

"Sebastien …" She gasps as she steps inside the villa. She turns around and stares at the building.

"I'm going to make this my home," I tell her. "As soon as I walked into the villa, it felt right. Maybe one day I might be lucky enough to be an uncle. I can see kids running through the vines, picking wildflowers, helping me in the gardens or tending to the animals," I confess. Family is everything to me, and I want this home filled with my family.

"Not your kids?" Quinn asks.

"Don't think it's in the cards for me," I tell her honestly.

Quinn frowns. "Do you not think you would be a good dad?"

"I'd be the best, but I know that being a chef I would be working long hours, especially running all this. I couldn't do that to my wife or kids leaving them to work in a kitchen all day and night," I explain.

"But it's your business. You could set the hours you want. Do you see yourself working such long hours for the rest of your life?" she asks me.

I shake my head. "No."

"Then you would have time for children. It's such a magical place. It would be wonderful to bring up a family here," she pushes.

"I'd have to meet someone first, then have time to date them. I have so much on my plate now with this show and the business. I won't have time to date. I don't have enough time to see my family and friends, add a girlfriend to the mix, and it doesn't end well for that relationship."

"Maybe you've been with the wrong women," Quinn adds.

"Why are you pushing me to get married and have kids?"

"Because you're old. Tick Tock," she says, giving me a cheeky grin.

"Hey, I'm in my prime," I argue, slightly offended.

"Yeah, yeah. Grandpa," she says, rolling her eyes.

The cheek of the woman. Next thing I know, I'm grabbing her and pushing her up against the wall of the villa. "Who's a grandpa now?" As my hand slams against the villa's wall, I press myself against her soft body. My dick begins to throb, coming to attention as it feels her warmth against it.

"Old men are usually all talk and no action, so …" she says, arching a brow at me.

Guess that's my green light to take things further. She can tell me to stop anytime she wants. I'm so thankful she chose a sundress today because my hand reaches out and lifts the hem of her dress and slides it up her thigh. She takes a shaky breath, making her breasts rise and fall before me.

"You can tell me to stop anytime you want, Quinn, but if you don't then I'm going to take what I haven't stopped thinking of since the moment I met you," I tell her through gritted teeth.

"You don't see me putting up a fight, yet," she answers breathlessly.

Fuck.

She wants this as much as I do. My hand slides between her thighs and my knuckles run along her underwear. A moan falls from Quinn's lips as I run a knuckle along her fabric-covered slit.

"Bet if I slide my fingers beneath your knickers you'd be soaked," I whisper against her skin. She subtly moves closer to me as if egging me on to find out how wet she really is. I move her knickers to the side with one finger as I slide another through her wet folds. A moan falls from her lips at the contact. "You're soaked, Quinn. You been thinking about what it would be like if I slide my dick between these pretty little folds, right here, right now? We're all alone on this mountain. No one could hear you screaming my name. It would be our dirty little secret. Wouldn't it."

Quinn nods and her teeth sink into her bottom lip as she tries to hide a moan from me.

"I want to hear how much you like my fingers sliding through your wetness, Quinn. Show me just how much you like what I'm doing to you," I command as I slip a finger inside her.

"Fuck, Sebastien," she curses, throwing her head back.

"I'll be happy to do that later, sweetness. First, I need you dripping over my fingers."

Quinn closes her eyes, and her head falls back against the wall as I slide another thick finger into her. Suddenly, her bag begins to vibrate, and my hand stills at the interruption.

"Answer it."

Quinn's doe blue eyes widen at the stern command as she tries to grab her phone out of her purse.

"It's my sister," she says, holding the ringing phone in her hand unsure what to do.

"Answer it," I say again.

She swallows hard and answers the phone. "Hey, Aspen, what's up?"

Her sister is silent. "Are you drunk?" she asks Quinn.

"No," she answers quickly.

My fingers curl inside of her which pulls a moan from her lips.

Her hand covers her mouth as her eyes widen and she tries to work out how to disguise that sound.

"Are you okay? You sound weird," her sister asks.

"I think I have food poisoning. I don't feel well," Quinn rushes out.

My thumb slides along her clit.

"Fuck," she curses as she tries to stifle a moan.

I'm a sadist, getting pleasure from torturing Quinn like I am.

"Was it Sebastien's cooking?" she asks.

My eyes narrow on Quinn, daring her to say something she shouldn't as I slide a finger against her hole.

Quinn's eyes widen, and she nervously shakes her head at me.

I raise a brow warning her to correct her sister that my food did not give her fake food poisoning.

"No, wasn't his. It was something I grabbed from the markets and didn't know what it was. Guess I won't do that again," she says on a chuckle.

"I've done that before. Have some ginger ale, that will soothe your stomach. I'll let you go. Rest up. And we'll talk again soon. Love you," her sister says.

"Love you, bye," Quinn says in a jumbled mess as she tries

to end her call. Once she has, she drops the cell back into her bag and then curses me out. "Fuck, are you trying to kill me? That was too much. Do you think she knew? That's embarrassing. Oh my …"

I cut Quinn's rambling off as I capture her lips against mine in a kiss. She melts against me, forgetting about the embarrassment of talking to her sister while my fingers were inside her. My hand continues to slide between her folds as my lips work hers over. I push her higher and higher until a flick of my wrist and a well-timed slide of my thumb around her clit has her coming all over my fingers and moaning in my mouth. I let her ride out her orgasm on my fingers as I slowly pull away from her lips. Those blue eyes stay on me as I pull my fingers from her, then place them in my mouth, sucking each one of my fingers clean of her sweetness.

31

QUINN

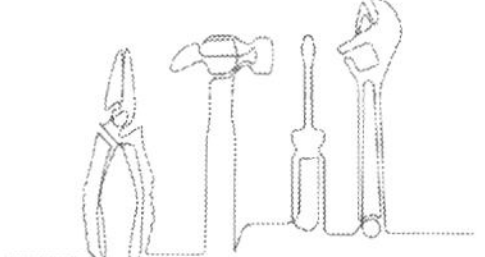

That was intense. Hot. Electric. Filthy.

Did he just lick his fingers clean of me? Do men do dirty things like that? He savored each finger as if it was the most delicious thing he has ever tasted, and the man is a chef so that's saying something. I don't know how to process what the hell just happened. And all he did was make me orgasm with his fingers.

Magic fingers.

I want to do it again. Not the phone call from my sister part, we can skip that bit. But the whole orgasm thing.

"Come on, there is more to explore," he says as he fixes his hard-on in his pants.

"Wait," I say, reaching to him. "That's it? You don't want me to, you know, help that out?"

"If you mean you want to help relieve that, we have time later. For now, I want to show you the rest of the home," Sebastien states seriously.

Can men even say no to hand or blow jobs? Thought it was impossible, yet Sebastien is. Was I not good enough?

"Aren't you in pain?"

He stills as a frown forms across his face. "No, my pants are a little tight, but I'll think about horrible things like peanut butter and jelly sandwiches, or spray cheese, and it will be down in no time."

Oh.

Sebastien must notice the confusion going on in my head as he reaches out and cups my face. "I want you, Quinn, but I want to finish showing you this house first. Once the tour is done, you can do whatever you want with me, okay?"

I nod still in an orgasmic daze. Sebastien takes my hand and pulls me through the rest of the home. There are five bedrooms, a beautiful old kitchen with antique-style tiles, a couple of bathrooms, a formal dining room, formal living, and an everyday living area. There is so much history in this building's veins, and I just want to consume it all. I'm envious that Sebastien has found this site because I'm in love with it. Maybe he might let me live rent-free in one of the other buildings in exchange for renovating his villa after the show is finished. Because I'll do it.

"What do you think?" Sebastien asks once we get back downstairs as he takes me out into the overgrown back garden.

"I'm so jealous. This place is something special. You should be so proud," I confess as we begin to explore the old gardens hand in hand.

"You and I are going to create something spectacular here over the coming months," Sebastien states as we continue to meander through the gardens that have views out toward the Garraf Massif mountains, which Sebastien pointed out earlier in our tour.

I stop and turn to him. "I don't want to mess this up for you," I tell him honestly.

"You won't mess it up. I have faith in you, Quinn. Everyone on this project has faith you can pull this off," he reassures me.

"I've never worked on a project by myself before. What

happens if I'm not as good as I think I am," I confess. It's a huge fear that I've been struggling with since arriving in Spain.

Sebastien reaches out and cups my face, grabbing my full attention. "I trust and believe in you, Quinn."

"But …"

He shakes his head. "No buts. These thoughts and fears sound like something Chad would have said to you over the years. And I will not have that man's words living in your mind rent-free any longer. You can do this. You don't need Chad to succeed. I promise you, Quinn, everything will work out in the end."

Aw. This man. I wasn't expecting him to get me like he has. And he's right. It's old wounds Chad left behind that I'm allowing to fester and open again. I've got this. If Sebastien believes in me and this is his dream, I need to start believing in myself.

Next thing I know I'm reaching out and kissing him. That man deserves a kiss. My lips are on his. Hungry, desperate, and needy as I begin to claw at him.

"I need you," I tell him.

"I need you too," he confesses, and like a match on a tinder box we ignite as his lips meet my neck and begin to kiss the sensitive skin, which is a direct line to my clit. My hand moves across the muscular planes of his back down to the hard globes of his ass, my fingers digging into his fleshy skin, pulling him closer to me. That was enough to make Sebastien lose his mind because the next thing I know, he's picking me up in his arms. He's sick of waiting too. My legs wrap around his waist as he moves across the garden until my back hits a wall. Then Sebastien's lips are back on mine again, erasing everything in my mind.

Electric white heat hits every nerve ending all over my body as if I've just had electroshock therapy. Thank goodness I had the fortitude to wear a dress today because this would be a lot harder. I can feel the stretched denim of his hard-on rubbing against me. The friction is a delicious heat, which slowly and steadily makes me feel like I might explode or go insane at any moment. I can't get enough of him as I continuously rub myself against his jeans like a damn cat in heat.

"Tell me what you need?" Sebastien asks as he grabs my face between his palms, his chocolate eyes molten with hunger.

"I want you," I tell him.

It's as simple as that.

He grins and kisses me again. He's just as hungry and needy as I am.

"Please tell me you have protection," I whisper awkwardly in his ear.

"Don't you worry, sweetheart, I've got you." He grins and moves his lips down my collarbone. Light grazes of teeth grip my flushed skin. His fingers work the top two buttons of my dress open, displaying the lace of my bra. He opens just one more button exposing my breasts to him. His hand reaches out and cups one, fingers digging into the plump skin. He's forceful yet gentle. His fingers find my nipple, and he proceeds to do his magic. *Who knew I could get off by nipples alone?*

His lips move away from mine and back down my neck, and this time he captures my lace-covered nipple in his mouth. The friction and heat are sending me wild as if I'm seconds away from crawling out of my skin. His teeth tug and tease, and I'm done for.

"You have the best tits," he mumbles against them as he proceeds to lovingly motorboat them. "They mesmerize me as they jiggle. I try, boy do I try not to look, but you …."

I am not sure if he's speaking to me or my breasts.

He shares the love between the twins until I can't take it any longer. My hand runs along the band of his jeans feeling his heated skin. One by one, I pop the buttons of his jeans and feel the strained fabric of his briefs, and he almost buckles with need. He feels so hard, long, and thick against my hand.

As much as I would like to tease him, in all honesty, I'm ready for the main event. My hands release him from his hold, and I wrap my palm around his velvety skin.

Well, Sebastien Sanchez, you most definitely have the goods to back that ego up.

"God, Quinn," he groans, followed by a slew of Spanish curses and pleas.

Next thing, his hand disappears into his back pocket, and he pulls out a condom. He rips the packet with his teeth, then rolls it along his sizable length. He nudges himself at my entrance covered by a pair of very thin, damp panties. His fingers run along my slit making my head fall back against the wall. I close my eyes and send a prayer to the gods. His knuckle moves the flimsy material to the side, then he drags the tip of his dick through my slickness.

Yes. Yes. Yes. I wiggle myself into position.

"You have no idea how many times I have pictured myself doing this to you."

Me too.

He drags the tip of his dick one last time through my folds before he plunges deep inside me. Both of us moan at the connection. I feel so full, and he feels so deep.

"I can feel your pussy strangling me, Quinn."

His dirty talk is on-point.

"Give me a minute."

He better not be a premature ejaculator because that would suck so bad, especially when he's all wrapped up in this handsome package. He moves us away from the wall, shuffles over to an old outdoor table, and lays me flat against it.

"Now, that's fucking better."

I don't even have time to give him a witty comeback before

his fingers dig into my hips, steadying himself as he pulls out of me and then thrusts hard into me again.

Shit.

I swear he's going to bruise my cervix if he keeps going deep like this. *Who cares? I'm sure I don't need it.* He finds a natural rhythm, and I'm just holding on for dear life.

Sebastien reaches out and pulls my bra down exposing my breasts. "I want to watch them bounce while I fuck you, Quinn."

Yes. Yes. All the damn yeses.

He feels so good. This feels so good. Why the hell have we not been doing this earlier?

Sebastien's face is intense as he screws me into kingdom come. Well, I sure as hell hope he makes me come again. I shouldn't have worried because this man has skills, major skills. His thumb finds my throbbing clit, and like a damn match, a couple of strokes, and he has me igniting, all the while continuing to screw my brains out.

"More, Quinn. I want more," he demands.

What? I just gave you an orgasm. I don't think I have another one to … oh, holy moly, there is no way he can pull another one from me this quickly. But he does. The pussy magician pulls an orgasm out of nowhere, and I'm floating, lost in the fog of bliss.

His fingers tighten, his rhythm becomes frantic, and every vein in his body pulsates while I wait for Sebastien to push himself over the edge. Moments later, he does, and he lets out a loud guttural groan.

That is the hottest sound in the world, and it sends tingles up my spine. We both lay there for a couple of moments, trying to capture our breaths.

"Wow." Sebastien grins down at me.

I'm still splayed along the outdoor table like a fancy table runner. "That was …" He has a smile on his face and hasn't tried to remove himself.

Reluctantly, I sit up on my elbows and stare at the handsome man before me.

"Please don't tell me this was a mistake?" he warns me.

"No. That's not at all what I was going to say."

"I don't regret what just happened. How could I when it felt so fucking right," he states as he pulls himself from between my legs, unrolls the condom, ties it up, and tucks himself back into his jeans.

I sit up further, pushing my boobs back into their holders and doing up the buttons on my dress.

"It did feel right, didn't it?"

Sebastien's shoulders relax as I agree with him. "I wouldn't mind doing it again, this time in a bed where I can explore every inch of your body."

Oh.

That wasn't at all what I was expecting.

"Is that okay, Quinn?" he asks, staring down at me with those molten chocolate eyes.

"Y-yes."

"Good." He holds out his hand for mine to take, and then he helps me off the table. I give myself a quick fix-up and take his hand that he offers me again, and we walk back through the villa to the car.

32

QUINN

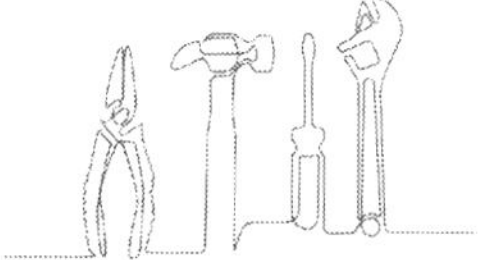

We arrive back home, and I thought as soon as we got back here, Sebastien would be pulling me up the stairs and going for round two. But instead, he stops me and hands me the house keys.

"You've inspired me, Quinn," he says excitedly.

I have?

"The entire ride my mind has been overloaded with recipe ideas for the restaurant, and I want to run to the market and grab some things. So head on up to the apartment, I'll probably be half an hour," he exclaims as he leans over and kisses my cheek. Then he's gone.

Never seen this side of him before, but I guess like an artist, when the muse hits, he's got to follow it. I wonder if that means he's going to let me taste his ideas because I'm starving.

By the time he returns, I've freshened up and am working on design ideas for the new areas we've been discussing all day. I've got paper and drawings all over the dining room table.

"You've been hard at work, too," he says. His arms are laden with bags and bags of produce which he places in the kitchen with a thud.

“Seems like you have been hard at work, too,” I reply, eying off the large amount of food he’s brought home.

“Today in the car on the way back home, when we were talking about the business and our new ideas, my mind started to race with the possibilities. The original ideas I thought I wanted from this project are now beginning to change and crystallize,” Sebastien says, his face lit up with excitement. “With this project, I think I may have been trying to recreate my past. Trying to regain back everything I lost in the divorce. Felt like I needed to prove to my friends and family in Spain that I deserved all of this,” he says, waving his hand through the air. “That, yes, my ex’s money may have been the foundation for my career, but it wasn’t the entire building of it.” Those chocolate eyes sparkle with newfound confidence. “I don’t need to be the best anymore. I’m not chasing accolades or fame. Been there, done that,” he tells me as he moves around his kitchen, unpacking his bags. “I just want to do what I love in a place that I love. I want everyone to have access to my food, not just those who can afford it. I want it to feel like they’re coming home.” He stops what he’s doing and grins.

“Sounds amazing.”

“I want to cook unpretentious food, rustic, earthy, homely. Just like the villa feels when I’m there.”

“You’ve had quite the journey today it would seem,” I say, twisting the pen in my hand.

Sebastien leaves the kitchen, rounds the island counter, and stops in front of me. He leans down and captures my face in his palms. Then he leans forward and kisses me slowly. There is no urgency. He takes his time exploring my mouth with his own.

“Um … what was that for?” I question him as he steps away from me.

“Because I wanted to.” He gives me a cheeky smirk and disappears back into the kitchen, where he spends the next couple of hours banging pots and making things.

The smells filtering through the apartment have me drooling while I've spent the last couple of hours going through architectural drawings of the original plans and the modifications we spoke about doing today. I spent a ridiculous amount of time creating Pinterest mood boards to show Sebastien the images I had in my mind, visualizing it for him. I know he sometimes gets a glazed look on his face when I get lost in explaining my ideas, so I think this will help.

"Quinn, come and try this. Here are some ideas I was thinking of adding to the menu," Sebastien says, laying out the items before me. "I've wanted to infuse my life in America with my life in Spain. Each country having a piece of my heart. So, I've added a Spanish twist to some American favorites."

What a brilliant Idea. I can't wait to taste it.

The first dish he pushes in front of me is collard green soup with Chorizo and a couple of slices of thick, crusty bread. I take my spoon and delve into the bowl, it's a little hot, but the flavors are there. I can taste the bell peppers and paprika, the smoky taste mixed with the greens, and then the salty, spicy Chorizo.

Sebastien grins at me when I give him the thumbs up.

Next, he moves in front of me a Spanish-style mac and cheese. No way.

"This is a little different from what we eat here. I've added Chorizo and Manchego cheese which gives it the Spanish twist," he explains.

I eagerly grab my fork and dig in. It tastes divine, and let's be serious, I don't think Sebastien makes anything that doesn't taste incredible.

"Love it. It tastes like home with my new home twist."

Sebastien grins and then shoves another plate in front of me. "We don't do toasted sandwiches much in Spain, but I thought I would upgrade the humble ham sandwich. This is a Manchego cheese, jamón serrano, and truffle sandwich."

I give him an 'are you serious' look, which makes him

chuckle as he pushes the interesting sandwich toward me. I take a bite, and it's absolutely incredible and not at all what I was expecting. The earthy tones of the truffle and the salty Spanish ham come through first. Then the cheese. It's perfect. Oh, so perfect.

"Love it. Love it."

Sebastien disappears into the kitchen. There's some more banging around, and then he brings out a side of steak for me to try.

"It's smoked paprika rubbed steak with Valdeón cheese which is a Spanish blue cheese."

Mmm, I am not the biggest fan of stinky blue cheese, but as it's currently melted all over my steak and the smell is out of this world, I'm going to take a chance. He's sliced the steak for me already, and it's cooked to perfection. I take my fork and skewer the slice, then pop it into my mouth—oh my, it practically dissolves. Wow! Just wow. I give him another thumbs up.

"Amazing. A … maz … ing," I tell him.

"Thank you for helping with the inspiration today." He smiles as he begins to dig into the leftover food.

"This was all you," I remind him because I haven't done a thing.

"You made me rethink things today. See my vision from a different angle … perspective. So, no, thank you."

I wave his praise away. I don't deserve it.

"If you keep feeding me like this, then that's all the thanks I need," I answer, then pop some more of the delicious steak into my mouth.

We finish our dinner, and after we've cleaned the kitchen, we grab a bottle of wine and retire to the terrace to talk more about the design elements of the project. This time, Sebastien joins me on the same daybed, where I have my computer ready and waiting to explain some ideas to him.

"After being at the vineyard today, I've played around with

some ideas for the extension." I open my AutoCAD software and show him the three-dimensional plans for the add-ons. "I found the architect's plans and tweaked them a little," I explain.

We spend the next couple of hours drinking wine and talking design until we are both way too tipsy, and our eyes are unable to stay open. I must have fallen asleep at some point because I wake to Sebastien carrying me to bed. Only this time, it's to his bed.

"What are you doing?" I groggily ask as he lays me down.

"Putting you to bed. What do you think I am doing?" he says as he pulls the sheets up over me. I watch as he rounds the bed and slides in beside me.

I turn over and look at him. "Why your bed?"

"Because I wanted you in it," he replies. His hand reaches out and pulls me closer to him.

"Just for tonight?"

Sebastien smirks as his hand pushes the hair away from my eyes and caresses my face. "I've decided I don't want to stop sleeping with you."

My eyes blink slowly at his words. "You've decided?" My voice raises just a little.

"Yes," he answers as if it makes a load of sense.

"Do I not get a say?"

Those dark chocolate eyes narrow onto my face as his thumb strokes my cheek. "I simply assumed you wanted this too after today."

Well, of course, what happened today was fantastic just thought that maybe he might be a little freaked out.

"I do. And you're okay with this?" I ask, waving my hand between us.

"Wouldn't have put you in my bed if I wasn't," he says with a grin.

"Just like that, we're sleeping together while living and working together?"

"Does that complicate things? Yes. But I think you and I know each other well enough now that if anything changes, we will talk about it," he says.

This is true. Is it really that simple?

"It's been a big day, Quinn. Let's just sleep on it, and we can talk about the logistics in the morning when my head isn't pounding from red wine."

He's right. We can talk about this in the morning. "Okay," I agree as I snuggle into him, and we both fall asleep promptly.

"Did you think you could reach for my dick in the middle of the night, and I wouldn't do anything about it." Sebastien's deep voice sends shivers down my spine as his lips glide across my skin. I then feel his fingers slide between my folds pulling a moan from my lips.

"This is the reason I want you in my bed every night so that you spend as much time as you can coming all over my fingers."

Never thought I would be a fan of dirty talk. Maybe it's Sebastien's accent that makes it ten times hotter or maybe he's just good at it.

I've never had a sex dream before. Who knew it would feel this real? Are female sex dreams called wet dreams? Or is that only for men? Would they be clit dreams? I hope Sebastien doesn't wake up and notice me dry-humping him in his sleep, that would be embarrassing. It's bad enough that I'm having a sex dream about it. He'd never let me live it down. That ego would be out of control.

"That's it, Quinn. Choke my fingers with your pussy."

That felt real. I shake my head not wanting to wake up but also hoping I'm not touching Sebastien while he's asleep. I want to be semi-awake to make sure I'm not making a fool out of myself.

Next thing I feel is Sebastien's teeth in my shoulder and the shock has my eyes flying open just as my orgasm hits its crescendo and I fall over the cliff with a moan.

"Such a good girl," Sebastien says which makes me jump.

"What the hell?" I squeal, moving away from him.

"Quinn, are you okay?" he asks. I can hear the concern in his voice.

"Yeah, just had a crazy dream," I say, trying to shake away the aftereffects of my orgasm.

"Were you asleep?" he questions me.

I roll over and nod. "I'm sorry if I did anything inappropriate with you."

"Quinn, I just had my fingers in your pussy all morning. I thought you were awake."

Huh. What did he say? I'm confused. It's too early, and my brain is foggy from the dream. "Wait, that orgasm was real? I wasn't dreaming?"

"You thought you were dreaming, Quinn?" Sebastien sits up with a concerned look on his face.

"I thought I was having a sex dream about you," I say, sitting up too.

Sebastien's eyes widen. "Sex dream about me?"

See, I knew it. His ego would be out of control if I told him that.

"Yes, it felt so real."

"That's because it was. You reached for my dick, gave me a handjob, and I reciprocated it back to you," Sebastien states.

Wait, what? I gave him a handjob in my sleep. "I was asleep till about five minutes ago."

"Fuck, Quinn. I had no idea," he says, raking his hands through his messy brown hair.

I don't mean to laugh. It's not really a laughing matter, but it kind of is. I was so hot for him that I tried to have sex with him while I was asleep. That is some intense chemistry, I think you'd say.

"What's so funny?" Sebastien asks, looking at me like I've lost my mind.

"I'm so sorry I don't remember giving you a handjob. I hope it was good?"

"Fantastic," he says.

"Hope I can live up to that next time I give you one awake. I might not be able to compete with sleeping Quinn. She might have skills that I don't have."

This pulls a smile across Sebastien's lips. "You're insane. I can't believe you were fucking asleep that entire time." He curses as he reaches out and pulls me over to him.

"Guess I really needed to get laid. Even sleeping Quinn wanted in on the action."

He shakes his head. "I'm going to go have a shower, then make you some breakfast, okay?"

Sounds like a plan. Not going to say no to breakfast being made for me.

"Something smells delicious," I say, walking into the kitchen. "It's a frittata," Sebastien says, placing the pan on the counter. He's dressed in low-slung pants and no shirt. I love coming into the kitchen and seeing his tanned muscles all glistening from exerting himself making food for me. Is that a new kink? I'll take it if it is.

"Everything is ready. Take a seat and relax," he says, handing me a plate before cutting me a slice of frittata. I dig into it while he then makes me a cup of coffee. I could get used to this special treatment.

Once I'm all set, he takes a seat beside me and digs into his slice, we eat in silence until we are both finished.

"You're spoiling me for other men with this treatment," I tell him as I clean up the dishes. "I'll have to hire a private chef when I get back home, I won't want to cook for myself ever again," I say with a chuckle.

"You are thinking of going home after the show?" he asks.

"I can't stay here forever, no matter how much I want to," I say, sliding the last plate into the dishwasher.

"Any thoughts on what you're planning on doing when you go back?" he questions.

I shake my head. "Haven't thought past the next three months. Anything can happen."

"Are you talking about us?"

I frown at his question.

"I like you, Quinn. Somehow you have crept into my life. You've come in and fitted perfectly into my life. You've smashed through my barriers and left your stamp all around me."

Well, damn, that's the sweetest thing.

"But I'm not looking for a relationship."

My stomach sinks at his words. *No. He's being honest with you, Quinn.*

"My life is about to be the busiest it has ever been. Once the show is finished, my life won't stop, Quinn. It will just be getting started. I have a business and a farm to get off the ground. Every waking moment is going to be taken up with this project. I can't offer you more than the limited time we have together on this project," he explains.

"I get it. But you're assuming I'm looking for a relationship. I'm not. I just got out of a horrific relationship. Do you think I'm ready to get back into another one?"

"I wasn't sure."

"Your life is in Spain, and mine is who the hell knows where, but it's somewhere."

"You saying you're only looking at this being a summer thing?" he asks.

"Yes. I like hanging out with you. And I very much like what happened yesterday and this morning. Even if I was asleep during it," I tease.

"I very much liked getting handjobs in my sleep."

"In my sleep," I joke.

"I like hanging out with you. We haven't killed each other yet living together so that's a bonus."

This is true.

"If we do whatever this is …" he says, moving his hand between us, "… there's an expiry date."

"Agreed."

"And we don't tell anyone," he adds.

"Fine, no Lettie," I say, rolling my eyes.

"And no sharing, especially not with Tyler if he's in town," he warns.

"Same goes for you and your chef groupies or any casual women you have flings with, for example, Sabine," I add.

"Easy. Done. No sharing," he says, agreeing.

"We keep sleeping together, but no one knows."

"Exactly. Are you okay with that?" he asks.

"One thing, does that mean you will still cook me things?"

My question cracks a smile across his face. "Yes, I'll still cook for you."

Sign me up. Orgasms and food, who would say no to all that?

"You've got yourself a deal," I say, holding out my hand for him.

"I can think of a better way to seal the deal, can't you?" he says, wiggling his brows.

"Last one to the bedroom comes last," I say, sprinting off quickly, laughing as Sebastien curses after me.

33

QUINN

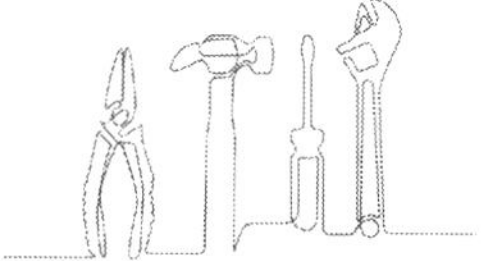

"My parents have invited you over for lunch today," Sebastien states as he lazily runs a finger over my stomach. We are curled up naked in bed together after another morning filled with orgasms. Not only are this man's fingers magic, but so is his tongue.

"That sounds great. I'm excited to meet them," I say, snuggling into his side.

"They are excited to meet you too. But you don't have to come if you don't want to," he adds.

I turn and look up at him with a frown on my face. "Do you not want me to come?" There's a little bit of disappointment that falls across me.

"No, not at all," he tries to reassure me. "We just agreed that no one should know about the two of us."

"Sebastien, I know the difference between meeting the family as a girlfriend versus as friends. Don't worry about me overstepping the line with you while we are there, okay?" I reassure him.

"Right, well then, we better get ready. My mama hates people being late," Sebastien says as he throws the covers off the bed and jumps up naked from the sheets. I watch his tanned firm ass walk into his ensuite.

"You coming?" he calls out from the bathroom.

Hastily, I stand and join him in the shower.

After another round of orgasms, we're ready to go. We jump into the car and begin to drive through the busy streets to the Pedralbes area of Barcelona, which isn't too far from where Sebastien lives. Apparently, once all his siblings were earning enough, they all pitched in and purchased their parents a gorgeous dream home in the elite suburb for them to retire to, which I think is incredibly sweet. He explained that they sacrificed for them to pursue their dreams, so they wanted to say thank you and give them something lovely in return.

Moments later, we're pulling into the underground parking garage of a large villa. Sebastien helps me from the car, takes my hand in his, and walks me through the garage and up the stairs, which brings me inside the home.

We take a couple of steps, and Joaquin is there, his eyes zeroing in on our hands clasped together. I try and break free, but Sebastien keeps a tight rein on them.

"I knew it," Joaquin says in Spanish. *"I knew you would screw her. You lucky bastard."* He goes to give his brother a high-five, but Sebastien doesn't meet his hand.

"Keep dreaming. You would have never stood a chance," I reply in perfect Spanish.

Both of them still.

Joaquin's face pales as he realizes I heard what he said to Sebastien.

"You speak Spanish?" Sebastien stares at me, dumbfounded.

"Si." I give him a shoulder shrug as if it's no big deal.

"Have you always been able to?" he asks. Clearly, he's shocked because he doesn't understand what he's just said.

"I didn't wake up today fluent in Spanish. I've spoken it for most of my life. I'm from Texas." As if that explains everything.

"Spanish is widely spoken down there. But certain words are a little different than your dialect because we lean toward Mexican Spanish rather than Spanish, Spanish."

Sebastien is still shaking his head in amazement before a glamorous older lady joins us. Her jet-black hair is pulled back into an elegant bun. She's dressed in a burgundy dress, and her figure is a knockout for a woman her age. Plus, she's rocking a pair of killer heels.

"Hola, Mrs. Sanchez. I'm Quinn Miller," I say, introducing myself as the boys are still too dumbfounded to speak. I hold out my hand to her, and she too, is stopped momentarily by my Spanish.

"So lovely to meet you, Quinn. I'm Alma." She takes my hand and gives it a shake. Then she greets Sebastien with a warm hug and multiple kisses on his cheeks. A striking older gentleman with salt and pepper hair greets us in the foyer.

"Sergio, this is Quinn. She is Sebastien's co-star in his new show," she explains to him.

"It's lovely to meet you, sir." His eyes widen at my Spanish before he shakes my hand.

"Come, come ... let's sit and eat." Alma ushers us into the dining room, where a beautiful table has been set up for us. A crisp white linen tablecloth, a pink floral centerpiece, and crystal glasses are arranged on the table.

"Please, take a seat here," Alma suggests, pointing to the chair beside where she will be sitting. I take the seat graciously while Sebastien takes the seat opposite me.

Alma offers sangria to the table, and she pours us all quite a liberal amount into our glasses. This could get messy. A plate of Escalivada—eggplant, bell peppers, and onions sliced and drizzled with olive oil served with anchovies, which is not my favorite thing in the world—is placed in front of me. I wait for everyone to be seated before picking up my fork.

The conversation flows easily as Sebastien's parents catch up on their sons' lives. Oooh, this sangria is so good. I take a large gulp to wash the anchovy taste from my lips.

The next course arrives, and it's a huge bowl of paella, which I shouldn't have been surprised about when the rich aromas fill my nose.

"This is a traditional Catalan version of the famous Spanish dish," Sebastien explains to me. *"Each region has its own style."*

This tastes delicious. I can see where Sebastien gets his cooking skills from—his mama.

"How is the project going?" Alma asks Sebastien.

"I took Quinn out to have a look before pre-production starts next week," Sebastien explains.

"What did you think of it, Quinn?" Alma asks, those dark brown eyes narrowing in on me.

"I love it. The views are some of the most magnificent I've ever seen. The old buildings are incredible, and I can't wait to bring them back to life."

"Quinn came up with some incredibly good suggestions while we were walking around, which has helped me look at this project differently." Sebastien looks over and gives me a wide smile.

I can feel my cheeks burning under his intense gaze.

"How so?" his mother asks, looking between the two of us.

"I didn't do a thing. It was all him," I add, uncomfortable with the praise.

"She made me realize what I truly wanted out of the project which wasn't what I thought it was."

The table falls silent at Sebastien's admission. I feel the entire dining table's eyes on me.

"I've decided to drop the pretentious fine-dining concept that I initially thought I should be doing, and now I want to concentrate on traditional, rustic cooking with a twist."

"Sebastien made me a sample menu once we got back home, and the food was stellar," I tell the table.

Everyone's focus is still looking between the two of us.

"I'm going to concentrate more on the farm-to-plate concept ... simple, fresh, good food. I realize now that I don't need the critics' approval anymore. I'm not chasing that Michelin star. I just want people coming back, learning, and enjoying what the winery has to offer."

Alma's face lights up. *"My sweetheart, I am so proud of you." She reaches out and taps his hand. "You know your father and I have always believed in you."* She grins. *"It's nice to see that you finally do, too."*

Sebastien and I talk more about our plans for the farm with his family as the wine flows more and more freely.

"Do you mind if I use the bathroom before we go?" I ask Sebastien.

He gives me the directions, and I head on through a little unsteady on my feet. This ended up being a rather boozy lunch, and I am all for that. After freshening up, I step out into the hallway and hear my name mentioned as whispered voices come from a room to the left of the bathroom.

"Is there anything going on between Quinn and yourself?" Almas asks Sebastien.

"No, why?" he answers.

"There seems like something is there, that is all," she explains. *"The way you talk about her, your entire face lights up. I see a spark of life inside of you again. It's just a mother's observation, that is all,"* she adds.

"Her life is in America, and mine is here. We would never work, so there is no point," Sebastien tells her.

He's right.

Still ...

"She speaks Spanish. Her life could be here if you both wanted it to be," Alma tells him.

"Mama, I love you. But please, don't worry about my love life. Quinn and I are just good friends. She's someone that I want to keep in my life, and the only way to do that is if we stay friends," Sebastien explains to his mother.

I feel the same way. I like him a lot and what we are doing may complicate things, but as long as we stay honest with each other about our intentions, I'm sure we can still be friends after it all.

"I worry about you, that is all. You can fall in love again after Maria. She wasn't the one and only for you," his mother tells him.

"I know. You should worry about Joaquin or Yvette's personal lives because they sure need your help."

She groans. *"Oh, please, we all know your brother. I worry about a scandal more than happily ever after with him. And Yvette ... she is too far away, so it makes it hard for me to be a pest. I just want my children to be happy. That is all."*

"And you want grandchildren too," Sebastien teases.

"You all better hurry up. I'm not getting any younger," she says, teasing him.

Leaving the conversation, I walk back out into the foyer and wait for Sebastien to emerge.

"Thank you so much for coming, Quinn," Alma says, kissing my cheeks. *"I don't think my son could be in safer hands with his project than in yours."*

Sebastien tries to keep a straight face, but unknowingly Alma has created a double entendre with her words.

"You are welcome anytime to the set," I tell her.

She embraces me again.

Then we say our goodbyes and leave.

"You might regret that offer of my mama coming to the set." Sebastien smiles as he takes my hand and escorts me back to the car.

"I think today went well, don't you?"

"They loved you," he tells me.

"I love your family, too. They are great. So much fun. Even though your brother is a dick."

Sebastien laughs and then proceeds to kiss my knuckles.

"My brother is young and dumb." I can feel his smile against my hand. "Thank you again for coming today. I appreciate it."

"You can thank me when we get home." I think the wine might be doing the talking in the moment.

"Is that right?" He turns and looks over at me, then puts his foot on the accelerator, and I push back into the seat making me laugh.

34

SEBASTIEN

"Hey," Quinn calls out sadly, walking into the kitchen.

"You okay?" I ask. Stopping what I'm doing in the kitchen, I pull her into my arms.

"I completely forgot that production organized a villa for me to live in."

This should have been the week Quinn would have arrived in Barcelona instead of the two weeks she's already had here.

"Oh." Realizing what she's getting at, I had declined the network's offer of a villa near the site because my apartment is only an hour's drive away, but now, I'm kicking myself.

"Check-in is today," she tells me. "I know this makes things a little more complicated, but it doesn't have to be. We can still hang out when we have the time." She tries to put a positive spin on it, but neither of us buys it. I've become used to her being in my space, but maybe a little space might be good for both of us as we are about to start working together.

"A car will be here in a couple of hours to take me to the villa."

Okay, so I don't even get to take her out there myself.

"I think we've been in a nice little bubble for these past

couple of weeks," she explains as she wraps her arms around my neck. "I think I forgot the reason why I'm here. And unfortunately, it looks like work is calling."

She's right. In all honesty, I had forgotten the reasons why we're here. The television show always felt like this thing we would do one day.

"You're right," I say as I nuzzle her neck, inhaling her scent of mixed berries, which I commit to memory. "Guess we need to put on our game faces." She nods sadly. "But not before I have my fill of you again."

I grin as I look down at her, pick Quinn up as she wraps her legs around my body, and rush her through my apartment to the bedroom. She giggles and squeals as she bounces against me. Then we tumble onto the bed in a fit of laughter. Quinn rolls herself on top of me, her thighs set on either side of my hips. Thank goodness she's in a dress, it's so much easier. Her hand runs along my chest, her nails digging into my shirt as she lifts it over my head. She leans forward and gently kisses her way down my bare chest, her teeth giving my nipples a gentle tug as she follows her well-worn path over my body. Her hands pull down my sweatpants and release me, and my dick slaps hard against my stomach. I hadn't had time to put on any underwear this morning. Again, easy access.

Quinn's hands run along my dick, gently stroking it.

I reach out and grab the hem of her dress to pull it over her head because I need to see her tits if she's going to be playing with my dick like she is. She's wearing a pink lace bra and matching panties today. That's one thing I've noticed about Quinn. No, it's one of the many little things I have picked up on about her, she loves lingerie and always wears a matching set. Something about that is the biggest turn-on.

Quinn reaches behind and undoes her bra. Her creamy breasts bounce free. Leaning forward, I capture her dusty pink nipples in my mouth. I know that my sucking on her nipples drives her wild. It's as if they have a direct line to her clit. Her hand moves over my dick, her thumb rubbing a bead of pre-cum over the tip sending shivers over my body. Quinn places a hand on my chest, moving me away from her breasts, forcing me to lie down and enjoy the view. I grab an extra pillow and stuff it underneath my head as her blonde hair falls around her shoulders when I feel the first swipe of her tongue on my dick.

"Yes, Quinn." I groan as her warm tongue swirls around the tip, and she starts teasing me. Then her greedy little mouth sinks over my cock, and I'm done for. This woman knows how to give head, and it seems she enjoys it too. She takes me deep to the back of her throat while my hips lose control and move off the bed. She hums her appreciation for my dick, and the vibrations drive me wild. I lose the battle, and my fingers lace into her blonde hair as my dick drives deeper and deeper into her throat.

"Fuck, yes." I switch to Spanish as my mind begins to stop translating. *"Take all of me down like a good girl,"* I growl at her.

She's bringing me closer and closer, and as much as I would love nothing more than to come down her greedy little throat, I'd rather come inside her.

Tugging, I reluctantly pull Quinn off my aching dick, flip her over onto her stomach, grab a condom from the side table, and sheath myself. Grabbing her hips, I pull her up onto her knees as I nudge her legs wider so I can slip between her folds. Inch by glorious inch, I sink inside of her, both of us hissing at our connection. I wrap her hair around my fist and begin to fuck her. I watch as I enter her sweet pussy over and over again, listening to her sweet cries as I find that perfect spot deep inside of her.

"So, fucking sweet," I curse in Spanish as I begin to lose myself in her, both of us coming closer and closer to the edge.

Her fingers slide over her clit as she helps me push her right on over.

"Yes, yes, yes," she screams as her orgasm takes over her, and I'm not far behind.

Slowly, we both come down from our high.

I slip myself from her and dispose of the condom. She's a crumpled mess against my sheets, her blonde hair fanned out all around her, her chest moving heavily, and her eyes are shut. I jump back into bed and pull her against me. I'm going to miss this, being able to have her anytime we want.

"That was … amazing." She sighs.

"Next time, we're probably going to have to be a little quieter," I warn her.

Quinn's eyes open as she looks at me. "We're going to have to get a little creative then." She grins.

Oh, hell yeah, I like her thinking.

"I'm sure we'll come up with something." I wiggle my eyebrows at her.

"Urgh … I have to go pack." She rolls her eyes, breaking the moment, and I let her go watching as she dresses again. She leans over, places a kiss on my lips, and then bounces out of my bedroom.

And my bed already feels empty without her in it.

"The car is going to be here soon," Quinn tells me.

Her bags are packed and ready for her move to the villa. She wraps her arms around my neck and kisses me slowly.

"I'll see you tomorrow for the production meeting," she reminds me.

"Guess we are going to have our game faces on then."

"Come on, it's not that bad." She grins. "I'm sure you can keep your hands to yourself for the day," she tells me.

"Um … no. You may not know this, but I think you're pretty cute." I kiss her. "And your ass is phenomenal." My hands grip her peachy posterior. "Your tits are mesmerizing." I cup one of them. "And when I look at your lips, all I can think about is watching them wrapped around my dick." She licks her lips driving me crazy. “Exactly, like that.” I point as my dick begins to rise to the occasion.

“I mean, you do make some great points.” She chuckles. “But we’re adults, and unless you want the fun to be taken away courtesy of gossip magazines and overzealous producers, then you’re going to have to keep all those thoughts locked inside here.” She taps my head. “I’ll make it worth your while.” Her hand grips my dick through my sweatpants.

Dammit, I want her hand to stay there forever.

Her phone buzzes, and we break apart.

“My ride has arrived.”

My stomach sinks as reality sets in. We kiss one last time because the next time we see each other, it’s not going to be the same.

With one final wave, she disappears out of the door.

A couple of hours later, my brother pops over by himself.

“What’s going on here?” he asks, walking into my apartment as he spies me madly working in the kitchen.

“Just playing around with some recipes,” I tell him as I wipe down the counter.

“Where’s Quinn?” he asks, looking around the apartment as if she’s going to jump out from behind the sofa.

“She’s gone to Penedès,” I tell him.

“Why? Did you guys have a fight?” he asks.

“What? No. Why would you think that?”

Joaquin shrugs his shoulders.

“We start pre-production tomorrow. So, she had to head up there to get ready. She was always staying up there during shooting,” I explain the situation to him.

“You two looked cozy at lunch the other day.” He grabs a beer from my refrigerator and passes one to me.

“And?”

“You are in sync,” he states, his eyes narrowing as he looks over the rim of his beer.

"We're friends," I add, repeating the same old spiel.

He nods. "The way you look at her … says otherwise." He adds, "You might want to get that under control before filming starts, unless—"

"Unless what?"

"Unless that is what you're going for. The whole will-they-won't-they storyline. Viewers eat that shit up." He grins.

"No. No, we are *not* doing that."

"Right. Well, then, you might need to do something about that because even a blind man can see you have a thing for her," he grills me.

"Just leave it alone," I warn him.

Joaquin holds up his hands in defeat. "Will do, brother. So, now that you're free, you wanna come out partying with me?"

"No."

"Boring," Joaquin teases. "You're happier playing with your bottles of spices than playing with beautiful women."

"Yeah, I am."

Joaquin's eyebrows raise high on his forehead with surprise.

"Go, have fun. I have work to do."

I kick him out of my apartment and get on with creating recipes.

35

QUINN

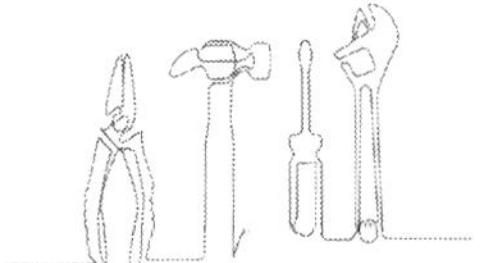

Not going to lie, I miss sleeping in Sebastien's bed. He called me later that night, and we chatted, but it wasn't the same. Urgh, don't be one of those girls, Quinn, who says they're all cool with a fling and then start catching all the feels. I miss the orgasms too.

Today is the day pre-production moves into town, literally. They have rented most of the accommodations available in the town. We have a meeting today with Kevin, the producer, to run through the next couple of months' shooting schedule. He wants to go through the different locations we will be filming and our side locations. Things like wine tasting, script outlines, running through the key lists of sponsors and advertising brands, and our social media including what and when we can share stuff. We have to talk with the stylists about our clothing as we have brand deals with certain companies.

Tomorrow we have a photo shoot for the promotional advertising for the series. So much stuff and my mind is already wondering how I'm going to react when I see Sebastien. I'm worried I might do something and give away what we have been doing behind closed doors. I know if anyone on the team suspects they are going to focus on it, and it will destroy the chemistry between us.

"Quinn, it's so great to see you again," Kevin greets me.

I've known him for several years as he used to work on *Farmhouse Reno* with Chad and me.

"You look positively glowing."

"Really?" Panic laces my skin. I feel like I have the words sleeping with Sebastien written across my forehead.

"Yes. The Spanish sun seems to agree with you," he says as he looks me up and down.

I hadn't told anyone from the network that I was crashing with Sebastien, just told them I was in a hotel, and thankfully, the paparazzi in Barcelona were respectful and left us alone.

"Really? Maybe the getaway is exactly what the doctor ordered," I tell him as I take a seat at the conference table. Kevin likes to have a one-on-one session first before bringing in the rest of the staff. He likes to iron out any problems, which I can appreciate.

"Can I speak candidly?" Kevin asks, and I nod in agreement. "Chad was a dick."

Well, that was the last thing I ever thought would come out of his mouth, and it makes me burst out laughing.

"They gave me a choice between you or him, and I chose you." His words make me smile widely. "I honestly don't know how you put up with him all those years. He was a diva."

"Also, this show is set in Spain, not Texas, so you know," I joke with him.

"True," Kevin agrees with a smile on his face. "Plus, I wouldn't have to put up with being screamed at like I'm an imbecile."

Hearing Kevin say that takes me back to when we worked with him on *Farmhouse Reno*, and I remember the fights they would get into. Chad used to tell me it was Kevin's fault. That he did this or that, and, of course, I believed him, thinking I could trust him. How wrong was I?

"I'm sorry, Kevin, for the way Chad treated you. That wasn't right."

"Oh, sweet cheeks, you do not apologize for that son of a bitch, you hear me." Kevin gives me a serious look. "I heard what he did to you. And when I found out about it, I told myself that I would do anything and everything in my power to make sure Quinn Miller would be number one on our network. And I want karma to eat Chad Bailey for breakfast."

"I do, too."

"Hell, yeah. That's my girl." He gives me a high-five. "Now, I'm guessing Sebastien is running a little late. I've heard traffic in Barcelona can be a bitch. But anyway, I can start on your side of the show. Now, what I want to say is this ... I trust you, Quinn. You have just as much experience on these reality shows as me. You know the drill. I also need you to trust me, too. Sometimes, I might have to make a call you might not agree with for reasons outside of what you might think. If that happens, pull me aside, and we will discuss it. Okay?"

"Sounds great."

"Now, I know you're totally prepared for this. You always are." He gives me another compliment. "The network and architect received your modifications on the second level and have signed off on them already. Honestly, that's a genius move."

"Thanks. When Sebastien walked me around the other day, it differed from what I had envisioned in my mind."

Kevin nods. "So, you've met with Sebastien since you've been here?" Kevin's brows raise at my little slip-up.

"I texted him when I arrived to see if I could have a look at the property before you all arrived. Thankfully, he did because we were able to make all those changes we sent through." My heart is beating frantically in my chest. I swear I have the words '*I've seen Sebastien's penis*' written across me.

"That man is hot as fuck," Kevin states, changing the subject.

"He's all right."

"Are you feeling okay?" Kevin questions.

"Yes, why?"

Goddammit, he knows.

I can't lie.

I'm so bad at this.

I could never be a spy.

I'm having a heart attack.

"Sebastien Sanchez is not all right. That man is a Spanish god." Kevin sighs.

Oh, that's all. Kevin thinks he's hot. He doesn't suspect a thing. Chill out, Quinn.

"And you got to spend one-on-one time with him all day." His eyes widen as if asking to spill the beans.

"Yeah, he's a nice guy. It was just work," I tell him.

"Boo, you're no fun, Quinn. Getting with Sebastien would be the biggest 'fuck you' to Chad," Kevin says with a grin.

Sebastien steps into the conference room right at that moment. His dark chocolate eyes bounce between Kevin and me. *Did he just hear that conversation?*

"What would be the biggest *'fuck you'* to Chad?" he questions.

Damn, he heard.

"I was just suggesting to Quinn that you two being together would be the biggest *'fuck you'* to Chad," Kevin elaborates.

Sebastien turns his head and looks over at me. I can read it on his face. He is like, '*What the hell has been happening in this meeting.'*

"It's all good. He's just making chit-chat," I explain to Sebastien in Spanish.

Kevin looks between Sebastien and me.

"Sorry, my English is not always good," Sebastien replies, putting on the thickest Spanish accent I've ever heard.

Kevin nods and smiles but can't stop staring at Sebastien.

"Is he okay?" Sebastien asks.

"He is mesmerized by your beauty." I giggle.

Sebastien looks very confused by the whole exchange as he takes a seat beside me.

"It's a pleasure to meet you, Sebastien. I'm a big fan," Kevin introduces himself.

"Kevin used to work on *Farmhouse Reno* a couple of years ago," I explain to Sebastien. "He thinks Chad's a dick."

Sebastien smirks as he greets Kevin.

"Right, well, back to work." Kevin claps his hands. "Sebastien, I wanted to let you know the network signed off on your kitchen staff being the on-site catering crew. So, they can begin in a couple of days."

Kevin then goes through each of our production lists one by one.

"Tomorrow, we have the photo shoot for the ads for the show. Layla will be in later to run through what the network wants you guys to wear," Kevin advises. "We need to run through the off-site filming schedules."

Kevin flips over the next sheet in his folder. "This Thursday, Friday, and Saturday, we have you filming in Champagne, France. This will be the episode about the differences between French Champagne and Spanish Cava," he advises.

"Both of us?" Sebastien asks.

"Yes. The network has decided they want you both to be thrown into each other's worlds. They want to see Quinn fishing off the side of the boat or milking a goat alongside you," he explains. "The audience is aware of her separation from Chad, and I thought instead of the public thinking poor her, I want them to see Quinn being her kick-ass self that I know she's capable of being," Kevin advises Sebastien.

Aw, that is so sweet.

"Chad is like the elephant in the room. They were much

loved by the public. Now, Chad is doing everything in his power to sell his show and his new relationship because, let's be serious, women are not happy that Chad dumped our gorgeous Quinn here. They identified with her. Women wanted to be Quinn living that Instagram farm life, and many connected with her on the whole cheating-spouse thing."

Sebastien's hand moves under the table and gives me a gentle squeeze on my leg to see if I'm okay about all this.

"I thought maybe if the average woman sees Quinn picking herself up and stepping out of her comfort zone, it might help some of them to do the same," Kevin adds.

"Aw, Kevin, that is really sweet," I tell him.

"Sebastien, you may not know this yet, but Quinn has a cult following," Kevin informs him.

Sebastien turns and raises a brow at me.

"You're not the only one with a legion of female fans," I state, making Sebastien laugh.

"See that …" Kevin points to us, "… that's the kind of interaction we want between the two of you. The back and forth. Maybe even a little flirting. Give the viewers something to mull over." Kevin continues giving us the rundown of all the crazy places we will have to visit and film.

Hours later, we're finally done with the meeting.

"Hey, Quinn … would you like me to give you a lift back to your villa? It's on my way," Sebastien asks in front of Kevin.

He looks up from his cell, grins, then goes back to whatever it was he's doing.

"If it's not too much trouble," I add.

"No, not at all. I'm going that way back to Barcelona."

Honestly, we are giving Oscar-worthy performances right here. "Thanks."

I turn to Kevin. "Sebastien's giving me a lift. I can't wait for us to start working together again," I say as I reach out and give him a big hug. "I'll see you bright and early tomorrow morning."

"You lucky thing, getting a ride home with Sebastien," he whispers in my ear. "It wouldn't be the only thing I'd ride." He bursts out laughing at his own joke, and I give him a grin then hastily make our exit.

Once we're in the car, I can finally relax.

"Okay, that was the weirdest day ever," Sebastien starts. "I'm not sure about Kevin."

I burst out laughing, the stress of the day finally getting the better of me.

"Are you okay?" Sebastien frowns.

"That was … *interesting*."

"You could say that," Sebastien chimes.

"I have so much nervous energy running all over my body, wondering if people could tell something was going on between us. I felt like I might have a heart attack at any moment," I tell him. "Before you came in, I said something about us coming up here to check out the place before today, and I thought Kevin had caught us out. Thankfully, Kevin is so mesmerized by you that he forgets about whatever it is he's talking about. That is your superpower. Use it wisely," I tell him.

He chuckles. "I missed you last night."

"It was one night."

"I know, but my bed was lonely, and so was my dick." He grins, and I bite my bottom lip. "Dammit, Quinn! Don't bite your lip like that unless you want me to pull over into this paddock and fuck you in my car."

That's hot. I wonder if he would. No, you don't know who from production is out and about. I'll keep my lip-biting under control until we arrive at my villa which isn't far.

Thankfully, there is no one around as we arrive, the car park is empty when we pull up beside the villa. As the talent, I got the biggest villa which is huge, but the best bit is the entrance to it is down a little laneway where I have an extra car space. So, when we step out no one can see us. It's private which is good because there are a couple of other villas near mine where people from the show are staying. And the last thing we need is for one of them to spy Sebastien visiting me.

Pulling my villa's key out as I step from the car, seconds later I feel Sebastien's warmth pressing against me, and I can feel how hard he is.

"Hurry up, Quinn, and open that door before I fuck you against it."

Gee, someone's testy.

Thankfully, my key eventually turns in the old lock, and the door swings open wide for us. Moments later, it's slammed behind me, and Sebastien is on me. We're both frantic with need as we begin to rip each other's clothes off.

"You're killing me in this dress," he growls as he tries to pull the offending material from my body.

"Do you not like me in dresses?" I ask as I kick my shoes off and drop my bag to the side.

"I fucking love you in dresses, but all I can think about is bending you over a surface and lifting up the hem and fucking you. They give me dirty thoughts," he confesses.

Note to self, wear more dresses. "Next time maybe you should."

"Maybe I will," he says, giving me a cocky grin before disposing of my dress to the side. "Fuck me, Quinn. You always wear the best underwear." He moans taking in the cream set I'm wearing.

I have a thing for lingerie. I like them to be matching, it makes me feel complete. Maybe it's an OCD thing.

"You drive me wild, wondering what color it's going to be today," Sebastien states as he kicks off his shoes and unbuckles his belt.

The fact that Sebastien thinks about what I have under my clothes gives me a thrill. My attention is pulled as he unbuttons his shirt and throws it to the floor, exposing his tanned skin and six-pack abs. I'll never get sick of looking at Sebastien Sanchez without clothes on. Those chocolate eyes narrow on me as he starts to unzip his jeans, and devilish smile falls across his lips as he slowly slides the material down.

Teasing me.

An ache throbs between my thighs as I bite my lower lip watching him undress for me.

"You want this?" he asks, raising a brow at me.

"You know I do."

"Get on those knees and show me how much you want my cock, Quinn."

He doesn't have to tell me twice. As I fall to my knees in front of him, normally I would feel self-conscious doing something like this, so open and exposed, but Sebastien takes me out of my comfort zone every time and I love it. Reaching out, I slide his jeans down and pull him from his underwear. His thick, long cock springs free and I lick my lips.

"Suck it," he commands.

And I do. I wrap my hand around his cock and slide my lips over him all the while looking right up into those dark molten eyes. They flare wildly as he stares down at me, neither one of us looking away from the other. He reaches out and cups my chin and smiles. As I suck him all the way down my throat. Sebastian curses in Spanish as his eyes close for a moment enjoying the sensation. His hand then moves from my chin and wraps itself around my ponytail. He pulls tightly, and I know what he wants. He wants to fuck my face. I love it when he takes over and becomes so wild with need that I just have to stay there and take it. He gives my hair a slight tug, giving me warning before he thrusts himself all the way to the back of my throat making me gag. He does it again and again, each time making my eyes water as he hits the back of my throat.

"Seeing you choke on my dick while those doe fucking eyes look up at me as you take each … fucking … thrust," he says, emphasizing each word with his dick down my throat, "like a good fucking girl, has me almost coming like a chump. I bet you're fucking dripping between those creamy thighs. Aren't you, Quinn?"

I mumble 'yes' around his cock.

"Slide those fingers between those pretty pink lips and show me," he commands.

And I do it. There isn't anything I wouldn't do for him when he talks to me in that commanding voice. Moving my thighs apart slightly, I push my hand into my underwear and slide my fingers through my wetness a couple of times before pulling them out and showing him.

Sebastien leans forward and sucks my fingers into his mouth, tasting me.

"Fuck, Quinn. You are always so ready for me. I can't decide if I want to come in your mouth first or have you come on my face first."

Either sounds good.

"Screw it. Get up," he says, pulling himself from my mouth. His dick glistens in the light from my saliva as he walks over to the sofa and lays back. "Come over and fuck my face, Quinn. I want to drown in your juices."

I love his filthy mouth. What girl can deny a request like that? I hastily dispose of my underwear and crawl up and over his face. We are in the sixty-nine position on the sofa, and before I even have time to get comfortable, he is grabbing my hips and pulling me against his face. The first swipe of his tongue against my throbbing clit has me almost launching myself off him. I steady myself as I lower my mouth back down over him and lose myself in the sensations that we are giving each other.

36

SEBASTIEN

Last night with Quinn was fantastic and not because of the explosive sex. I don't think I will ever tire of making that woman come. It was great being able to relax around each other again without the worry of production's well-trained eyes on us. My apartment feels empty now that she isn't stomping around it anymore, and last night I hesitated to go back to it because I wanted to stay in bed with Quinn, who was all soft and snuggly. Couldn't blow our cover on day one though, so I did the right thing and went back to Barcelona.

Today we have the show's promotional photo shoot for the network to splash around everywhere, and I'm in a mood because I didn't get to wake up with Quinn this morning.

"Good morning, Sebastien," Kevin greets me as I enter the studio space they have set up in one of the old buildings. There are sheets and wires everywhere. They have created a green screen backdrop, and Kevin explains they will be creating glossy background images behind us. I look around the set and notice Quinn hasn't arrived yet. Maybe I should have gone and picked her up on my way in.

"This is Tanya. She will be looking after your hair and

makeup today," Kevin introduces me to an older brunette woman. "The first look today is you in your chef whites," Kevin tells me as Tanya asks me to sit in a chair and gets to work.

Once I'm all made up, I head over to the set. Quinn's there doing some solo shots. I can see on the monitor the different backgrounds they are putting her against as they scream different poses for her to do. She's dressed in what looks to be Farm Girl Barbie, with the American-style red and white checkered shirt, which is opened way too low for my liking. They have her in the tiniest denim cut-offs with cowboy boots. It looks like she's wearing a blonde wig too. They have transformed her back to the old Quinn Miller, the one who was with Chad.

She's with me now. That image isn't her anymore. What the hell are they thinking?

"Great. Sebastien, you're here." The photographer then points and tells me to stand in position near Quinn.

"Morning," she greets me through gritted teeth.

"What the hell are you wearing?" I ask her as I take my position beside her.

"What they told me to wear." She shrugs and poses.

"It's not you," I tell her. "I mean, it's the old you, but not the new you." Getting myself tongue-tied, my anger gets the better of me.

"I know. But it's the character I'm playing," she tells me.

"I don't like it," I grumble.

"Sebastien, stop scowling," the photographer yells at me.

"It's okay, really," she tries to reassure me.

"Is this what you want? To always be compared to Chad's version of who you are?"

She stills and turns to me, her jaw a little slack with surprise.

"What the hell is going on, you two?" the photographer yells.

I flip him off.

"Guys … is there a problem?" Kevin joins in our private conversation.

"Yeah, Kevin, there is." Turning my glare to him, he takes a step back under its intensity. "I thought you said yesterday that you would do anything for Quinn to break out of the shadow of her former life with Chad?" I question him.

"Of course," Kevin agrees.

"Then why the hell is she dressed like Farm Girl Barbie here?" I say, pointing at Quinn. Kevin turns his attention to her, and it's as if he's seeing her truly for the first time. Quinn is wriggling nervously under our scrutiny.

"Guys, take five," Kevin yells at the photographer who curses as he storms off the set. "I see what you're saying, Sebastien," Kevin finally agrees with me. "What do you suggest?"

"What do you mean?" I look between Quinn and Kevin.

"You have some strong ideas about this, I would like to hear them," Kevin says as he folds his arms across his chest and waits for my answer.

"I … um … well …" I take a moment to gather my thoughts. "I see her ditching the farm girl chic and being more relaxed. Maybe in a sundress?"

"And what do you think, Quinn?" Kevin asks.

"I have to agree with Sebastien," she answers.

Kevin looks between Quinn and me again.

"Sweetheart, why did you *not* speak up?" Kevin asks.

"I don't know … I'm so used to going with the flow and not wanting to rock the boat that I did what you wanted me to do."

Kevin shakes his head. "No, that won't do, Quinn. I need you to be honest with me. If you don't like something, speak up. Okay?" Kevin tries to reassure her. "Now, Layla …" he calls for Quinn's stylist who rushes in from the back area. "Wipe this red lipstick off. We are going for a more natural boho vibe instead of slutty farm girl. Okay?"

Layla nods, and Quinn follows after her.

"Thanks for looking after Quinn like that," Kevin whispers.

"I didn't realize how much control Chad had over Quinn. She's stepped back in front of the camera and fallen back into her old routine. It might take a little bit for her to break the habit and adjust, but I think she will, especially with you by her side," he says, patting me on the shoulder.

"Places. Let's take Sebastien's solo images while Quinn's getting changed," Kevin yells out to the workers.

The shoot eventually ended up going well. Quinn dropped the fake smiles and gritted teeth and relaxed in front of the camera, even when they made me kiss her cheek for twenty minutes as they had us completing various poses.

"That's a wrap, guys." Kevin claps his hands, and everyone begins to unpack. "That was brilliant," he enthusiastically tells us. "The network is going to love these shots. The chemistry between the two of you leaps off the screen." He grins. "Sebastien, the contractors arrive tomorrow to start on all the preliminary building works."

Apparently, one day on a renovation show is one week in filming days, Quinn explained to me.

"Have you double-checked all of the plans, and everything is signed off?" Kevin asks.

I went through them all last night with *my* project manager, Lucien, who I've known since school, and is the only person I would trust with this project. He agreed everything looked good. The network has its own project manager, but Lucien is site manager, and that's for a reason. Trust means everything to me.

"Yep, good to go," I reply.

"Great. Well, I guess I'll see you in France then." Kevin waves his hand dramatically in the air.

Tomorrow we're off to France to film our champagne tasting, I'm looking forward to it as Quinn is so excited. I'm hoping there is time for Quinn and me to have some alone time while there. I hate being this close to her and not being able to touch her. I got used to being able to touch her anytime I liked while she was staying with me. Now I have to consciously tell my hands not to reach out and touch her.

Once I've wiped off all this hideous makeup they applied, I run into Quinn who's waiting outside for me.

"Thank you for today," she says as she walks with me to my car.

"You don't need to thank me."

"But I do. You were my voice when I needed it, and that means a lot to me," she says as we arrive at my car.

Running my hand through my hair, I try to think of the words that explain how I feel. "I didn't like it, Quinn. I hated them trying to recreate what you were like with him. You're not with him anymore, you're with me."

Shit.

I realize what I've just said.

Quinn's mouth falls open at my confession. "If being with you means you have my back then thank you," she says, brushing off my comment. "I didn't think being back on set would feel so weird. I assumed the new and improved Quinn would be the one stepping onto this show, that I wouldn't be reverting to the old one. Who sat there and never spoke up," she says, letting out a heavy sigh.

"You've got this," I tell her.

"I do with you by my side."

We stand there in silence, both of us saying more than we should, knowing we are dancing a little close to a line that neither of us is interested in crossing. This isn't permanent. No matter how great it feels, there's an expiry date on us. I just have to keep reminding myself.

"I've got to go pack for France. Thanks again for having my back," Quinn says, stepping away.

"That's what friends do."

Quinn's brows pull together at my comment before she looks around to see if anyone is around. There are workers on the horizon but no one close. She gives me an awkward thumbs-up before turning on her heel.

"Quinn," I call out.

She stops and turns around.

"I can give you a lift if you need one." Please say yes.

"Thanks, but I have some things to finish here before I go home. Drive safe, and I'll see you at the airport tomorrow," she says.

Maybe it's for the best we have a break tonight, especially when we are saying things we shouldn't.

37

SEBASTIEN

Last night sucked not spending it with Quinn. Getting up early and going to the airport was hell too. When I got on the private plane, Kevin and Quinn we already sitting together chatting away. I didn't like it. I assumed we would be sitting together. When I stomped onto the plane, Quinn looked up, wished me a good morning, and then went back to her conversation with Kevin. Did I make things weird with my slip-up yesterday? I think it's common for people who spend all this time together to say things they mean, but it doesn't mean I'm declaring my undying love for her. I like her … a lot, but that's all.

As soon as we landed in Champagne both of us were whisked away to separate areas to get ready for the shoot. That's how I find myself sitting in a bright red Citroen DS 19 Cabriolet, a classic French car, driving along a graveled road toward a towering chateau in the distance. There's a dude with a camera right in my face and a drone flying above us as I drive carefully. I pull up out the front of the chateau, which the network has hired for us to film in, and open the car door. They want to create a magical night in Champagne.

"We need you to get out, walk through the front door, and out to the back where Quinn is waiting," Kevin advises me.

After I've driven the same driveaway several times, once I've got the scene perfect, I do as I'm told and walk out the back of the chateau. Quinn is sitting by the pool, wearing an oversized hat sipping on a glass of champagne, in a yellow sundress. Is she trying to kill me?

"You look hard at work." I say my line.

She turns ever so dramatically as her fingers push her sunglasses down her nose, so she can look at me over the rims and says, "I'm doing research, Sebastien."

"Cut. Perfect," Kevin screams.

Both Quinn and I burst out laughing, which breaks the uneasy tension that has been there between us since yesterday.

"I need a drink. They made me drive up and down the entrance to the chateau five times." I moan as I grab her glass of champagne and throw it back.

"I had to pretend to get lost in the maze, like a bimbo after one too many champagnes. They thought it would be cute," she says, pretending to gag.

"You're going to veto that in edits."

"Hell, yeah I am," she says with a grin.

"I like your dress," I say. Looking down at her, my eyes trail along her sun-kissed skin as she lazes on the sun lounge.

Quinn shakes her head at me, those blue eyes wide with fear, as her hand comes up and taps the tiny microphone on her chest.

Shit.

I nod in understanding. "It matches the sunflowers in the fields," I add, so if anyone heard my earlier compliment, they would hopefully not think anything of it.

We shoot various locations with images of us riding bikes through the vineyards, walking through them, and then having conversations about grapes. We are then taken on a tour of a winery, where we learn how they make champagne. Quinn and I tried one too many glasses, much to the annoyance of Kevin as we kept stumbling over our lines. The girl filming the behind-the-scenes content for the digital platforms loved it.

I'm guessing we might regret that later.

Now, I'm dressed in a tuxedo for dinner with Quinn. Kevin's production team has set up an intimate dinner underneath the stars in the chateau's gardens. Fairy lights are draped from the gazebo. The table has been set for a romantic dinner. A gorgeous floral arrangement in the center of the table consists of red roses. Real subtle, Kevin. Candles are laid everywhere along a gravel path to the chateau.

The whole thing screams—I'm part of the Rose Ceremony on *The Bachelor.*

"Quinn, we're ready to go. Sebastien, stand at the end of the path, please." I hear Kevin in my earpiece, so I do as I am told. There are a couple of moments of silence, and then I hear a door creak open and heels click-clack across the terrace. Quinn appears around the corner, and I'm blown away.

"Oh, wow." Realizing I've said that out loud and everyone can hear me talk through my mic, I take a deep breath and try to steady myself. I can't slip up with all these people listening to me. Quinn looks incredible like a princess descending from her castle. She's dressed in a black, off-the-shoulder evening dress with a dangerous high thigh split showing off her tanned, toned legs with each step she takes toward me.

Her blonde hair is pulled up into an elegant bun, and her neck is dripping in diamonds as are her wrists and ears. She gives me a tentative smile, and just as she's about to reach me, her heels dig into the gravel, and she twists her ankle and comes crashing down. I'm too far away to catch her in time, but I watch in slow motion as she goes down.

Everyone rushes toward her.

Quinn is doubled over in a fit of laughter from the floor.

"I'm so sorry, guys." She giggles as tears stream down her face. "Heels and gravel really don't mix."

I put my arm around her and lift her out of the dirt.

Layla gets to work brushing the dust off her gown.

"Well, we got a decent amount of footage," Kevin tells her. "Let's get you fixed up and start filming your dinner."

A little while later, Quinn is back looking as if her stumble never even happened. I hold out the seat for her, then take my own.

"I'm so embarrassed," she whispers.

"That was a pretty epic fall." I grin at her.

"Stop it!" She hisses, trying to keep her fits of laughter inside.

"Places, everyone," Kevin screams in our ears. "Dinner's being served."

A waiter dressed in a black and white suit comes out and pops a bottle of champagne dramatically for the camera, and the cork shoots off into the garden. He pours us both a glass before another waiter brings out a silver cloche and sets it down in front of us. The waiter pulls the cover away from our meal, and a plate of snails is laid out before us.

"Please don't tell me these are snails?" Quinn looks up at me.

"Escargot is a French delicacy," I tell her.

Kevin has totally set this up for her to freak out over.

"It's been cooked in butter, garlic, and herbs." I take one out of its shell and pop it in my mouth while Quinn stares at me horrified. "Come on, you can do it. Try it. You might like it."

She shakes her head a couple of times, then looks off-camera and sees everyone waiting around for her to do it. I take another snail and place it on my fork and hold it out for her to take. Her doe blue eyes open wide, and I mentally see her working herself up to do it. She leans forward and takes the morsel off my fork. She tries to keep a straight face while not gagging as she eventually chews and swallows.

"How was it?" I ask.

"Not as bad as I thought. I've had worst things in my mouth" She says, as she picks up her glass of champagne and begins to wash the bite down.

I try not to burst out laughing at her comment. "I'm guessing everything tastes better with champagne," I tell her.

She nods in agreement.

"Perfect," Kevin calls from the darkness. "All done for the night. Everyone, let's pack up. Room service is available for dinner tonight. Do not order the lobster, Craig. I know it's something you would do," Kevin warns one of the sound guys.

We are eventually un-miced and Layla, the stylist, takes Quinn's jewels before she tells us she will be over in the morning to collect our clothes. We wave goodbye and head back inside.

"Want to grab dinner together?" I ask Quinn.

"Sounds great. Let me get out of this and freshen up, then I'll be over." We leave each other on the grand staircase, her room is at one end, mine is at the other.

A little while later, there's a knock at the door. I open it, and Quinn is nervously looking down both sides of the hall. She jumps in as soon as the door is open.

"Hey," I say. Walking over and grabbing her face with my hands, I kiss her passionately.

"Hey, you …" She smiles as she wraps her arms around my neck.

"Can I just say you looked absolutely gorgeous this evening until you crashed and burned at the end of the path."

She playfully hits my chest, giggling. "I'd like to see you try and navigate that. High heels and tiny stones don't mix." She groans.

"I was also very proud of you for eating the escargot," I tell her.

She makes a funny face. "Look, I know in chef land they might be nice, but to my mouth, it's a big nope. All I could think about was that I was eating 'Turbo' the snail." She twists her nose up in disgust. "But I will say the butter and garlic helped." She grins, then her stomach makes a loud growl making us both laugh. "Sorry, pretty sure my stomach isn't happy that I fed it snails."

"Well, we better get you some proper food, then." I call down to reception and order us dinner.

Eventually, it arrives and is placed in the seated area of my room.

"This is a lot of food. What on earth did you order?" Quinn takes a seat and opens the cloches to see what I have chosen. There's nothing crazy but something that pushes her out of her comfort zone.

"Oh, my goodness, this looks beautiful. Hold on, I need to add it to the Gram." She takes a couple of pictures of the food with her camera.

"Okay, we have La Joute, which is vegetable stew."

Quinn looks up at me a little surprised.

"You didn't think I would put your taste buds through any more torture tonight, did you?"

She shrugs.

"We also have a selection of cheeses, and of course, a bottle of champagne."

We dig into our food and chat about our day, just like we always did back home. Everything feels right again in my world, where it's just the two of us and nobody else.

38

QUINN

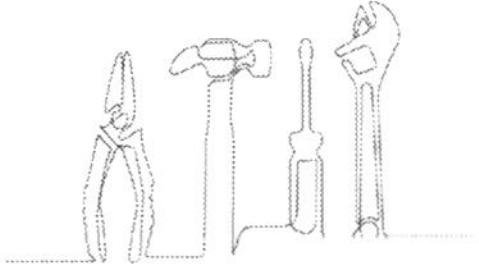

The sun streams through the curtains waking me up. There's a warm lump beside me. Sitting up in bed, I turn and look at a disheveled, naked Sebastien beside me.

"Wake up." I push him.

He rolls over with a groan. "Why are you waking me up? You exhausted me last night," he mumbles.

This is true, champagne always makes me frisky.

"Oh my god, what time is it?" Looking over at the bedside clock, I scream out, "Shit." I jump out of bed and frantically try to find my clothes.

"Why are you freaking out?" Sebastien asks me.

"One, because I slept over here in your room last night, which we both agreed we wouldn't have sleepovers while filming because we didn't want to get caught. And two, Layla is coming to pick up the clothes in like two minutes, and if she sees me here like this, our little late-night orgasms are over." I point at him as I pull my underwear up and throw on my dress, then pull my hair up into a messy ponytail.

I lean over and kiss him. "See ya later." I poke my head out the door to double-check the coast is clear, which it is, then I step out of Sebastien's room and try and act cool as if I haven't fallen asleep in my co-star's bed.

I get to my door and twist the knob, but not before I hear my name.

"Quinn."

"Ahhh …" I squeal at Layla's voice right behind me.

Where the hell did she come from?

"You scared me," I tell her, holding my chest.

Layla looks me over, her eyes narrow.

"Are you just getting home?" She raises a brow in my direction.

"What. No. Ha ha." I chuckle. "I went for a walk," I tell her.

"Must have been a pretty short walk from Sebastien's room to here." She grins.

Busted!

"This might sound utterly unprofessional, but high-five, girl."

Um. Wow!

"Don't worry, Kevin's not going to find out from me. My lips are sealed, but be careful the corridors have eyes," she whispers. "And if Kevin finds out, that little romantic stunt last night is going to get worse," Layla warns me.

I knew it.

"I really appreciate your discretion, Layla," I tell her.

She shakes her head. "Most people are rooting for you after the whole Chad thing. You deserve better. Anyway, I'm here for your dress, please." I dash inside my hotel room and grab all the items she needs, then give them to her. "And don't worry, I never saw a thing." And with that, she turns on her heel and disappears down the hallway.

As I close the door behind me, I grab my cell and quickly text Sebastien. Moments later, there's a knock at my door. I open it, and I'm surprised to see him standing there. I nervously look around to make sure the coast is clear before letting him inside my room.

"What are you doing here?" I ask.

He reaches out and kisses me slowly.

"What was that for?" I ask, pulling myself away from him.

"Just trying to calm you down." He grins.

"I'm glad you think this is funny." My tone turns serious which makes him frown. "I mean, as a man in the media, a sex scandal won't harm your reputation at all."

Sebastien's eyes widen at my words. "I don't think this is going to turn into a sex scandal. By the sounds of it, Layla isn't going to say a thing."

"But she might for the right price or someone who isn't as nice as her will. You do realize how this all works? You realize the number of people who probably sold you out on your show to the media." These words give him pause.

"You think someone on my show sold me out?" His shoulders slump a little.

"The stories about things that happen on set, or with people from the set … how do you think the media finds out?" I raise a brow at him.

He rakes his hand through his dark brown hair, taking in my words.

"I didn't think I was that big of a celebrity to have that happen." He seems genuinely confused, so I reach out and touch his arm.

"You're on a TV show. No matter how big or small it may be, your personal life is gossip fodder," I explain to him.

"I'm sorry, Quinn. I thought you were stressing out for no good reason."

"Producers and networks also release info if it means building attention for the season. It's all about *their* best interests, definitely not ours."

Sebastien looks over at me, he takes a couple of steps, then kisses me again.

"I'm all-in," he tells me.

What?

"If they find out about us, I'm all-in."

I don't understand what that means. He must see the question written on my face. I thought we had an agreement?

"If it gets out, I'm not going to hide us. I'm not going to tell the press that it's fake news. I'm going to say that Quinn Miller barreled into my life, and I'm so much happier for it." He kisses me again. "Unless you aren't comfortable with that, then I can sprout fake news." He grins.

"I thought …"

He shakes his head. "I'm finding it hard to keep my hands off you."

"Me too," I say, biting my lip. "But we agreed that whatever this was had an expiry date."

"It still does."

Oh. I'm confused.

"If we are found out I won't deny it. But I think everyone knows that it wouldn't last between us. My life is in Spain, and your life is in Texas. They will be happy that you are using me to get over Chad and once you head back to the states, they will forget all about our summer fling."

Everything he says makes sense, but why does it hurt my heart hearing him say it's just a summer fling?

39

QUINN

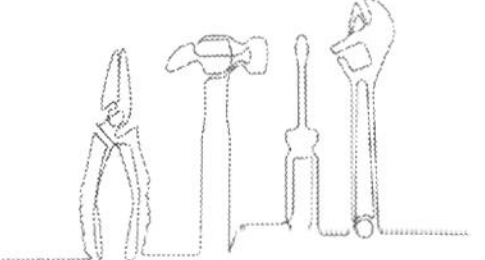

We are back in Spain, and this time we are filming on a goat farm, which isn't as glamorous as a chateau in France. This is my segment learning about where some Spanish cheese comes from. They bring out the baby goats, and I lose my damn mind. They are the cutest things. The farmer hands me a bottle, and I get to feed them, and I'm dying from cuteness overload. What a great start to the day.

"You need to buy baby goats," I tell Sebastien while they hop all over me as I sit on a bundle of hay.

"I don't think you would finish my renovations if I did that." He grins, playing to the camera. He's probably right, though.

"Or maybe it would help me work better since my endorphins will be firing on all cylinders because I will start with my morning baby goat cuddles."

Sebastien laughs and shakes his head.

Don't worry, he bought the goats. We are filming that little project next week, where I create the most gorgeous barn for them.

The farmer then takes us to the dairy, where we see how it's set up, all the machinery, etc. This is something Sebastien is extremely interested in. He and the farmer talk about the milk and the cheeses he makes with it.

"Quinn, would you like to milk a goat?" Sebastien asks.

Of course, there's one waiting for me, a metal bucket to sit on, and the camera crew ready to go.

"Sure. I'll give it a go," I say, taking my seat, and the farmer explains exactly what to do. I put on a show about touching the nipple then start to milk. *Go me!* Sebastien leans over to inspect my work, and I squirt him with the teat. His face is covered in milk as he splutters about. I'm laughing so hard that I actually fall off the bucket I'm sitting on. But it was worth it seeing his spluttering face. Kevin tells us that it is television gold right there.

Sebastien and I continue our nightly routine of walking around the property together, checking the crew's progress. I know Sebastien's friend, Lucien, is working on the hidden villa, which isn't being used for the television show and things are starting to come along nicely there. They cleaned up the old garden and cleaned out the house to see what needed to be replaced. The villa has all new electricity and plumbing which ended up being a huge task having to update the old lines. I joke that he could move into the villa now that it has the necessities, saves him driving back to Barcelona each night. Sebastien is thinking about it. It means we could sneak away to his villa instead of mine. The crew is not allowed there as it's not part of the show.

Most nights, Sebastien still drives me home after filming under the guise that it's on his way home. And no one bats an eyelid as it's become commonplace. If it's early enough, he cooks dinner for us, and we sit out on the back terrace with a wine in hand and look out into the darkness where the stars are our only source of light. We usually chat about what happened that day, and what's happening the next day, it's nice, domesticated even.

And I know with each day and night we spend together the feelings of like I have for him are increasing. As much as I try, I can't help myself. When you spend so much time with someone and then spend all your nights with his head between your thighs it's hard not to fall. We made a pact that we wouldn't fall for each other, and if someone did that, we would tell the other, but I don't want what we have to end, and I know if I tell Sebastien that I've fallen for him, he is going to hightail it. So, I do what any self-respecting woman does and push those feelings down inside of me and pray that he doesn't notice. I already know I'm on the road to Heartbreak Town with a population of one, but I don't want to get off, not yet anyway.

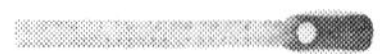

"I'm Quinn Miller, a hometown Texas girl who loves renovating old farmhouses."

"And I'm Sebastien Sanchez, award-winning Spanish chef …" He pauses.

"And together, we are working on the biggest project either of us has ever taken on."

We say, reading our lines.

"All while, *Under the Spanish Sun*," Sebastien adds.

"Perfect, guys," Kevin calls from the sound studio. "We will insert bits and pieces of what we have filmed while on location, and the intro to your show is ready to go." He grins. "Now, Quinn, we need you to film some DIY scenes for us this week. If you can go with Layla, that would be great, and Seb, you have some on-location cooking pieces to do," Kevin explains.

Sebastien and I give each other a look as we are both pulled in different directions.

"Right, so today we have you in these super cute denim dungarees, a white tee, and these awesome bright pink safety boots," Layla explains.

"Oh my gosh, I love them," I say, admiring the safety boots. *Why shouldn't women have cute work gear?*

"If you love the boots, the network has also got you your own pink tool belt with your own set of pink tools, including a tape measure, hammer, hard hat, and so on."

I squeal with delight like a little girl at Christmas. I've always wanted the pink gear, but Chad said it looked unprofessional for me to be walking around with them.

Screw you, Chad! On Wednesdays, I wear pink workwear.

I walk onto set. They have set me up in one of the buildings that is finished but isn't part of the show—it's my little DIY heaven.

"Oh my god," I scream. Staring back at me is an entire toolbox wall set up in pink. I rush over and run my hands over the drawers and drawers of metal tools in all different shapes and sizes. It looks like any man's dream garage tool area, just in pink. "How?" I ask, turning to Layla.

"You can thank Kevin for all this."

I can't believe it. Everything is exactly what my dream tool shed would look like. It's totally over the top, but I love it.

"He wanted to showcase that building is not a man's domain and that women can dominate, too, while looking cute if they want to," Layla tells me.

Love, love, love.

Holly, the girl who's running digital behind the scenes asks if she can snap me posing with some of the products.

Jo, the associate producer and Kevin's right-hand woman, walks into my she cave. "Do you love it?" she questions.

"Yes, yes, yes," I reply, which makes her laugh.

"Great. I know the company is talking with your manager, Carmen, about maybe being the face of the product. She wanted to see what you thought of the products before saying yes to them," Jo explains.

When Chad left me, he took my entire crew including my

agent, Tammy. Thank goodness Lettie put me onto Carmen, who is a boss bitch, and is working overtime securing whatever endorsement deals she thinks are necessary. Her goal is to make me the highest-paid female on the Lifestyle Network. My goal is to recoup all the money Chad stole from me.

So, I spend the next couple of weeks filming DIY segments. We did one on upcycling wine barrels which I turned into a fire pit, coffee tables, bar benches, a swing, cooler, and bedside tables. Then I repurposed the old Cava bottles we found in one of the barns that the vineyard used to produce and turned them into lamps. I also found a heap of old corks and added tiny LED lights into the core and clumped probably about one hundred of them together to create a gorgeous chandelier. Found old, rusted animal troughs and turned them into benches. Cowbells into lights, old industrial equipment into items for the accommodation. Anything I could find that was going to be thrown out, I turned into something that could be used. I've missed these types of projects, and it's been good to get back into the swing of making items the way I want them to be and not being told how to do it.

Unfortunately, at the moment, Sebastien and my schedules have not been the same. He has been traveling around Spain filming his segments about the gastronomic delights of his home for the past three weeks while I've been toiling away at the property. We've been able to catch up with each other every night briefly before we collapse into bed, exhausted from the long days.

I've missed him.

Really missed him.

But so has he. He said it first, and I agreed. At least we're on the same page regarding that. The feelings I have for him keep getting stronger, and I'm finding it harder to hide them.

It's been almost two months since I packed up and came to hide out in Spain, but honestly, it feels like I've always been here. The longer I'm in Spain, the more it's beginning to feel like home. And I'm not sure if I want to leave when my time is up in a month.

I've finished filming and decided to head down to Sebastien's hidden villa on one of the golf carts to see how it's coming along. It's been a little over a month since work started. I pass rows and rows of vines on either side of the road. The striking mountain ranges are in front of me, and behind are bright blue skies. It's gorgeous. I have a sense of coming home the closer I get to the villa.

When I turn the corner, I'm amazed at how much work has been done. The overgrown gardens have been cut back, exposing the beauty underneath. The vines that had begun to grow over the building have been torn away, exposing gorgeous sandstone color stone walls with old wooden shutters covering the windows. *Who knew they were there?* The terracotta Spanish-style roof tiles have been power-washed, and people are fixing the tiles that have broken over the years of neglect.

I wave to them as they work away in the hot sun.

Pushing open the front door, the sound of power tools fills my ears. Dust and chaos are everywhere inside the home, but so much progress has been made. I walk around the workmen and head outside to the garden, so I won't be in their way, and before me is a large hole in the ground where there once was a frog-filled pool. It's been drained and cleaned out, resurfaced, and tiled. It's going to be gorgeous out here next summer, and that pool is going to be so inviting. My stomach sinks knowing that I won't be here this time next year, I have no idea where in the world I am going to be. And I hate that I won't get to see this place as often.

"It looks pretty good, doesn't it?" Sebastien's voice comes from behind and surprises me, making me jump. His arms reach out to steady me, I turn around and look up into his handsome face.

I've missed him.

My heart flutters wildly in my chest. He reaches out to caress my face, and we are lost in our own little world. It's been too long. We ignore the workmen moving around us as they all but disappear, all I see is him.

"I've missed you, Quinn," he confesses as those chocolate eyes turn molten as he stares down at me. He then leans forward and kisses me on the lips in public. I'm surprised by the public display of affection and wasn't expecting it. He then wraps his arms around me, pulling me closer to him. My chest hits his as his mouth against mine makes my knees weak.

"Wow, that was a greeting," I say as I smile up at him.

He places a kiss on my forehead. "I'm so happy to see you again. I feel like I've been gone forever," he says, picking me up and swinging me around in his arms which, of course, makes me giggle.

"It does feel like forever. I've missed you, too." I chuckle as he places me back down on unsteady feet. "Your home is really taking shape, and it looks amazing. Thought I'd pop down and check up on it since I've finished working. I didn't think you were coming back till tomorrow?"

"We finished early. Thought I'd check up on the work too before coming to find you. Why are you not working?" he asks.

"Because I'm awesome at my job and don't have to do too many takes." I grin.

"I've seen what you've been up to on the socials. I can't believe you made all those things out of old wine barrels."

"I found so many old farm machinery parts, too. They are my next project," I tell him. "How did you go exploring with Kevin?"

I laughed when I found out Kevin was going to be his location producer. I wonder who assigned him that job?

"We had fun, he's a good guy. A little full-on, but nothing I can't handle."

"Aw … I bet he offered to keep you company at night?" I say, running my fingers up his chest one by one.

"Jealous?" he says with a grin.

"Yes."

Sebastien chuckles at my honesty. "The only thing that kept me company was my hand and your socials. Quinn Miller in workwear gets my dick hard," he teases. "Now, come on, let me take you home. My hand is sick of me," Sebastien says, grabbing me by the hand and pulling me back through the villa.

Someone's in a hurry to get lucky, and I can't wait.

40

SEBASTIEN

"We did it!" Kevin raises his glass high in the air. "I cannot thank you all enough for making this project the success it is and will be once aired," he says, looking out into the crowd a little teary-eyed.

Today was the last day of filming, and tomorrow the Americans all pack up and begin to head home. Quinn and some of the set design crew have set up for our farewell dinner in the restaurant for the first time. They have moved all the tables together to make a couple of large, long tables down the middle of the restaurant. The chandeliers made out of twisted wine barrel metal have been hung in pride of place down the center of the room. They almost look like sculptures.

At first, when she pitched me the DIY stuff, I thought it would look cheap and homemade, but Quinn proved me wrong. It's beautiful and elegant and saved me a load of money not having to fit out the restaurant with overpriced art and design.

"Quinn … Sebastien," Kevin calls us to the head of the table. "Sorry, I know you're busy in your new kitchen, but please join me." He grins. "Now, I have to give these two a very big shout-out because if it weren't for them, none of us would have spent the summer in Spain.

The crowd nods and cheers in agreement.

"This was such a special project, and one I think we can all agree was the best we have all worked on."

The crowd goes crazy again. I think the copious amounts of empty bottles on the tables means the crew has enjoyed the evening, and it's well-deserved.

"Now, I don't want to toot my own horn ..." Kevin states, and the audience laughs, "… but I think we have a ratings winner on our hands here, guys." Kevin wraps his arms around Quinn and me. "We are taking this show all the way to the top," he screams, and everyone hollers before he hands Quinn the microphone.

"Wow, Kevin. Not sure how I can follow that," Quinn starts, and the crowd chuckles. "But I'll keep it short and sweet." She looks out at the crowd, all happy and smiling. "This show, and y'all … every single one of you …" her eyes land on me, "… ended up being the biggest surprise in my life. Months ago, I thought my life would never be the same. I was wrong." Tears begin to well in her eyes. "I was broken, alone, and didn't know which way was up."

Kevin cuddles her as the tears begin to flow more freely.

"Then, y'all came into my life …" she looks at me fleetingly, "… and put me back together again."

The crowd gives her a noisy and almost incomprehensible hip, hip, hooray.

"Sorry." She turns to Kevin and buries her face into his chest.

"You did good, kid," he tells Quinn, then turns back to the crowd. "Let's all get fucked up."

The crowd raises their glasses in agreement.

Kevin rushes off to join his team, leaving Quinn and me together.

She surprises me when she wraps her arms around me in front of everyone. "Thank you for putting me back together again, Sebastien," she whispers in my ear before releasing me and making her excuses to leave.

Shit.

I need to check on the kitchen, but Quinn's left the building in tears.

"I'll go check the kitchen. You go after her," Layla says as she walks past me, giving me a knowing wink. I mouth *'thank you'* as I rush out after Quinn. It's dark outside, and it takes a moment for my eyes to adjust.

"Quinn," I call out into the night sky.

"Sebastien?" I hear her sniffle my name.

There she is huddled around the corner.

"What's the matter?"

She shakes her head. "I'm being emotional."

"It's okay. It's been an intense three months of working long hours, now that it's over, all that stress is coming out in tears," I tell her as I wipe them away.

"It's not just the show that's making me emotional," she says, looking up at me.

I swallow hard. I know what she's saying.

"I don't want to leave," she whispers into the darkness, and I know that sentence ends with 'you' on the end.

Leaning forward, I place a kiss on her forehead and breath in her scent. The memories of everything we have shared these past months flood my mind, and the thought of her leaving and never being in my life again ….

"Fuck it," she says, cursing. "I've fallen in love with you, Sebastien. And I know I promised you I wouldn't. But I did. And now whatever this is between us is ending, and I don't want it to. I want to give what we have a try. I want to wake up with you every morning in the villa you slept with me in for the first time. I want to continue to work on helping you complete these renovations. There are so many left to do and the thought of not being a part of all this pains me. I love it here as much as I love you. Ask me to stay, Sebastien and I will."

Silence falls between us as Quinn lays everything on the line for me. And I want it. I want it all with her. Knowing tomorrow might be the last morning I wake up with her fills me with dread. When I think about this place, it always has her in it. I see her blonde hair blowing in the breeze as she stands on the terrace and looks out over the vines. It's her reaction I look for when I create a new recipe. This place has so much of Quinn built into it that everywhere I look I see here.

How can I ask her to give up everything to come live with me on top of a mountain while working twenty-hour days, seven days a week to bring my dream to life? What about hers? I never want to be another Chad. She deserves to find out what she wants in this life, not have her happiness tied to another man with a dream that isn't her own.

"I can't ask you to stay, Quinn."

As soon as I say those words, she takes a step away from me, and I already feel her loss. Her heart breaks in that moment, and I feel like the world's biggest asshole for being the one to do it. I promised I wouldn't hurt her, yet here I am doing just that.

"Even though I want you to," I confess.

Those doe blue eyes glisten with her tears as she stares at me, confused.

"This is my dream, Quinn. I can't ask you to give up on yours for mine."

"It's become mine too."

I shake my head. "I'm the guy you have a summer fling with before you go back to your life and meet the guy that can give you everything you desire."

"You weren't a rebound, that was Tyler ." She sniffles. "You're the man that put me back together. You're the man that mended my broken heart when I never thought there was a chance of it ever being mended again."

"That's what the rebound guy does. That's all I'm good for, Quinn. I can't offer you anything more than a good time."

She shakes her head as tears fall down her cheeks. "You are worthy of being more than someone's fling. I'm in love with you, Sebastien, and no matter how much you push me away, nothing is going to change that."

"I'm not pushing you away, Quinn. It's the truth. There is no future for us. Maybe as friends but nothing more." I know I'm being cruel to be kind, but she will thank me for it. Her life isn't here in Spain. It's back in the states as the network's brightest renovating star. It's knocking Chad off his high horse and taking his self-proclaimed title of the most popular talent at the network from him. There is more waiting for her than being by my side running a vineyard.

"I've got to get back to the kitchen, Quinn."

"That's it? That's all you have to say to me. After everything we have had this summer that's all you have to say," she yells at me.

I hate seeing her in pain like this, but she'll get over me, they always do.

"There's nothing more to say. There was always an expiry date, we both agreed. And that time's come."

"You're a fucking coward. I loved you with all my heart, and still, it's not enough for you to take a chance on love again. After everything I've been through, here I am laying everything on the line, and you can't do the same for me."

"I'm sorry, Quinn. I wish you all the best back in the states. You're going to be a great success." With that, I head back to the kitchen, each step away from her widening the hole in my heart.

41

QUINN

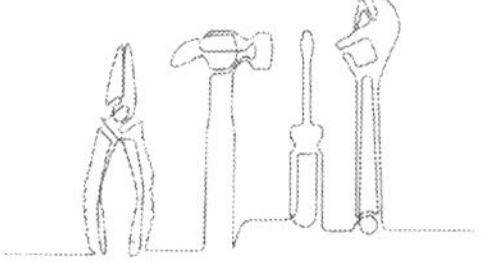

Month One Apart

I was so angry with Sebastien for leaving me in the darkness in tears and with a broken heart. Thankfully, Layla found me in a heap and helped put me back together again, enough for me to celebrate with the production team.

Stupidly I waited a week in Spain, hoping and wishing that Sebastien would change his mind. That he would tell me he made the biggest mistake of his life by letting me go that night because he was scared of the real feelings we had between us.

It never happened.

I jumped on the next flight out of Barcelona to Los Angeles leaving a piece of my heart in a city I had fallen for. Lettie was there waiting for me at the airport like a true friend. She never pushed me to explain what had happened. She just held me while I broke down.

Lettie cracked it after seeing me spend another day watching renovations shows on her couch with a pint of cookie dough ice cream. She signed me up with a therapist the very next day and told me if I was going to be living under her roof, I needed to sort my baggage out. And she was right. I probably should have done therapy after my breakup with Chad. It's been good going and talking to someone.

Derrick and the Dirty Texas girls called me when they heard I was back in town and invited me over for family barbecues, but I just haven't felt up to it, especially as they are Sebastien's friends and I think that would be weird.

One month down since leaving Spain and ….

1,390 times I've stalked Sebastien's socials.

2,163 times, I've picked up the phone and listened to his old voice notes.

---

831 times I've picked up the phone to call him to tell him something and remembered I couldn't.

Don't need to count how many pints of cookie dough ice cream I've consumed. We all know it's not a sane amount.

42

QUINN

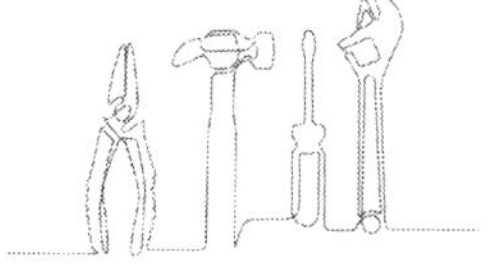

Month Two Apart

All that time spent crying on Lettie's sofa with a pint of cookie dough ice cream probably wasn't the greatest idea, especially as the network wants to start advertising the show before the fall season opener. And when one of my favorite dresses won't do up, that's when I know I have to ditch the ice cream and get my life back on track.

Lettie and I have been keeping busy going to the gym, to Pilates, and yoga.

I finally said yes to catching up with the Dirty Texas crew, and that was great. Derrick did pull me aside and tell me he had spoken to Sebastien, and he eventually cracked and told him what had happened between us and that he feels bad for breaking my heart. Not bad enough to call me. He also explained why he thought Sebastien did what he did. He filled me in on his marriage to Maria, a famous Spanish socialite and how they were the crème of Barcelona society, he with his restaurants and her with her being a famous actress, as well as having a famous family. When Sebastien found out she was sleeping with her co-star he ended it. He didn't realize, like me, that she owned everything he had built because of her initial investment set up by her trust. Because she was rich and was able to afford the best lawyers, Sebastien couldn't fight it. He had to walk away from it all and start again. *Very similar to me.* When the divorce was finalized, Sebastien was shunned by her influential friends, and it took him a long time to rebuild his image. I'd heard bits and pieces of his story but not all this. Derrick told me to not lose hope, that the thick-headed idiot would realize he's still madly in love with me, but he thinks he's doing something noble in letting me go so I can spread my wings and soar. They sound more like Derrick's words than Sebastien's, but I understand the sentiment. Still think he's a coward for not telling me all this.

I've been keeping myself busy lately, thanks to Carmen who has been negotiating some brand ambassador deals for me which has been exciting. I was lucky enough to get the pink workwear gig. It netted me a lot of money. It was exciting getting my first solo multi-million-dollar deal. It made me feel like I've accomplished something.

This month things got easier.

Only stalked his socials 590 times.

Picked up the phone to call him only 405 times.

How many pints of cookie dough ice cream did I eat? Not as much as last month so I'll take that as a win.

How many times have I called him? 0 times.

But I did text him.

Quinn: The promo images of the show are up online. Heaps of great comments about the show. People seem excited by it which is good.

Keep it professional, Quinn.

I don't hear back from him all day until just before bed and my phone beeps. My heart races as I see his name flash across the screen.

Sebastien: They used the image of me feeding you escargot and the horrified look on your face.

That wasn't at all what I was expecting him to write back. It's how we used to communicate with each other.

Quinn: I will still stand by they taste nothing like chicken. They also used the image of us having a flour fight in your kitchen.

Sebastien: Having that mess in my kitchen was torture.

Sebastien: I hear congrats are in order for your brand deal.

How did he hear about that? Has he been keeping track of me? No. I bet it was Derrick.

Quinn: Thank you. I heard you had some of your own too.

Derrick told me about them.

Sebastien: Not going to say no to a famous knife company supplying my kitchen with an unlimited number of knives for a year. They are expensive.

I find myself smiling while reading his texts. And the texts keep coming and coming. We talk about the most mundane things. He keeps me in the loop with the farm and shares photographs of the progress on the villa. And each time I hear from him, the hole in my chest becomes wider and wider.

Until it's a gaping chasm.

43

QUINN

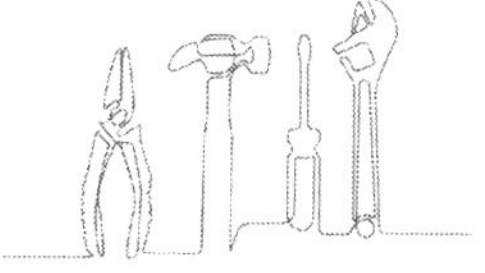

Month Three Apart

Our texts soon turn into phone calls of the nightly kind —well, my night, his day. He calls me on his way from his apartment to the farm. He excitedly talks about everything that's been happening. He's even been sending me updates on the goats and their new enclosure. We've fallen back into our old ways. It just happened naturally, and I look forward to our nightly chats.

Sebastien purchased some chickens for the upcycled chicken coop I created. He sent me a video of the pool at the villa being filled with water, and it looks incredible, especially with the mountains in the background. The roof has been restored in the villa, so he's preparing to move in full-time next week when he returns from LA.

My stomach twists in knots because he arrives next week to attend the premiere of *Under the Spanish Sun*. It's part of the fall lineup premiere season that week. Each night a different show is launched to the media and influencers, hoping to drum up some last-minute support for the shows before they go live to the general public.

After that, we will start our national talk show tour. I'm excited but also worried because Sebastien and I will be forced to spend time together again and we will have to try and bring back that rapport that we had all those months ago and that everyone is now seeing on their screens. And I'm not sure if my heart can cope with flirting with him again, knowing he doesn't want me.

Last night, it was the premiere of Chad and Danika's new show. The critics slammed it. I feel bad for the people who worked on the show, but I don't feel sorry for Chad at all. The critics didn't think there was any chemistry between Danika and Chad. That everything felt forced and too set up. Comments were made that Chad was trying too hard to be someone he wasn't, and they didn't like the way he spoke to Danika.

Tonight is the premiere of my show, and I pray we are not slammed like they were. I'm a bundle of nerves for the show and for seeing Sebastien again. I'm excited, elated, nervous, worried—every emotion you can feel, I'm feeling it right now.

What happens if he has met someone else? Derrick reassures me he hasn't messed around with anyone since I left, but who knows? Sabine is probably lurking in the wings.

He may see me again and realize, actually yeah, we are better off as friends. That his life back in Spain is perfect as it is.

Can I be just friends with him? Maybe. There is a whole ocean between us and given time … who am I kidding? No. I can't just be friends with him, my heart won't allow it.

"Are you ready?" Lettie asks as I take one last look in the mirror to check that I don't have lipstick on my teeth. "Stop stressing. You look gorgeous."

I've gone for a cute, white sequined mini dress with long sleeves and a low-cut back. It's a little daring for me, but I think the occasion calls for something sexy.

"You're professional, Quinn. And I promise when we get home, if things don't work out there are pints of cookie dough ice cream in the freezer waiting for you."

She's the best.

We jump into the waiting limousine and head toward the studio.

"Everything is going to be okay," Lettie says, reaching out and holding my hand. "He is going to take one look at you and fall to his knees."

Yeah, I wish.

"What happens if the spark isn't there anymore? What happens if it was just the Spanish sun that worked between us?"

"Come on now, Quinn. You can't think like that. You two are always on the phone with each other these days. Men don't talk that much unless they're into you," Lettie tells me.

Maybe she's right.

The LA traffic is a nightmare, but we eventually make it to the studio a little later than we intended.

"Take a deep breath and put on that winning smile, Quinn Miller," Lettie says.

I suck in a deep breath and blow it out, calming myself down as someone opens the limousine's door. It's Kevin. He's there dressed in a suit holding out his hand for me.

"Thank you," I say, noticing my hand shaking in his.

"You've got this. You look beautiful tonight. Now, let's rock this red carpet," he whispers.

I nod in agreement and push my shoulders back, trying to muster up as much confidence as I possibly can. The red carpet is a blur as I twist and turn and pose. I answer the same mundane questions over and over from reporters. My cheeks hurt from smiling as I step off the carpet and into the studio space that has been set up with cocktails for the show.

"You did good," Lettie says, giving me a reassuring look.

I'm distracted because all I could think about was running into Sebastien on the red carpet. I didn't, but now my anxiety is at an all-time high as my eyes scan the room looking for him.

Kevin's phone goes off in his pocket. "Shit," he curses when he looks at it. "Sebastien's flight's been delayed. He won't get here till the end."

I relax ever so slightly at his words.

"The bigwigs are going to hate this, but it is what it is, can't bring an airplane in any faster. I've got to go," Kevin says as he scurries away to fight that fire.

"Drinks, then?" Lettie asks.

"Oh, hell, yes." I relax for the first time tonight.

It's go-time, and Kevin calls me up on stage with the rest of the crew, minus Sebastien. He introduces us to the room, which receives a rousing round of applause. He waffles on for a bit, then he excitedly lets everyone know the show is now live. The room erupts, and the introduction to our show starts. I can't watch, so I disappear and find myself somewhere to have a quiet drink and pray that we beat Chad.

"You look so beautiful tonight, Quinn."

That voice.

That deep-timbered accent, the one that's embedded into my everything is here and talking to me. I don't dare turn around because I don't want him to see the tears already welling in my eyes.

"You still smell like berries," he whispers, his lips touching my skin ever so gently that my body practically combusts in that moment.

Slowly, I turn around and see his handsome face. He looks a little tired and may have lost some weight too. His dark hair is disheveled, he hasn't had time to shave, and his jaw is covered in dark prickles. I reach out and touch his cheek, just to see if he's actually here, and it isn't a figment of my imagination.

"You're really here." The words tumble out of my mouth as my fingers feel the prickles against my skin.

"Yes," he answers quietly, his eyes closing as my fingers run over his skin. The world seems to stand still—it is as if time itself has stopped.

"I've missed you, Quinn."

Everything stills.

"You have?"

"More than you could ever know," he tells me.

My heart bursts at his confession as the first tear falls down my cheek. His face softens as he watches it roll down before he reaches out and wipes it away.

"I've missed you every waking moment since the day you left. I haven't stopped thinking about you, no matter how often I told myself I had to let you go. I've been a fucking idiot, Quinn."

Well, damn.

"I should never have left you," I confess.

"You had to. I didn't want to hold you back. You've accomplished so much since coming back here."

"It means nothing to me, all of this," I tell him.

Sebastien's brows rise.

"I did all of this to distract me from you."

"From me? I thought you were happy?" he asks.

I shake my head. "I'm finally happy now. Right here with you beside me again."

"Quinn?"

"You pushed me away because you thought you were doing the right thing. That you thought you knew what I needed. But what you didn't understand in that thick head of yours was that I was exactly where I was supposed to be. With you, on that mountain, with the goats and chickens, creating crazy designs from things lying around the farm. Helping you build your dream. A dream that is mine now. I can't stop thinking about you and the life we could have had at the villa."

"I've ruined everything. I thought I was doing the right thing letting you go," he says, running his thumb over my cheek.

"You should have spoken to me instead of pushing me away."

"I'm hopelessly in love with you, Quinn Miller. I knew if I asked you to stay that you were it for me. I was done. I knew I wanted to turn the villa we were rebuilding into our home and fill it with all our children," he confesses.

A gasp falls from my lips at his admission.

"I needed to give you a chance at experiencing life before being stuck with an old man like me," he says, giving me a smirk.

"I thought old men were supposed to be wise," I say with a smirk.

"I guess not," he says with a shrug. "Has my stupidity ruined things for us?"

I let his question hang between us. He pushed me away for months because he thought he was doing the right thing and as hurtful and stupid as it was, it made me realize what I wanted out of life, and I guess he was right in sending me away. Because I've never been surer than I am in this moment, being with Sebastien Sanchez is where I'm supposed to be.

I shake my head letting him know he hasn't ruined things.

Those chocolate eyes widen. "Are you serious, Quinn?" he asks in disbelief.

"Deadly. It's you. It's always been you, and I want everything you said before. The villa. The kids. The life on the farm. There isn't any other life I could see myself living," I say as I wrap my arms around his neck and pull him in closer.

"I don't deserve you, Quinn Miller," he says.

"Think there are a couple of ways you can make it up to me."

"Is that right?" he asks, raising a brow at me.

I nod, giving him a knowing smile.

"Fuck it, come with me," he says, unwrapping my arms from his neck and pulling me down the corridor. He tries a couple of doors until he finds an empty meeting room. He slams the door behind us and has me pushed up against it in two seconds flat. The only light shining in the room is from the streetlights outside —so we are bathed in shadows.

"I need to be inside you, Quinn," Sebastien whispers into my ear as he kisses my neck. "It's been too fucking long."

"Yes," I hiss.

"I want nothing between us," he growls into my neck.

"I'm on the pill."

He grunts at my admission, and the next thing I know he's kicking my legs apart and his finger is inside of me. Testing. Teasing.

Yes. Yes. Yes.

How I've missed this.

Then, it's gone and replaced with his dick in one long thrust. I feel full as he takes me against the door, his lips on mine as he does, both of us needing the release. Sebastien dirty-talks me in a slew of Spanish curses as he pushes me higher and higher until I fall over the edge.

His teeth sink into my shoulder as we both come quickly.

It takes us a couple of moments to come down from our high.

"I've missed you." He tenderly kisses my shoulder as he pulls himself from me. I turn around, and I can feel the evidence of our lovemaking.

Sebastien realizes and says, "Stay there. I'll be right back." Then he opens the door and disappears as I try not to move. A little later, he's back with a box of tissues and hands them to me, and I clean myself up the best I can.

We both burst out laughing at the absurdity of it all.

I wrap my arms around his neck. "You're stuck with me now, Mr. Sanchez. I hope you're prepared for it," I tell him.

"Bring it on, Miss Miller, I'm man enough." He grins.

After a quick stop at the bathroom to freshen up, we walk back into the room arm in arm as the premiere episode finishes. Suddenly, the crowd erupts, and the entire room goes crazy. Kevin rushes over to us.

"Sebastien, you made it just in time." His eyes lighten, then he notices that we are arm in arm. "Tell me you two are finally together?"

"We are," Sebastien tells him.

Kevin starts jumping up and down and then engulfs us both in the biggest bear hug known to man.

"This is brilliant news. But even better news is … it was a smash hit, baby," he screams.

Wait! What?

"The viewers love the show. Suck it, Chad," he says then disappears off into the ecstatic crowd.

"You heard him. Suck it, Chad," Sebastien says with a chuckle.

"I love you, you fool." Pulling him to me, I kiss him in front of everyone.

EPILOGUE

QUINN

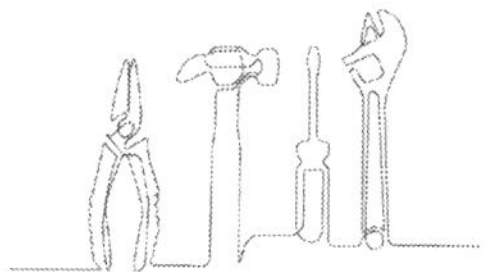

Five Years as Mrs. Sanchez.

That's right, he put a ring on it!

Sebastien proposed to me the night the villa was complete, and we moved in together.

I said yes, of course.

Under the Spanish Sun was a network hit. They then offered us a ridiculous amount of money to continue with the franchise, and we agreed, provided we had some control over production. They said yes and gave us Kevin full-time.

Both Sebastien and I made the USA Today and New York Times Best Sellers Lists with our published books—he for his recipe book and mine for my renovation book. We even collaborated on one together.

I've also created my own lifestyle brand including furniture and décor.

Sebastien has also created his own line of kitchen products.

A year after the show premiered, the restaurant officially opened its doors to the public. That same year we harvested our first grapes to create our own Cava line, which we launched two years later, and the wine is still thriving to this day.

We also married that first year once the summer season had stopped because we were insanely busy with so many fans popping in to have a look. We had a beautiful intimate winter wedding with our friends and family at the villa. It was nice to be able to show them our little world away from everything.

Then surprise, one year later, we welcomed our first child, Matias.

Two years later, we welcomed Gabriela to the family.

And as they say in showbiz…. *That's all, folks!*

Oh, yes, I forgot one crucial detail.

Chad.

Whatever happened to him, you may ask?

Well, his show was canceled. His girlfriend left him for a famous football player. He lost all his money on some crazy business scheme, and now he's a YouTube star trying to recapture his prime.

Karma wins again.

THE END!

ACKNOWLEDGMENTS

Thanks for finishing this book.
Really hope you enjoyed it.
Why not check out my other books.
Have a fantastic day !

Don’t forget to leave a review.
xoxo

ABOUT THE AUTHOR

JA Low lives on the Gold Coast in Australia. When she's not writing steamy scenes and admiring hot surfers, she's tending to her husband and two sons and running after her chickens while dreaming up the next epic romance.

Come follow her

Facebook: www.facebook.com/jalowbooks
TikTok: https://geni.us/vrpoMqH
Instagram: www.instagram.com/jalowbooks
Pinterest: www.pinterest.com/jalowbooks
Website: www.jalowbooks.com
Goodreads: https://www.goodreads.com/author/show/14918059.J_A_Low
BookBub: https://www.bookbub.com/authors/ja-low

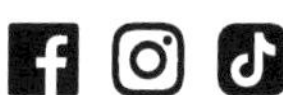

ABOUT THE AUTHOR

Come join JA Low's Block
www.facebook.com/groups/1682783088643205/

JALow Books Website
jalowbooks@gmail.com

Subscribe to her newsletter here

ALSO BY JA LOW

If you would like to see Sebastien before he meets Quinn you can find him in the Dirty Texas series.

The Dirty Texas Box Set

Five full length novels and Five Novellas included in the set.

One band. Five dirty talking rock stars and the women that bring them to their knees.

Wyld & Dirty

A workplace romance with your celebrity hall pass.

Dirty Promises

A best friend to lover's romance with the one man who's off limits.

Bound & Dirty

An opposites attract romance with family loyalty tested to its limits.

Dirty Trouble

A brother's best friend romance with a twist.

Broken & Dirty

A friend's with benefits romance that takes a wild ride.

One little taste can't hurt; can it?

If you like your rock stars dirty talking, alpha's with hearts of gold this series is for you.

ALSO BY JA LOW

Spin off Dirty Texas Series

Paradise Club Series

Paradise - Book 1

Lost in Paradise - Book 2

Paradise Found - Book 3

Craving Paradise - Book 4

ALSO BY JA LOW

Connected to The Paradise Club

The Art of Love Series

Arrogant Artist - Book 1

ALSO BY JA LOW

Playboys of New York

Off Limits - Book 1

Strictly Forbidden - Book 2

The Merger - Book 3

Taking Control - Book 4

Without Warning - Book 5

ALSO BY JA LOW

Spin off series to Playboys of New York

The Hartford Brothers Series

Book 1 - Tempting the Billionaire

Book 2 - Playing the Player

Book 3 - Seducing the Doctor

ALSO BY JA LOW

Bratva Jewels

Book 1 - Sapphire

Book 2 - Diamond

Book 3 - Emerald

ALSO BY JA LOW

Connected to The Bratva Jewels

Italian Nights Series

The Sexy Stranger - Book 1

Made in the USA
Columbia, SC
28 July 2024

38966058R00170